D0438824

Social Blunders

ALSO BY TIM SANDLIN

Sorrow Floats

Skipped Parts

The Pyms:
Unauthorized Tales of Jackson Hole

Western Swing

Sex and Sunsets

THE GROVONT TRILOGY

Skipped Parts (1991)

Sorrow Floats (1992)

Social Blunders (1995)

Social Blunders

TIM SANDLIN

HENRY HOLT AND COMPANY
NEW YORK

Henry Holt and Company, Inc.
Publishers since 1866
115 West 18th Street
New York, New York 10011

Henry Holt® is a registered
trademark of Henry Holt and Company, Inc.

Copyright © 1995 by Tim Sandlin
All rights reserved.
Published in Canada by Fitzhenry & Whiteside Ltd.,
195 Allstate Parkway, Markham, Ontario L3R 4T8.

Library of Congress Cataloging-in-Publication Data

Sandlin, Tim.
Social blunders / Tim Sandlin.—1st ed.
p.   cm.
I. Title.
PS3569.A517S6 1995   94-43193
813'.54—dc20   CIP

ISBN 0-8050-1628-7

Henry Holt books are available for special
promotions and premiums. For details contact:
Director, Special Markets.

First Edition—1995

DESIGNED BY PAULA R. SZAFRANSKI

Printed in the United States of America
All first editions are printed on acid-free paper. ∞

1 3 5 7 9 10 8 6 4 2

The lines excerpted from "The Theory and Practice of
Rivers" by Jim Harrison (copyright © 1985, ALL RIGHTS
RESERVED) are used with his permission.

I wrote this
for old Fred, young Kyle, and loyal Flip;
in memory of Richard Koeln and Mimi Levinson;
and because of Carol

Acknowledgments

As usual with my books, this was a group effort. Teri Krumdick and Vici Skladanowski helped with the research. Tina Welling, Yana Sue Salomon, and my mom read earlier drafts; their comments were vital to the process. Drs. Sandy Chesney and Bruce Hayse showed me the ropes of disease and death. While Mark Wade and Grant Richins at Valley Mortuary assisted with funeral arrangements, those fine professionals are nothing in any way, shape, or visualization similar to the funeral directors I created in this novel. Competence doesn't go over well in fiction.

I spent an interesting morning at the Red Hills Ranch kitchen table, listening to Sarah Sturgis and Paula Lasson talk about winter in the mountains beyond the reach of plowed roads while a guest stitched up a slice in Paula's son's hand. As the Kiowas used to say, nothing was wasted.

Bert and Meg Raynes are my role models.

Special thanks go to Les and Maggie Gibson at Pearl Street Bagels for daily cranking me up on coffee, and Steve Ashley, owner of Valley Books, who gave me sanctuary.

The days are stacked against
what we think we are:
it is nearly impossible
to surprise ourselves.
I will never wake up
and be able to play the piano.

—JIM HARRISON,
"The Theory and Practice of Rivers"

Love is having to say you're sorry
every fifteen minutes.

—JOHN LENNON

Social Blunders

Prologue

Maurey reached for my Coke and drained it. "They shaved me again."

"I thought that was only for abortions."

"Doctors must shave every time they poke around down there. I might as well start shaving myself like Mom, save them the trouble."

Maurey looked awfully chipper, considering she'd just broken her leg and had a baby. Her hair was brushed shiny, and her eyes glittered blue with interest at the baby stuck to her breast. A surf of love rolled over me, only more for Maurey than the baby. The baby was still a little abstract.

She held out a Bic pen. "Want to sign my cast?"

Her encased left leg hung by this pulley-and-hook deal. Her toes were gray.

"Does it hurt?"

"Itches like king-hell, but doesn't hurt."

"You never said king-hell before."

Maurey smiled, which was neat. "You're rubbing off on me."

"Holy moley." I signed—Yer pal, Sam Callahan.

"Is the baby eating breakfast?"

Maurey parted the hospital gown to give me a better view of the baby's mouth clamped to her nipple. She looked asleep. "Her name is Shannon."

"That's pretty, I never heard it before."

Shannon's cheeks sucked in and out and the eye I could see opened, then closed slowly, like a tortoise.

"Can I touch her?"

Maurey looked worried for a second. "Okay, but be gentle. Babies aren't footballs."

"They don't travel as far when you kick 'em."

Maurey didn't like my joke a bit. For a moment I thought I'd blown the chance to touch my baby. We hemmed around and I apologized and Maurey asked me when was the last time I'd had a bath, which she knew full well was the warm springs.

"You didn't mind yesterday."

"Yesterday I was different."

I sat on the edge of the bed and touched my daughter on the back of her leg, above the plastic ID anklet thing. She was soft as a bubblegum bubble and, I imagined, just as delicate. I had created this. These toes and eyelids and all the potential for greatness and badness and beauty had come from me. I started hyperventilating and had to bend over with my head between my knees.

"I hope she grows up to have my looks and Dad's brains," Maurey said.

"How about me?"

"She'll have your hair."

PART ONE

North Carolina

1

"Traumatic events always happen exactly two years before I reach the maturity level to deal with them," I said, just to hear how the theory sounded out loud.

"Two years from now I could handle my wife running off with an illiterate pool man. Two years from now I will have the emotional capacity to survive another divorce."

Hints that I might not survive the crisis cut no slack with my daughter. In fact, I wasn't even certain she had heard my little speech. Shannon seemed totally absorbed in aiming a garden hose at the front grill of her Mustang. As she rinsed soap off the gleaming chrome, her eyes held a distracted softness that reminded me more than somewhat of the softness her mother's eyes used to take on following an orgasm. Now, there's an awful thought. According to the two-year theory, a day would come when I could accept my daughter having orgasms, but for now I'd rather drink Drano.

"They say divorce cripples men more than women," I said. "Women cry and purge the pain while men internalize and fester."

Shannon raised her head to peer at me through her thick bangs. "You've never internalized pain in your life. Heartbreak to you is like garlic to a cook."

"Who told you such nonsense?"

"Mom. She says ever since you saw *Hunchback of Notre Dame* you've been looking for a Gypsy girl to swoop down and save. Then later you can die for her and feel your life wasn't wasted."

Secretly, I was pleased Maurey had seen the parallel, although I'd always related to the hunchback more from the tragic outsider aspect than as a savior of Gypsy girls.

"Do you and your mother often discuss my psychic makeup?"

"Everyone discusses your psychic makeup—Mom, Grandma Lydia, Gus. Hank Elkrunner says you're an egomaniac with delusions of inferiority."

"I suppose Hank figured that out by throwing chicken bones."

Shannon shrugged the way she did when I was being too unreasonable to argue with and went back to her chrome. It was evening in October, the silver light hour when thousands of male Southerners all across the Carolinas stand back and toss lit kitchen matches at lighter fluid–soaked mounds of charcoal.

Shannon said, "You'll be mooning over a new woman within a week. Why not save me some teenage anxiety and find a nice one this time? Hand me that T-shirt."

"Isn't this my T-shirt?" It was lime colored with GREENSBORO HORNETS in white over a yellow cartoon hornet swinging crossed baseball bats. "Wanda was nice."

Shannon stopped rubbing the headlights long enough to stare me down—one of those how-dare-you-lie-to-me stares women inherently pass on to one another. Shannon looks so much like Maurey, it's almost enough to make you believe in virgin birth. Where were my genes in this person who called me Daddy? Both my women had thick, dark brown hair, except Shannon cut hers short, collar length, while Maurey's hair hung down her back. Long neck, small hands, cheekbones of a Victoria's Secret nightie model, teeth that had never cost me a dime over checkups and cleaning—the only difference was Shannon had brown eyes while Maurey's were sky blue. And Maurey had a scar on her chin from a beating she once took at the hands of a man.

I said, "Okay, she wasn't so nice, but she had potential. Remember her crab salad."

"You don't marry a woman over crab salad. Wanda was a dysfunctional stepmother, a stereotype of the Cinderella, Hansel and Gretel ilk."

Ilk? "My God, who have you been talking to? Are you dating a psych major?"

Shannon reddened along the neck behind her ears. Fatherly intuition strikes again. The only question was whether the blush came from sex fantasized or sex completed. Shannon rubbed my T-shirt across the windshield with all her might. When she spoke, her voice sounded like she was hitting someone.

"You can't save every fucked-up woman you stumble over."

"I'd rather you not talk that way when I'm close by."

She turned the hose dangerously close to my tennis shoes. "You made fun of me when I said dysfunctional."

"Let's try neurotic."

"Okay. You find these neurotic women, God knows where, and you think that if you accept them as they are, out of sheer gratitude, they'll change."

Not a bad analysis for a nineteen-year-old. Of course, I couldn't admit that; never let a daughter know she might be right. "Why is it children always oversimplify their parents?"

Shannon smiled at me. "I doubt if it's possible to oversimplify you, Daddy. That's why I love you."

Tears leapt to my eyes. Wanda's leaving had turned me into an emotional sap, to the point where I'd cried the day before when I heard the neighbor kids singing "Happy Birthday to You." Because the picture on the front of the jar reminded me of a young Shannon, I'd stuffed a hundred-dollar check into the muscular dystrophy display at Tex and Shirley's Pancake House.

Shannon either ignored or didn't notice my poignant moment. She stood back to admire her shiny, clean Mustang. It was ten years old, creamy white with a black interior and a LICK JESSE HELMS IN '84 bumper sticker. I'd given it to her for high school graduation.

"One thing for certain," Shannon said, still looking at her car

7

instead of me. "That woman wasn't worth a heart attack. Why not get drunk and chase women the way you did before?"

"Because I married this one. The grief process is different when a marriage breaks up."

Her eyes finally came to mine. "Heck, Daddy, you're only grieving because you think that's what Kurt Vonnegut would do in the situation."

"Don't lecture your father on grief. I was miserable before you were even born."

Shannon stuck the hose in my pocket.

I flee to my Exercycle 6000 and ride fifty-five miles at high tension. Depression must be avoided, no matter what the cost. Depression is lying on the Edwardian couch for six months, too tired to unlace your shoes. Depression is awakening each morning feeling as if someone near and dear and closely related died the night before. Bad news. Don't tempt depression. Far better to pump a stationary bicycle for six hours, full speed, dripping sweat into your eyes and hurling curses at women not present.

Starting with Wanda. Wanda of the black braids, tiny tits, and ferocious tongue; Wanda who said my intelligence and ability to articulate caused her crotch to tingle with slurpy anticipation; Wanda who said "I do"; the very same Wanda who stole my Datsun 240Z and ran off with the pool boy—the pool boy for Chrissake. No matter how long or how hard I pump the Exercycle 6000, I can't get around it. She left me, the author of *The Shortstop Kid* and *Jump Shot to Glory*, for a boy with BORN TO LOOSE tattooed across his left shoulder blade.

My housekeeper, Gus, has no pity. "Wanda was a tramp. You just falling apart 'cause you think that's what a man does when his wife leave."

"But she left with a boy who can't read."

"So what he can't read." Gus is six feet two inches tall and black as a Milk Dud. When I piss her off, which is often, she leans back with her hands planted on both hips and glares down her nose at me. "She don't want his brain any more than she want yours. What she wants is his Peter."

I stop pedaling. "Is that what she wanted from me?"

"You, she want money, fool."

I ride with a fury—ten, twelve, fourteen hours a day. Sadistically, I screw the knob that increases the tension in my pedals until my quadriceps and calves scream in pain. When Shannon said it's not worth a heart attack, she wasn't speaking metaphorically. My chest pounds like a train. I can hear each gush of blood spurting through my temples. Sweat trickles from the ear where Wanda's tongue once licked. The saddle digs into my butt, raising blisters on the cheeks where Wanda's fingernails used to rake.

After five or six hours of riding toward a wall, the brain forgets there was ever a before the bike or may ever be an after the bike. I enter a zone without time, pain, or exhaustion. Some call it coma. If the deal works right, I forget the tongue and fingernails for a moment and reach a point of being so thoroughly wrung out that I sleep.

Before I discovered frenetic exercise, I only knew two other methods of avoiding depression. The first—getting drunk and staying drunk. That's not my style, and besides, when alcohol fails it fails big time. The second—sleeping with someone else as soon as is humanly possible. That is my style.

Here's my past pattern: I'd say to myself, next time out, tonight, I'll choose an impossible woman, an obvious trollop with whom I could never connect in any way outside the crotch. An airhead or a drunk or a married woman, anyone just so she's impossible. And I'll be safe.

Only the sex turns out not so empty and I wind up trying to save a lost woman who'd rather not be saved. Starting with the beautiful and wonderful Maurey Pierce at the age of thirteen, I had systematically, purposefully, made certain each woman was worse than the one before, in hopes of protecting myself in the clinches, and finally, upon reaching what I took as the rock bottom of women who could cause me pain, I married Wanda.

2

Maurey Pierce telephoned.

"You sound out of breath."

"I've been riding the bike."

"Gus tells me the slut ran out. Congratulations, sugar booger."

"Maurey, my marriage just blew up. That should call for a little sympathy."

Pause. "Your marriage was the family joke, Sam. Both your marriages. Nobody's going to fake sympathy when they blow up."

"That's what Gus said."

"How much did she take with her?"

"The 240Z and my baseball card collection. Me Maw's jewelry, but I guess I gave her that anyway."

"You gave her your dead grandmother's jewelry?"

"We were playing 'How much do you love me?' one night in bed. She said 'Do you love me enough to give me everything you own?' and I said 'Yes.'"

"Sam."

10

"It was foreplay. I didn't mean her to take me literally."

Maurey was quiet a few moments, obviously disgusted. "How's my baby?"

There was news, but I wasn't certain how to break it. "I think Shannon lost her virginity. She didn't come home Friday night."

"Sam, Shannon lost her virginity after a Carolina-Duke game two years ago."

I almost dropped the phone. "How do you know?"

"She told me. She bet her virginity on Duke and lost. She was planning to sleep with the geek anyway and figured if she did it on a bet there'd be no strings attached. Doesn't that just sound like a daughter of ours?"

I looked from the Exercycle to a painting on the wall of some Indians killing a buffalo, then back to my hand on the phone—all those years of protecting my daughter from the rancid gender down the tubes. I muttered, "She's so young."

"She waited four years longer than we did."

"And look how we turned out—maladjusted ambiverts unable to sustain the simplest relationships."

"Ambiverts, my ass, my relationship is fine." I shut up on that one. Maurey's relationship with Pud Talbot was a sore point with us, so sore that when she first took him in, Maurey and I stopped speaking to each other for eight months.

In the silence, Maurey said, "Before you go off the deep end could you spare a couple thousand? The drought burned half our grass and we'll have to buy feed this winter."

"You must think I'm made of money."

Another sore point—my money. "You're made of horseshit, Sam. God knows everyone here at the TM Ranch appreciates our allowance; we're just tired of doing backflips to yank it out of you."

I didn't say anything. The first days after your marriage dies, people should cut a little slack. The women in my life don't know the meaning of *slack*.

"I'm sorry," Maurey said.

"I'm sorry too." I listened to Maurey breathe, but she didn't say anything more. "How many lost souls am I supporting this week?" I asked.

"Three, counting your mother. I've got a recovering junkie out haying with Hank, and an unwed mother who's supposed to be teaching Auburn French, but so far all she's done is cry. And Petey called, he's coming in Wednesday. God knows why."

"I thought Petey hated all things rural." Petey is Maurey's brother. He's never much liked me and vice versa, although we keep it civil. I never called him a derogatory name, either to his face or back, but he once said I was a *screaming heterosexual.*

"All I know's what the letter said—meet him at the airport Wednesday. I suppose you'll be the next to drag your ass home. Pud wants to change our name to Lick Your Wounds Ranch."

"I better stay put for now. Wanda might come back and she'd worry if I was gone."

Maurey made a snort sound. "She's a bitch, Sam. The woman doesn't deserve to suck the mud off your sneakers."

Back to the bike. Now I have two traumas to flee—my botched marriage and my daughter's lost virginity.

To say that my life began with Shannon's birth is not the overblown remark you might think. I was thirteen when Shannon was born, three weeks short of fourteen. How much that matters can happen to a person before his fourteenth birthday? Mostly I took care of my mother, Lydia, which is another thing I discovered when I reached what passes for adulthood. Parents are supposed to take care of children, not the other way around. Lydia told me it was normal for a child to cook meals and wash the clothes. How was I supposed to know different? She had me balancing her checkbook when I was ten years old—the ditz never wrote down dates and check numbers—and these days she complains continuously because I won't let her handle money. I mean, good grief, already.

Lydia now runs the only feminist press in Wyoming. She's stopped drinking and stopped smoking, and she jogs the county roads wearing a sweatshirt, tights, ninety-dollar sneakers, and a headband that, if you circle it from ear to ear, reads MEN CAN BE REPLACED BY A BANANA.

Oothoon Press publishes books such as *Mother Lied* and *The Cas-*

tration Solution. Lydia's authors call me, the one who pays their bills, a pig and a villain simply because I have a penis and most of the pigs and villains down through history have had penises. Hell, I don't like the male sex any more than Lydia's authors, only I make an exception of myself.

When Maurey gave me the Russell print of the Indians killing the buffalo, she said it reminded her of me. I'd recently ridden several days and several hundred miles directly into the scene, and I still didn't get the connection. One Indian is shooting the buffalo with a rifle, and one Indian is shooting him with a bow and arrow, while a third waves a spear in the air and shouts Indian stuff. Meanwhile, the buffalo is goring the hell out of a fourth Indian, who is either dead or dying, and stomping the hell out of the fourth Indian's white horse. The painting is dramatic, what with two animals and a human dying and three humans and an animal killing, and everyone caught up in your basic here and now.

After Maurey said Wanda was unworthy to suck the mud off my sneakers, I rode eighty miles, staring at her painting. I've never been one to get caught up in the here and now, myself. I can't remember a single scene I've been in where one part of me wasn't standing off to the side, figuring how to word it when I told the story to a woman, and conceptualizing her reaction, then my reaction to her reaction and so on until we wound up in bed or married or whatever. Call it the curse of the romantic writer—even the romantic writer of Young Adult sports novels. So far I have the temperament of Scott Fitzgerald and the following of Dizzy Dean. Reach out for an understanding of that one.

Did Maurey think of me as the Indians killing the buffalo? Or the buffalo itself? Maybe she was saying I'm the last of a dying breed, valiantly raging in a futile battle before ultimate death. That didn't really sound like my Maurey. Or maybe I'm the dead or dying Indian who got himself reamed by his prey.

She'd more likely think of me as an Indian than a buffalo. I'm not bulky or hairy enough to compare to the buffalo. She probably thought of me as an Indian—wild and free and prone to running around without a shirt. Lydia's boyfriend is an Indian. Hank Elkrunner does most of the actual labor at Maurey's ranch. I don't know how Hank puts up with my mother's never-ending narcissism. Lydia passionately cares about the condition of her nails and the worldwide fight for feminist awareness, only she doesn't put much stock on details in between, like family and friends.

Mostly Hank looks inscrutable and stays out at the ranch until he's summoned to take care of her banana needs. Hank Elkrunner is the only male person I've ever been able to stomach for the long run. Shannon says my anti-male bias is the character flaw that dooms every aspect of my life, such as women. I don't agree with her, but many hours of cranking an Exercycle while fleeing demons is a good time to question basic assumptions.

The neat thing about physically pushing yourself above and beyond endurance is that after exhaustion comes second wind, then after second wind you slide into bizarre, disconnected thought processes. Bizarre, disconnected thought processes are followed by third and fourth winds during which the brain goes to lands even drugs can't take it, and finally you start to hallucinate your ass off.

I heard hoofbeats; the buffalo snorted and blew steam and red foam from his nostrils; the horse screamed as its back was broken. The wall framing the painting thrummed with the low breathing of a sleeping beast. Hallucinations can be cool, or they can scare the living bejesus out of person.

Women's faces swooped at me—Lydia, Maurey, Shannon, Gus. Then bodies—beautiful bodies with elbows, shoulder blades, the backs of knees, necks, feet, and fingers—all the parts that I love. Like bats, crotches began swooping out of the buffalo's head, straight at my own. Here came the wispy blond tufts of Leigh, the stiff-as-a-hairbrush bush of Janey, Wanda's crotch shaved smooth like a volleyball. Darlene, Karlene, and Charlene. Sweet Maria. Linda the raw oyster.

Before Wanda, I was rarely able to hold a woman longer than two menstrual periods. Rejection came soon after copulation, but there for a while copulation came with rapid-fire regularity. Call it the conquest-and-loss syndrome. It was nothing I did or deserved. Any non-jerk who is young, fairly well off, and single—and has a beautiful daughter—can find short-term romance. Plus Maurey taught me how to get the girls off every time. That helps.

I leaned forward with my eyes closed, sweat dribbling off my chin onto the handlebars, concentrating on the parade of crotches. I could taste each woman's juice on my tongue and the back of my mouth. A sound came like water on concrete, and I opened my eyes. The Indians had been replaced by five men who stood in a circle with their penises out, aimed at the buffalo, who had turned into a woman I couldn't recognize. She lay on the floor with her dress torn and her back bare and bleeding while the men urinated on her.

3

I found every last one of them," Shannon said as she blew into the kitchen the next morning. She was wearing white shorts and a teenage wench top that reminded me of Paw Paw Callahan's undershirts. A boy followed several paces behind, assuming the demeanor of a well-trained spaniel.

"This is Eugene," Shannon said. "Eugene, my dad."

The boy stepped around Shannon to shake my hand. I stayed seated in front of the red beans and biscuits Gus insists I eat every morning of my put-upon life.

"Pleased to meet you, sir," Eugene said. His hand was the texture of deep-fried tofu. In my day, we didn't go around touching the fathers of girls we boffed.

I looked past him. "Where were you last night, little lady?"

Shannon ignored my question as she poured herself and Eugene mugs of coffee. Eugene had that classic psych major look—receding hairline, dribbly chin, canvas shoes. Shannon put Sweet'n Low in his coffee without asking. She wrinkled her nose flirtatiously at him, then turned to me and said, "It only took four hours at the library. You could have done it years ago."

"Forms must be maintained," I said. "If you're going to stay out all night I demand the courtesy of being lied to."

Shannon reached in her day pack and pulled out a nightgown. I scowled at Eugene, who hung his head and grinned. If he said "Aw, shucks," I meant to plaster the kid—red beans right up the snout. Beneath the nightgown, Shannon found what she was looking for—a letter-size envelope and a larger manila envelope.

She came over and dropped them on the table next to my *Greensboro News*. "Names and addresses of all your fathers."

"What?"

"Greensboro only had three high schools in 1949. All we had to do was find the yearbooks."

"Your black father took the longest," Eugene said.

I lifted the letter envelope and four photographs fell out. "Where did you get these?"

Shannon opened the refrigerator and peered inside. "Don't be dramatic, Daddy. Where do you think I got them? You were moping around like a wounded bear over Wanda the witch, so Eugene and I decided you needed something to do. And anyway, I deserve to know who my grandfather is."

I stared at her with all the anger I could pull off, but since her head was in the refrigerator, my anger was neatly deflected. "You and Eugene decided I need something to do?"

Eugene smiled and nodded his head. "I said you should transfer your obsession to a suitable substitute other than your abject failure as a husband, and Shannon told me about the football players who group raped your mother and made her pregnant. That must have been a tremendous burden on your ego during the formative years—to know your very being is based on humiliation."

"So I opened the safe and borrowed the pictures," Shannon said. "Now, it's your turn."

I stared at the four photos. Five football players. Numbers 72, 56, 81, 11, and 20. Seventy-two and fifty-six were in the same picture. Big boys with burr haircuts and square heads. Eighty-one was thin and wore glasses. Eleven had the confident smirk of a high school quarterback. Twenty was black. He was noticeably shorter than the others and the only one grinning at the camera.

"What do you expect me to do?" I asked.

Shannon brought out the remains of a strawberry pie. "Those men violated Lydia. As her son it's your duty to wreak vengeance. Destroy their wives, ravish their daughters, shame their sons, drag them publicly in front of the media and show the world what scumbags they are."

Eugene smiled and nodded again.

"That was thirty-three years ago, Shannon. They were just boys then."

Shannon focused on me with the fierceness of her mother. "They raped Lydia, for Godsake. They stood in a circle and pissed on her torn body. You can't just pretend it didn't happen."

"I can't?"

Shannon, with Eugene in her wake, left for wherever women in the prime of their youth go in the morning. By eleven she had a Saturday lab class at UNC-G, where she was majoring in anthropology. I have no idea why she chose anthropology; maybe nobody knows their kids.

I stared at the manila envelope a while, then walked to my room to fetch the Grape-Nuts I kept hidden for times when Gus fixed breakfast and disappeared into her rich personal life that I know nothing about. She's been with us ten years, and she still won't tell me if she's married or has children of her own or anything. Shannon probably knows.

Back in the kitchen, I poured two-percent milk over the Grape-Nuts and ate without looking in the bowl. Two-percent milk is another of those decisions the women had made for me. When you don't have money, you think people who do have money can do anything they like. Don't believe it.

Finally I stood and washed the cereal bowl and spoon, but not the beans plate or pan—the subterfuges we have to scheme through in our own home—and walked back to the table. The envelope held one sheet of paper from a yellow legal pad.

William Gaines
   147 N. Glenwood
Skip Prescott
   14 Corner Creek Drive
Cameron Saunders
   16 Corner Creek Drive
Babe Carnisek
   1212 W. 23rd
Jake Williams
   2182 Bronson

The father thing has caused me a lot of discomfort late at night when thoughts range out of control. As a kid, I used to make up scenes where my real father was a famous baseball player or a CIA spy or something—anything, so long as he had an excuse to deny me up until the point of my daydream.

"I was being chased by the Mafia, son, and if anyone found out I had a boy, you would have been in the gravest danger."

"I understand, Dad."

In school when I should have been studying geography, I drew pictures of Dad. Mostly he looked like Moose Skowron who played first base for the New York Yankees. Sometimes he looked like John Kennedy.

But then Lydia spilled the beans about the group rape thing, and I had to face the fact that I am a child of violence. When I first started writing stories, I wrote the scene over and over.

"Try this on for size, you slimy slut," the quarterback growled as he shoved his throbbing missile into Mom's pubic mound.

"Smack her again," laughed the tackle. *"Make her beg."*

"Let's hold her nose and pour more vodka down her throat," the black guy said as he unleashed a gush of sperm into Mom's hair.

I wrote a thirty-page version of the evening that ended with Lydia near death, crawling through vomit and come into the bathroom where she passed out with her fingers reaching for the spermicidal jelly.

Maurey says the truth about my roots is why I hate men.

"I don't hate men. I just don't trust the dirtbags."

19

"Face it, Sam, you're a male-aphobe."

"If I hate men, then I hate myself."

"That's the point, dildo."

My own mother claims I'm a latent homosexual. "All men who can't stand men are denying their sexuality," she said. "The thought that you're queer makes you sick, so you deny it by overreacting. Why don't you behave like Petey Pierce and let the door swing whichever way it swings."

"I'm not gay, Lydia. If I was, I'd say so."

"No, you wouldn't."

My personal theory is I'm a Lesbian trapped in the body of a man.

Let's analyze this deal: I am alive because of a monstrous crime. I enjoy being alive. I wouldn't want it any other way. Which means I must be pleased these high school prick football players got Lydia drunk and forced their penises into her fourteen-year-old body. I must be pleased they stood in a circle and peed on her bloody, torn crotch.

Following this logic, whenever I think of the rape, which is all the time, I can't stand myself for being pleased it happened and I'm alive. I can't stand men for the physical power they possess over little girls. Therefore, I avoid contact with the male sex and I cannot resist giving oral orgasms to women, generally low-class women, although my standards vary with availability.

I popped open a Dr Pepper and wandered the house without energy, room to room, looking at the corners where the walls and floor came together. My grandfather, Caspar Callahan, had been semi-old New York money, and when he met and wed Lucille Weathers, semi-new Durham money, he founded the Caspar Callahan Carbon Paper Company and built the rich Yankees' dream of an in-town plantation home. Not a scrap of carpeting in the house. Painting from the Sir Walter Scott school of chivalry. Natural-wood chiffoniers and hutches and a Lincoln rocker I wasn't allowed to sit in that must have been as old as Lincoln himself. The library was full of bound books I hadn't read and a very large globe of the world as it appeared in 1948. The den was filled with paperback books I had read and a stereo system that could vibrate the columns out front.

The only major change I'd made downstairs in the fifteen years since Caspar's death was to convert the salon into a home gym, with Nautilus equipment, a climbing wall, and a Sears Exercycle 6000 that faced the Charlie Russell painting of Indians killing a buffalo killing an Indian.

It's odd owning a house, especially a big son-of-a-bitching house like mine. You tend to think in terms of *my stuff*. Those Chinese paper trees on the wall are *mine*. The glass-fronted gun case without guns in it is *mine*. After a while you think you deserve this stuff.

From day one Caspar viewed my mother as a pretty little lame-brain—the traditional Southern attitude toward rich girls. Lydia balked at the genteel lamebrain mold, opting for the rebellious lamebrain, which meant fighting Caspar night and day and entering numerous self-destructive scenarios simply to prove he couldn't stop her from self-destructive scenarios. So, when the strokes finally nailed Caspar, he left me the house, the money, and the carbon paper company—which I almost instantly turned into the Callahan Magic Golf Cart Company. Caspar also left me the game of trying to control Lydia by controlling her cash flow. Pissed Lydia off no end.

Upstairs are eight bedrooms and four and a half bathrooms. I opened and closed the doors of each one, just to see if someone I didn't know was living with me. It could happen. Shannon has a way of bringing home lost pets and people. Takes after her mom, although Shannon specializes in out-of-work blues musicians, where Maurey mostly takes in drunks.

The last door on the left side of the north hallway was Wanda's private sanctuary, where I'd been forbidden to set foot the last year. Maybe that room was the one I'd intended to explore all along, and the others were just circling the subject. When she first moved in, Wanda insisted on a space. Her word. She'd seen the cover of Virginia Woolf's book in the den and decided a room of her own was the strong woman's due. Wanda had gone out and charged various decorative items, including a wet bar, a Smith-Corona typewriter, a two-drawer file cabinet, and a Stanley padlock, and hauled everything into the room I used as a fort when I was growing up.

She claimed to write in there, but I don't know, as I saw nothing she ever wrote. That's how we met—at a writer's conference on Okrakoke Island. I was the token Young Adult sports action novelist, and she gave me grief for not being Saul Bellow.

I was sitting in the bar, discussing minor league baseball with a sci-fi writer from Montana, who, like me, was waiting to get laid. Writing conferences have a sexual pecking order: The poets and agents are chosen first, followed by serious artists with vision, followed by writers who actually make money. Us genre guys must wait for what's left, which often means the first two days are spent drinking and watching ESPN in the bar.

A short woman with jet black hair and soft cheekbones shouldered in between me and the sci-fi writer. "I heard you at the panel discussion today. You wrote *Bucky Climbs the Matterhorn.*"

I shrugged and stayed neutral. The panel subject had been "Commitment of the Writer," and I didn't consider myself an expert on commitment. Whenever the moderator called on me I quoted Günter Grass.

She picked up my glass and took a drink. "Why waste your time on drivel? Why write if you aren't serious?"

I was impressed how she didn't ask before stealing my drink. And I liked her lack of cleavage. The last woman I'd involved myself with was tall with mazumbas you could smother between. I'm always drawn to what the last one wasn't. "Have you ever read *Bucky Climbs the Matterhorn*?"

"I only read literature."

"How do you know it isn't serious just because my book is demographically aimed at fourteen-year-olds reading at a sixth-grade level?"

"No book *aimed* at an audience is honest."

I looked over at the sci-fi writer, who raised an eyebrow in her direction. I don't know why Wanda didn't choose him. He had a three-book contract with a possible movie tie-in.

"Are you a writer?" I asked, knowing the answer. Everyone in North Carolina is a writer.

Wanda clicked down my drink and glared fiercely into my eyes. "You better not hurt me."

"I haven't hurt anyone yet. No reason to think I'll start with you."

"When I give myself, it's total. I believe in taking risks and putting my ego-center out there on the line."

"I admire your frankness."

"Honesty is all that matters. I won't accept the hidden agenda."

"My agenda is visible."

"Sure."

The Montana writer excused himself and went to the bathroom. Wanda and I spent the next two days eating room service food off each other's genitals.

The lock was putty to the man with a Swiss Army knife. Two screws in the door and two in the door frame and here's the lock in my hand. The first thing I noticed inside was a twin bed covered by my grandmother's quilt. A bed hadn't been among the charged items when Wanda outfitted her writer's sanctuary.

The rolltop desk and typewriter sat in a film of dust. Left of the typewriter, a ream of paper collected its own evidence of non-use. On the right, a single sheet had been typed on: **My heart screams into the black Void of an uncaring Universe.** Not a bad start. A number of possibilities leapt to mind for a second sentence. Piles of *Cosmopolitan* magazines and *National Star* newspapers lay scattered on the floor, the *Cosmo* covers more breast obsessed than *Playboy* ever was, the *Star*s announcing miracle diets, ugly behavior by the famous, and bizarre copulations between aliens and lower-middle-income children. The *Star* on the bed, which must have been the last one Wanda read, featured a pair of New Jersey twins who had sex in their mother's womb and the little girl twin was born pregnant.

The top file cabinet held a half-smoked pack of Chesterfields and two empty peppermint schnapps bottles. Wanda smoked Virginia Slims. I thought of her face. She had these tiny creases of dimples that you wouldn't notice except when she laughed. Her chest was freckle laden down to the top of her bathing suit. Below that line she was white as a kitchen sink. Her pubic hair had been eight ball black and only slightly wavy, not curly like other women I'd known. Six months ago she'd shaved herself down there. Said it made her feel cleaner.

In the bottom drawer of the file cabinet I found a litter of used condoms. They lay amongst the colored cellophane of their torn wrappers. Some had leaked come out the top onto the dark green of the drawer. Others were tied off at the mouth, like balloons.

I closed the drawer quietly, walked over to the bed, and sat, facing the wall. She'd hand lettered meaningful quotes from writers and tacked them up at eye level.

> The one way of tolerating existence is to lose oneself
> in literature as in a personal orgy.
>
> FLAUBERT

> We need myths to get by.
>
> ROBERT COOVER

> Writing is turning one's worst moments into money.
>
> J. P. DONLEAVY

What did this intellectual dither have to do with screwing the pool man and God knows who else in my family's home?

I worked open the window and looked down on my backyard, with its magnolias and Georgia hackberry trees sloping to the liver-shaped pool that I would probably never swim in again. The worst of it all was they stood in a circle and urinated on her. What was that supposed to signify?

I lifted Wanda's Smith-Corona and carried it to the windowsill, where it balanced, keys facing inward. Ever since the third grade, when Lydia gave me her Royal portable, typewriters have been my sacred objects, magic machines that produce beauty a thousand times greater than the sum of their parts. A typewriter can actually give birth.

"Sayonara," I said, then I pushed her out the window. She bounced off the roof of the screened-in veranda, broke into two sections, and

24

tumbled down the sloping lawn, coming to a rest in the grass, well short of the swimming pool.

My own room had wagon-wheel lamps, a Two Grey Hills Navajo rug, a Molesworth desk, and twin antelope heads mounted on the wall. I lay on top of the Hudson Bay four-stripe bedspread with my shoes on and stared at the ceiling. I thought about baseball for ten minutes— the '59 Dodgers, my favorite team of all time—then I rolled over and telephoned Lydia.

Hank answered, which was out of the ordinary. He's usually out at the ranch, irrigating and pulling calves.

"Your mother is in jail," he said.

Why wasn't I surprised? "Who did Lydia kill?"

"She threatened the President's dog."

Lydia blamed Republicans for everything from urban blight to fluoride in skimmed milk, and she'd never bonded with dogs, but this was beyond cranky feminism.

"Ronald Reagan's dog," Hank added unnecessarily. "His name is Rex. She sent a telegram saying if Reagan didn't appoint a female attorney general, she would assassinate Rex."

I looked from one antelope head to the other. As a teenager, I'd written a short story in which my antelopes' eyes hid cameras that recorded Lydia's movements for a team of former Nazi scientists studying defective frontal lobes in white mothers. An editor at *The New Yorker* rejected the story with a personal note saying I lacked subtlety.

"Is anyone working on getting her out?" I asked.

"Maurey won't lift a finger—says a woman who threatens dogs deserves prison. Pud and I performed a ghost dance last night."

"I mean bail. Lawyers. Reality."

Hank made a deep chuckle sound. He and Lydia have been a couple for twenty years, a relationship held together by Hank taking whatever Lydia says or does as humor.

"They'd let her out on her own recognizance," Hank said, "but she won't go."

"Because Thoreau refused to leave jail?"

"Because the women's cell has a black-and-white TV and the men's is color. Lydia organized a sisters hunger strike for equality."

Here's a problem I could deal with. There are so few, I like to jump on them when I can. "Look, Hank, call Sheriff Potter, tell him I'll donate a color TV to the women's cell."

"Lydia will claim you cheated."

"For God's sake, don't tell her."

4

I telephoned Dyn-o-Mite Novelty Co. and ordered a custom bumper sticker that read AS GOD IS MY WITNESS, I'LL NEVER BE MONOGAMOUS AGAIN. Then I extracted Wanda's Dodge Dart from the garage full of golf carts. Wanda took my Datsun 240Z. She said I owed it to her.

"It's the least you can do after everything I gave up to support your vapid dreams the last fourteen months," she said.

"What did you give up?"

Wanda tossed me a look of intense pity and sped off into the Carolina humidity.

I drove the Dart up Wendover Avenue through a high school parking lot to an open-ended football stadium where boys in full uniforms and helmets were running steps. Football practice is what I do whenever I'm worked up over life. I sit at the top of the bleachers and imagine the players raping Lydia. I choose five typical teenage boys and picture them on top of her, behind her, in her mouth. I picture them urinating on her nude body.

The coach stood at the bottom, wearing gym shorts and a cast on his left arm, shouting epithets of failure at the players. I got the idea they'd lost a game the night before and had been sentenced to a Saturday afternoon of running up and down the stadium stairs. The coach called the boys "girls," meaning it as an insult.

A fat kid dripping sweat missed a step going up and fell, barking the holy hell out of his shin. He rolled on his back in intense pain, then sat on a wooden bleacher seat and looked glumly down at his bleeding leg.

The coach threw a wall-eyed hissy fit. Charged up the steps and got right in the kid's face guard and screamed at the top of his lungs.

"You stupid homosexual pussy!" the coach screamed. "You pitiful excuse for whale shit!"

The kid didn't react. Just sat there looking at his leg. If I'd been the fat kid I would have pushed the coach backward down the stairs and broken his other arm.

The coach slapped him. "Look at me when I talk!"

"Hey," I said. I was sitting twenty feet or so away, atop the bleachers. "That's no way to treat a human."

The coach stared up at me. "This is none of your business."

"Touch the kid again and I'll make it my business."

Now the kid was staring like I was a Martian.

The coach's face wrinkled up. "Are you in administration?"

"I'm in humanity and you're impolite. You're an ape."

The fat kid made it upright. "Don't call my dad an ape."

"Your dad?"

"He yells because I deserve it."

My eyes passed between the two. There was a nasal resemblance. "You're his father?" I asked.

The coach beamed with pride. "I don't show no favoritism."

A funeral procession blocked the intersection at Battleground Avenue, so I turned off my engine and waited. The cars were all big, new, and American, except for a couple of Mercedes being driven by women. I have a religious belief that dead people can read nearby minds for four days after they die, which means I'm careful at funerals. If this dead person was reading my mind as the hearse drove by, he or she, or by now it, I suppose, overheard some pretty confusing thought processes.

I was parked next to a Christian bookstore with a Kinko's copy shop on one side and a Baskin-Robbins ice-cream parlor on the other. Two pregnant teenagers sat on a bench in front of Baskin-Robbins, eating goop out of banana split boats. We're talking third trimester here—beached whales.

I turned right into the Baskin-Robbins parking lot but missed the drive and jumped the curb and knocked off my muffler, which caused the girls to burst into spontaneous giggles and the Dart to roar like a sick lawn mower.

As I retrieved the bent muffler, one of the girls said, "We oughtta call the Mothers Against Drunk Driving hot line."

The other one stopped her spoon in midair to check me for signs of drunkenness. "We're not mothers yet."

"I'm still against drunk driving. Have been for over four months."

They were both short and gave the impression they had been chubby well before pregnancy. They had silver hair with black roots and dimples at the elbows that winked as they spooned triple sundaes. The only difference was complexion—the girl against drunk driving was pink and the other one came off as a dull bamboo color.

"I'm not drunk," I said.

This made the girls laugh, and I liked them immediately. For being so large, they seemed in remarkably good moods.

"If you're not drunk, you got no excuse," the pink one said.

I walked over to the guardrail Baskin-Robbins had put up to keep people from driving through their plate-glass window. "I don't have any excuse."

"What if I'd been standing on that curb," the pale one said. "You'd have hit me and I might have gone into premature labor."

"Shoot, Lynette, I don't know about you, but I'd be happy as a peach to go into premature labor."

"*Babs.*"

"I'm tired of being pregnant."

29

I sat on the rail with the muffler in my lap. "Can I ask you a question?"

The girls spooned ice cream and considered how to deal with me. Lynette was eating hot fudge on three various forms of chocolate while Babs had separate toppings—butterscotch, caramel, and something red—on what appeared to be strawberry, butter pecan, and creme de menthe. I immediately critiqued their personalities based on ice-cream choices and decided I'd rather be involved in Babs's problems over Lynette's, but they were both interesting.

"I'll give you each fifty dollars to help me with an ethical dilemma."

"Cash or check?" Babs asked.

"Check, but it's good. Here, look at this."

I talked while they studied my check guarantee card, then me. "You see, there's this decision I have to make where I must choose right over wrong and not doing anything is a decision unto itself. I'm usually real firm about right and wrong, but this time I can't figure out which is which. I'm lost."

"Are you selling insurance?" Babs asked.

"Good Lord, no."

Lynette said, "Insurance agents always start off with that innocent question stuff and before you know it they're in your kitchen."

"Insurance agents don't pay fifty dollars for an answer," I said.

That gave them cause to think. An ambulance blew by on Battleground going the opposite direction the funeral procession had taken.

"Just don't tell Rory," Babs said. I had no idea what that meant, but it seemed like agreement.

I folded both hands on the muffler and tried to figure a way to word the problem. "Let's pretend the fathers of your babies did something awful. They're both no good sons of bitches."

Lynette could relate. "That don't take no pretending. B.B. Swain is the evilest snake in Broward County."

"Great. Now pretend he doesn't know you're pregnant."

That's when I lost Babs. "But Rory knows I'm pregnant. He married me in church."

"Just pretend."

"That's easy for Lynette, but my Rory is an angel. He rubs my feet when I'm tired."

Lynette's lower lip swelled up. "She's so smug about her having a husband and I don't, it makes me want to throw up." She turned on Babs. "It's your fault I'm preggers in the first place."

"Don't blame me. You're the one sold yourself cheap."

"B.B. would have been perfectly happy with a hand job till he heard you going at it like a cat." Lynette made her voice high and trilly. *More, more, I'm ready. I'll do anything for you, Rory.*"

"You should have used protection," I said. I'm big on protection. Some call me promiscuous, but no one calls me a thoughtless lay.

Lynette blinked real fast. "B.B. told me he was impotent."

Babs made a gesture like waving flies off her ice cream. "Never believe anything a boy with a hard-on says."

"That's God's own truth," I said.

Lynette started to sniffle and her eyes glistened up. "Now you got me so sad I'll have to buy another sundae." She stared accusingly at me. "We were having a perfectly nice time till you had to jump the curb."

Babs said, "Yeah."

"Let's make it an even hundred. Each."

Babs put her arm around Lynette. It took a minute, but Lynette finally made a sound like sucking tears back into herself and said, "Okay. We're pretending our babies have rotten fathers."

"And the fathers don't know about the babies."

"Why not?" Babs asked.

" 'Cause you never told them."

"That don't make no sense."

"Just pretend."

"This is easier for me than Babs," Lynette said. "I have an imagination."

"I have an imagination too."

"No, you don't."

Trying to talk to two women at once is exponentially harder than trying to talk to one. The nuances go on forever.

I interrupted. "Now pretend your baby has grown up."

"How old?" Babs asked.

"Thirty-three."

"That's how old Jesus was when he died."

"Hank Williams was thirty."

"Your baby is thirty-three."

They stopped and looked at me funny. "No need to raise your voice," Babs said.

"I'm sorry."

"We're pregnant. Not deaf." I'd heard that before.

"Here's the question."

Lynette tipped her boat so the melted chocolate slop ran to one end. "I thought we'd never get round to the question."

"Should your baby who is thirty-three reveal himself or herself to his or her father?"

Lynette slurped down the goop while Babs screwed her mouth into a thoughtful line. I was charmed by them both.

"That is a question," Babs said.

Lynette spoke with a chocolate mustache. "I'd want my baby to beat the tar out of B.B. Swain."

"How about you, Babs?"

"Is your father rich?"

"It's not for me. It's an imaginary person."

That got the girls back into a good mood. Women love to catch a man in a lie.

"Okay, it is me and I don't know if my father is rich or not. The whole deal is complicated."

A light came on in Babs's face. She'd found a way to relate to the problem. "On 'One Life to Live' a boy got hit by a race car and he needed a transfusion and the only person he could get it from was his real daddy." She turned to Lynette. "Remember?"

"He was a blood type only one in a million people have."

"Only his mama had never told anyone, not even his real daddy, who he was."

Lynette jumped in. "So she had to tell and everyone got totally PO'ed and the real daddy's real wife ran off to France with the man who up till that day thought he was the real daddy."

"They were having an affair beforehand," Babs said.

"But the boy died anyway."

"Does that answer your question?"

"Yes."

The drive home was so loud I had to roll up my windows, but then fumes seeped in from under the Dodge and I rolled them down again. People pointed at me. Children stuck fingers in their ears.

I found Gus in the kitchen, listening to the phone. From her benignly amused expression, I knew who was on the other end.

"Lydia?"

Gus nodded.

"Is she out of jail?"

Gus flared her nostrils, which is a trick I've tried and failed to learn for years. "You be nice to your mama."

"I'm always nice to my mama."

Lydia doesn't say hello. Her way of starting a conversation is to dive in like a hawk on roadkill. "They'll be breaking down the door soon," she said. "Why aren't you here to defend your mother's honor?"

Mother's honor—the classic oxymoron. "Did you tell me everything you know about my fathers?"

"You'd have been so proud, sugar booger. I stood up for women's rights and the male-dominated hierarchy capitulated."

"The TV thing?"

"How'd you know about that?"

"The reason I'm asking about the fathers is Shannon found those photographs you kept hidden in the panty box when I was a kid."

"Sam, you are not listening. Your mother is on the lam. I expect federal agents will crash through the door at any instant."

"Hank said they let you out on your own recognizance."

"That was before they heard about my little social blunder."

I waited. Lydia's social blunders range from minor affronts to major felonies, but what they all have in common is sooner or later they cost me money.

"It's your friend Maurey's fault. Right from the start I said 'Do not trust that Maurey Pierce.' Instability runs in her family."

"Pot calling the kettle black. What'd Maurey do?"

"She tattletaled."

"People over twenty-one don't tattletale. They rat."

"She ratted. I'm an innocent victim, trying in my own meek way to transform the Earth into a better, more feminine planet."

I changed the phone to the other ear. "Are you going to tell me what you did that was so innocent?"

"Nothing. I did nothing."

"Okay, don't tell me." Lydia generally won't release information until someone tells her not to.

"As a joke, I FedEx'ed Rex a poison chew toy."

"Rex, the dog?"

"Hank told Maurey and Maurey called the Secret Service."

I considered the implications—cost times bother times time. "How do you poison a chew toy?"

"Soak it in Raid for two days, then sprinkle on some crushed d-Con."

What could I say? My mother thinks she can improve the world by assassinating famous dogs. "This is all very interesting, Lydia, but about my fathers."

"Forget the phantom fathers, your actual mother needs sympathy. Now."

"Remember when you drove Maurey and me up from Rock Springs after she almost aborted Shannon, you told us this story where Caspar was supposed to come home Christmas Eve, only he didn't, so you invited some boys over for a party and they got drunk and raped you over and over and urinated on you and that's how I was conceived."

There was a long silence, which is weird for Lydia. Lydia abhors silence. "What's the point?" she said.

"What I want to know is, did you know the names of the boys who raped you?"

She didn't answer.

"You told us one was the brother of a school friend," I said, "so you must have known their names."

"God, Sam, it happened over thirty years ago. How am I supposed to remember the names of stoolheads I only met once thirty years ago."

"Those stoolheads are my father. At least, one of them is. I'd think if a boy rapes you and makes you pregnant, his name would stick out in your memory."

Another silence, followed by an impatient exhalation. "Mimi's brother had a silly frat boy kind of name—Sport or Slick, something like that."

"Skip?"

"That's him."

"You told me Mimi's last name was Rotkeillor, but the Skip on Shannon's list is Prescott."

"What are you, Perry Mason? Maybe I mixed up my Mimis. All I remember is he had a syringe he used to shoot vodka into oranges."

"Was another one named William?"

"Why, at your age, are you suddenly obsessed by sperm donors?"

"Shannon looked through old yearbooks and came up with five names and I need to be certain they're correct."

"Why for God's sake?"

I had no answer. "Why didn't you tell me my fathers' names?"

She made a bitter laugh sound. "Hell, Sam, you never asked."

Good point. "I'm asking now."

"There was a Billy. And Jake. A big kid named something like Bubba."

"Babe?"

"That's it."

"How about Cameron?"

"Maybe."

"I have to be sure."

"One of them was named Cameron." She paused. "Sam, what difference can it possibly make now?"

It's my theory that most humans only make two or three decisions in a lifetime. The rest is random luck. At that moment, I made a decision.

"Lydia," I said, "it's time I met Dad."

5

Saturday morning I fell into a clitoral fantasy at Tex and Shirley's Pancake House. Over cheese blintzes I discovered Linda Ronstadt sitting next to me while my hand under the table dipped into her silken panties. As I rubbed lightly, side to side across the top, Linda lifted a section of orange to her mouth and with dainty teeth bit off the very tip. Drops of orange juice sprayed across the fine fuzz on her upper lip. A low, Spanish moan rose from her breasts. I went into my world-renowned fingertip figure-eight maneuver.

"More coffee?"

"Sure."

"I'll bring your check." I hate reality. There's nothing so deflating as a waitress pulling the plug on a daydream. It's almost worse than not finishing the real thing.

Linda Ronstadt has been a regular part of my erotic imagery for almost twenty years, and she only grows sweeter as the time passes. I take pride in my loyalty toward dream lovers. No jumping from rock star to movie star to cover girl for me. What I do is find an unknown, a starlet on the brink of fame, so I can be the first before every college kid with five fingers and a jar of Vaseline claims a piece of the action. This might be another revolt against my gang-bang heritage.

After the waitress cleared breakfast, I spread a street map of Greensboro on the table and drew five Magic Marker stars on the addresses of the five fathers. High school sports heroes, as a rule, don't wander. It's the big fish–little pond syndrome; once you get used to being treated like you matter, it's hard to uproot and move somewhere where you don't.

After I added one more star for my own Manor House, the pattern on the map was not unlike the six stars on the front of a Subaru. Skip Prescott and Cameron Saunders lived next door to each other in the Starmount Forest development, which surrounded the Starmount Country Club—home of the Bull Run model golf cart—and meant big money.

William Gaines was just off the west edge of Starmount Forest, not three blocks from Tex and Shirley's Pancake House. It was a sharp edge, cashwise, but still respectable enough to mean his life hadn't been a bust. Babe Carnisek lived south of downtown. Men in his neighborhood drove American pickup trucks sporting South-Shall-Rise-Again bumper stickers and worked by the hour for people they didn't like. A number of my golf cart welders came from West 23rd.

Jake Williams's star sat dead center of a black neighborhood I'd never actually driven through, although not so much because it had a reputation as dangerous. The area just hadn't come up.

Time to move. I wished I could arrive in my 240Z, or at least a Dodge Dart with a muffler, but some days you've got to take action now, to hell with the conditions. You wait for conditions to be right and nobody'd ever do anything. Twenty years after first hearing of my fathers, I was finally going to meet them. As Shannon said—more than once—the night before, it was about damn time.

A man with glasses was kneeling in a garden in the side yard of 147 North Glenwood. The man didn't look like a rapist. Rapists don't garden. The house was one of those two-story red brick jobs that sprang up like hives across the South after World War II. A screened-in porch ran the width of the front, through which I could make out a figure at a table.

As I climbed out of the Dart, the man in the garden looked over and waved. I waved back and walked up the crushed rock walkway to the front door. The whole scene felt domestic, as regular as hell. When I knocked on the screen door, a tenor voice barked. "What?"

Inside the porch, a teenage boy sat at a card table, writing furiously in a store-bought journal. As I slid through the door, his face kind of jumped out. He stared at me with anger and said, "Nothing can happen more beautiful than death."

I said, "Walt Whitman."

He said, "Nine out of ten men are suicides."

I said, "Benjamin Franklin—*Poor Richard's Almanac.* You're going to have to do better than that to beat me at death quotes. When I was your age, I knew them all by heart."

The boy was dressed in black. He stared at me with what I took as a tragic sneer. His neck had the rose speckle of recently cleared-up acne.

"Don't worry," I said. "You'll get over it."

"Are you here to fix the freezer?"

I tried reading his journal upside down, but all I made out was his name—Clark Gaines—in the top left corner and the word PUTRID, underlined three times.

The boy's forehead puckered into a series of folds. "I'm dying. Did you know I'm dying?"

"I hope it's nothing genetic."

Obviously not the response he'd hoped for. "Genetic?"

"Inherited. I hope you didn't inherit whatever you're dying from."

"What difference does it make what anyone dies from? I'm dying, you're dying, the whole planet is rotting like a dead cat's eyes gorged with tiny white worms."

I saw the picture. "Then you're dying as in 'We are all dying every day.' You're not dying as in knowing when or how."

39

"Do you realize all the humans on Earth are loose excrement, including you?"

There's nothing sadder than a Southern male poet. "This is a stage, Clark. Someday you'll grow out of it and look back and gag that you were ever like this."

"Who are you to say I'll outgrow death?"

Who indeed? But I considered myself an adult, and one of the duties of an adult is to tell the young that when they grow up they won't be miserable anymore.

Time to bring the conversation back to my mission. "William Gaines?"

The boy nodded toward the man in the side yard. "Saint Billy is tending his garden."

"Why is he Saint Billy?"

"Old Billy Butch believes we live in the best of all possible worlds. Religion to him is garden tomatoes and calling his mother Miss Ellie. The sap would be hilarious if he wasn't my father. Have you read *Nausea* by Jean Paul Sartre?"

"When I was considerably younger than you are now."

The kid seemed surprised. "Then why haven't you experienced suicide?"

"Sartre didn't know his ass from an avocado."

Clark's forehead rippled like he expected me to hit him. Or wanted me to. I swear, tears appeared in his pained eyes. I decided it was time to talk to Saint Billy.

He had a face like Dennis the Menace's father—the TV show, not the funny papers. He wore cotton gloves and sturdy shoes that L.L. Bean makes especially for people who work in dirt. As I approached, he stood up with a small spade in his right hand.

"Thank God," he said.

"Why?"

"You're here for the freezer."

I didn't say anything. There's an awkwardness to telling a man he may or may not be your father. What if he tried to hug me?

Billy said, "Come on, then," and pulling his gloves off as he walked, he led me around the house. I watched him for signs of me. He was thin, like I am, but also tall, wore glasses, and had straight hair—no matches. Billy probably wasn't the one, and, if so, did I have the right to bring back an act of violence from years ago? Maybe I should fix his freezer and go home.

"Two days ago when Daphne opened the lid, it made a whistle sound and the motor quit," he said. "We've kept it closed since, but goods are beginning to thaw."

We stepped into the back utility room, which held wasp repellent, used flower pots, a washer and dryer, and a chest-type freezer, what grocers call a coffin case. Billy stood looking at the freezer as if something might happen, then, after a short pause, he opened the top and a wave of warm air drifted into my face. Fish—the warm air carried fish and a hint of spoiled milk. In the freezer, rows of butcher-papered and neatly labeled foods leaked on each other.

"I did not come to fix your freezer."

He looked up from his soft fish. "I'm losing a lot of meat here."

"Do you remember a girl named Lydia Callahan? You knew her in high school."

He folded his gloves and stuffed them into his back pocket. "No, I don't recall a Lydia Callahan."

I counted to three and jumped in. "Lydia is my mother. She says you and four other boys had group sex with her on Christmas Eve 1949." I couldn't bring myself to say *rape.* "I was born nine months later, so there's a five-to-one chance you fathered me."

Silence. Billy's facial color dropped a shade, but other than that I saw no physical reaction. He blinked a couple of times, watching me.

"That night was an unfortunate mistake," he said.

"For everyone but me."

Billy took off his glasses and looked down at them in his hands. "I shouldn't have been there."

Sometimes it's best to shut up. Billy seemed lost in memory, not really seeing me or the open freezer or anything. I suppose he was reliving the ugliness, wishing he could change the past. I suppose.

"Have you told the others yet?" Billy asked.

The door to the house was open and I couldn't help but wonder if Clark had slipped in to listen. "You're the first."

"Mr. Prescott isn't going to like this."

"Skip Prescott?"

He nodded. "He owns Dixieland Sporting Goods. I'm in charge of footwear."

"Why should Skip Prescott not like this any more than the rest of you?"

Billy turned to face outdoors. It was a nice backyard—magnolia tree, wicker swing, brick barbecue. He took good care of his stuff.

"What do you expect me to do now?" he asked.

"I don't know. How do you feel?"

"How am I supposed to feel?"

"A possible son has appeared from nowhere. That should make you feel something."

He blinked twice more. "I already have a son."

"I met him. He seems interesting."

"Clark is a sensitive boy." He let it go at that. "What's your name?"

"Sam Callahan."

"What do you do?"

Interesting question. "I make golf carts."

We fell back into silence and mutual staring at the melted meat in the freezer instead of each other.

"Maybe we should have lunch or something," Billy said.

"Or something."

"How is your mother?"

"Lydia runs a feminist press in Wyoming."

He blinked some more. I tried to picture Billy Gaines battering his dick into Lydia, but the image wouldn't come. I wasn't angry at this man. I'd expected to feel wrath or revulsion, maybe even honest hatred, but all I felt was sorry to have bothered him.

"If I was you I'd throw out the fish and pack ice around the rest," I said.

Billy seemed to wake up. He put his glasses back on and turned to look at me. "I suppose you're right."

I walked back around the house, past the screened-in porch, and on to the Dart. At the Dart I turned to see Clark, standing behind the screen with his arms crossed over his chest. I couldn't see his face, but I imagined he was thinking about death.

6

The Prescott house was this fairly large, white monstrosity loaded with balconies and gables and triangular windows way up on the third floor. If they gave a test measuring tastes of the well-to-do, I guess we'd all fail, but at least I know I have bad tastes and don't buy anything without the counsel of women. Skip must have designed his house after a tour of Southern train stations.

I went up the steps, rang the doorbell, and waited, watching the automatic sprinkler system drench the lawn; but no footsteps sounded inside. No imposing butler laid open the door. I rang some more, and after a while a severe black woman in a white uniform came out on the second-floor balcony to glare down at me. I asked a couple of questions on the lines of "Is anyone home?" but she wouldn't speak. Normally when I see a new woman I imagine how she would taste and how she would sound when she came, but this woman had a posture that nipped fiction right in the bud.

The house next door was also Deep South gaudy, but at least the place looked lived in. A volleyball net was stretched across the freshly mowed lawn, and a kid's Sting-ray bicycle leaned against a flower box with some late violets or pansies or something in it. Purple flowers anyway.

The door was answered by a short person in an Extra Terrestrial costume.

"Get lost," he said.

"Phone home," I said. I knew he was E.T. and E.T. said "Phone home" because the last night Wanda and I made love was the night we drove to Carolina Circle Mall and saw *E.T.*, the movie. That was two months before she ran off with the pool man, my 240Z, and Me Maw's jewelry. I, personally, had been sexually dormant the full two months before and six days after she left. I should have known Wanda couldn't go that long without a salami.

The boy looked behind me at the Dart. "You're a Jehovah's Witness," he said.

"No, I'm not."

He yelled *"Mom,"* then ran down a hall and disappeared, leaving me at the open door. Taking this as an invitation, I walked on in and followed down the hall. One door opened on a formal parlor, the kind of room no one enters except to dust once a month. In the Old South, when you died they stuck the open casket up on sawhorses in rooms like this and left you overnight while the women and darkies cried and the men drank whiskey.

The other door opened on two women sitting on a couch, drinking General Foods International instant coffee.

"You're not a Jehovah's Witness."

"No, ma'am."

"Don't call us *ma'am*, darlin'," the other woman said. "If you're not a Witness, who are you?"

"Sam Callahan." The women were dressed country club casual—expensive golf shirts, white shorts, and tennis shoes. The one who'd spoken first had red painted fingernails. The little one who'd called me *darlin'* had a big diamond on a chain around her neck and her hair in a ponytail.

She had the challenging steel-gray eyes of a woman who rates herself by her allure. "Are you the mystery boy Billy Gaines tele-phoned all in a dither about? He described you as much younger."

"I'm surprised to hear he was in a dither."

She leaned her compact body toward me. "Billy said not to talk to you until Skip has a go, but Skippy and I live next door, so why come here if you want Skippy?"

She would probably talk through the entire orgasm—*No. Yes. Oh, God. Yes. Yes.* I don't care much for women who talk and come at the same time.

"You're Mrs. Prescott?"

"Katrina to you. This is Mimi Saunders."

Mimi said, "Katrina, I see no call to flirt with the young man." Mimi had a really long neck and her hair in a bun. I hate to be mean, but she didn't strike me as a woman who has orgasms.

"I'm not flirting." Katrina drilled in with the eye contact. "Am I flirting with you?"

"I'm not good at recognizing flirting when it happens."

"Well, this isn't flirting. I'll tell you when I start to flirt."

Both my hands slid into my pockets. "Thank you."

"Now sit and tell us why we can't talk to you until Skippy gets first go."

Mimi set her coffee cup down with a click. "He didn't even present his card. If we're not supposed to talk to him, I don't think we should."

"Oh, hogwash, Mimi. If it's something Billy Gaines doesn't want us to know, of course we've got to find out. It's our job."

I sat on an ottoman footrest with my hands still in my pockets. The women watched, relaxed in their upper-crust lives. Mimi wasn't certain she wanted me rocking the boat, but Katrina was bored silly by the privileged life and dying for anything to happen. You can tell these things if you've spent any sober time around men's wives.

Katrina studied me. "I don't suppose you're a Mafia debt collector out to break Skippy's legs?"

"No." I stopped myself on the edge of *ma'am.*

"One can only hope." She looked disappointed and reached for the coffee box on the glass-topped table, through which I could see her legs crossed demurely at the ankles. A lot of time and money had gone into those legs.

She stared at the box. "Must be a dark, disgusting secret from the past then. I always knew Skippy was hiding his shame."

"Yes."

Mimi inhaled and raised one hand while Katrina held her breath and lowered both hands. I clarified. "Except I doubt Skippy is hiding the shame from you because I doubt he knows."

Katrina's face broke into a smile. "This is great."

"It is no such thing," Mimi said. "He's a shyster, Katrina. Look at that silly grin. Pretty soon he's going to ask for money."

"No, I'm not," I said.

Katrina slid toward me on the couch, which made her shorts ride up. "Tell us the secret this minute or Mimi and I shall take you down on the floor and torture you."

I decided she was a fireball. Certain somewhat small women are fireballs and they make me nervous. Being tortured by this particular fireball might be interesting—or if she was my stepmother it could spill over into weird—but I didn't see any reason to keep secrets. I mean, the men raped Lydia. If fallout came from exposure, I sure wasn't the one to stop it.

I tried to meet her eyes. "Mr. Gaines, Mr. Saunders, and Mr. Prescott were part of five football players who, uh, had group sex with my mother and created me."

A girl appeared in the doorway that led to a back patio type place. She was tall, big boned, and in her early twenties. I couldn't tell you how she would sound, but I knew she tasted like lemon meringue pie.

"I'm headed for the pool, Mom," she said. She had light blond hair, which I don't normally go for, and wore a white terry-cloth robe open at the middle to show a sky blue one-piece bathing suit.

I turned to see which woman she was calling *Mom*. The girl looked at Mimi, who had her lips puckered as if she'd eaten something rotten.

"What's wrong?" the girl asked.

Katrina recovered first. "This boy says he's your half brother, Gilia."

"Might be," I corrected. "The odds are one out of five."

Gilia studied me with frank, blue eyes. Shannon could pull off that honest yet wanting nothing look. Must be an attitude the new generation of women developed because I don't remember it from my day.

She said, "I didn't know Daddy was married before."

Mimi made a choked sound. "He wasn't. It's a scandalous lie. This villain has come to destroy our home."

I said, "That's a classic overreaction, Mrs. Saunders. I'm not here to affect your home in any way."

Her face was awful. The woman had lost all reserve. "How dare you make accusations at Cameron. My husband is an honorable gentleman."

"I'm sorry, Mrs. Saunders."

Katrina suddenly stood up. "Don't be sorry. Skip has a scandal coming. That pinhead's been dipping his wick ever since I married him."

I glanced over at Gilia. She stood uncommitted as a fence post.

"I don't see any call for scandal," I said.

Katrina laughed. "I can't wait to see how Mr. Wheeler-Dealer handles this. First, he'll offer you money to change the story." She grabbed my arm. "Don't take it."

"I don't need money."

"Then he'll threaten you with hired violence. Skip's too wimpy to touch you himself."

Mimi's voice was up near hysteria. "Cameron does not dip his wick."

"Oh, he does too," Katrina said.

"And Cameron does not deserve scandal. You. Leave my house this instant."

I stood up from the ottoman, but Katrina didn't release my arm. "I'm sorry to have upset you," I said.

"*Out.*"

Katrina's fingernails dug into my skin. "Don't make him go. I want all the sick, ugly details of how your Cameron and my Skippy soiled this poor boy's mother."

At the word *soiled*, Mimi buried her face in her hands and sobbed. I hadn't expected to have this effect on people. I hadn't thought beyond the fathers and me, but now it sank in that others were involved—innocent strangers who'd never raped anybody.

"I better go," I said.

Gilia looked from her mother to me.

I said, "Nice to have met you."

Her lips parted, but she didn't speak.

"You ain't my kid, you're too scrawny."

Babe Carnisek was big—big as Billy's coffin case. Even leaned back in a recliner with his hands curled in his lap he appeared in the upper-six-foot range and near three hundred pounds. He hadn't gone to fat, either. A well-dinged free-weight set and lift bench filled the gap where the breakfast nook should have been.

"But you did have relations with my mother," I said.

"I humped her, if that's what you mean. I was number two behind that bastard Skip, before she got wore out."

Babe's wife, Didi, came in from the kitchen, carrying three ice teas on an A&W Root Beer tray. "Who got wore out, honey?"

"His ma. A bunch of us screwed this junior high chick and PeeWee here says we got her pregnant. Says I might be his dad." Babe was paying more attention to the Washington-Detroit game on TV than to his wife or me. Washington was up 21–8—not so close a game as should have pulled him away from the possibility of a son.

Didi offered from the tray. "He's too shrimpy, Babe." She put a finger on her chin and studied me like a Food Lion steak. "You couldn't be his father; unless your mama was a midget. Is your mama a midget?"

"No, ma'am. She's about the same height as you."

"I wish you was his boy. Babe always wanted a son, but we cain't have any, on account of the steroids."

"Look at that pussy block," Babe said. "I can block better'n that, without my knees."

Didi sat down from me on the vinyl-covered couch. "Babe had a scholarship to Virginia Commonwealth University, until he ruint both knees playing softball."

The tea had enough sugar to send a horse into diabetic shock. "If you aren't my father, which one do you think is?"

The Detroit quarterback fumbled the snap. "God almighty," Babe said, "I hate quarterbacks. Every ratty little one should be horse-whipped." He looked over at me. "Skip Prescott or the nigger, I imagine. Other than them we're all linemen."

"Billy Gaines was an end."

"Tight end. And high school teams didn't pass much in the fifties. Guilford County ran a T formation with Billy blocking the left side."

"Was he any good?"

Babe snorted. "Billy's blind as a bat. Mostly he stood in people's way."

"So you think it's Skip or Jake."

"I was you I'd hope for the nigger. I'd rather have a nigger daddy than Skip Prescott any day."

"You don't like Mr. Prescott?"

Babe went back to the game, but Didi clucked a couple times and gave the explanation. "Skip hired Babe the first summer out of high school, then said he'd fire him if he didn't play on the Dixieland Sporting Goods softball team."

"And Babe blew his knees," I said.

I looked at Babe, who was pretending to watch the game. But I could tell he was thinking about what might have been.

Didi sipped her tea. She was pretty in a Kmart kind of way. I'll bet she'd never been gone down on in her life. "Then Skip told Babe if he took these blue pills he'd grow strong and be able to play football again."

"Steroids," I said. "I didn't know steroids existed back then."

"We didn't know what they were," Didi said. She gestured at the game. "Now all those players on TV take steroids and not a one of them will ever have children. Babe says if he sees Skip again, he'll break his neck."

"I know where Skip lives."

I think Babe wanted to change the subject, because when he spoke it was louder than before. "Your mama was a pistol, boy. I have to admit, that girl was a pistol."

Seemed a weird thing to say about a girl you raped and urinated on. "She runs a feminist press in Wyoming," I said.

He frowned. "Lesbo?"

"I don't think so, she has a boyfriend."

"Lesbos scare me. They was one in Woolworth's the other day buying shotgun shells. Said she was going to shoot her husband."

"You didn't tell me that," Didi said.

"How did you know she was Lesbian if she had a husband?" I asked.

"Short hair and a fuzzy mustache."

Didi protested. "Italian girls have mustaches and none of them are Lesbo."

"Wasn't no Italian. I can tell Italian women."

Subject closed. We sat drinking tea and watching the game while the Redskins scored two more touchdowns. Babe didn't seem to have any more to say about fatherhood. Partway through the third quarter he had Didi fetch his hand squeezer exercise coils so he could watch TV and build up his wrists simultaneously.

"So, you're sure you aren't my father?" I said.

He shrugged without looking away from the game. The Lions were finally mounting a drive. "Hell, anything's possible. Maybe you're just a runt."

"I think I'll be leaving now," I said.

Babe ignored me. Didi took my glass. "Come back any time," she said. "We always have plenty of tea. Babe won't drink beer. Too many former athletes drink beer and let themselves go."

Babe sat in his recliner, flexing his wrists. Lord knows what he did for a living. What does a person whose life is his body do when the body lets him down?

"Good-bye, Mr. Carnisek," I said.

His eyes brightened, as if he'd received an idea. "Tell you what, come Father's Day, you can send me a card."

"I'll do that."

"I always wanted a card on Father's Day."

7

I stopped in my yard to watch a one-legged robin hop around the grass. She seemed as stable as the next robin—didn't tilt to one side or wobble or anything. Reminded me of a three-legged dog a neighbor of ours owned back in GroVont. Next to my pecan tree, the robin pulled a worm out of the ground. It was a long wienie and it didn't want to give up its grasp on the earth, but the robin kept pulling and hopping back on her one leg until the worm popped free. Then she flew off, south.

Since the World Series when Wanda left, I hadn't been seeing past myself. I hadn't noticed how the maple leaves across the street were a deep Mogen David wine color, and the air smelled like refrigeration. The neighbor's black cat lay curled on the hood of their Lincoln Town Car. I saw the girl Gilia in my mind and wondered where she might be swimming, so I could go there and watch. In Wyoming this was swimming temperature, but I figured the country club pool was drained by now. Maybe she was one of those people who takes swimming seriously, as opposed to a social tanning session. She had interesting eyes.

Inside the garage, a Vicksburg golf cart hummed into the plug in the ceiling recharger. Five other models named after Civil War battles were lined up, facing the double doors. I sat on a bucket of pool-cleaning chemicals and stared at the gardening tools mounted on fiberboard on the back wall. Each hoe and hammer sat in brackets and fit into an outline of itself drawn in yellow paint on the board—like the outlines they draw around murder victims found on the sidewalk.

I had no reason for being in the garage, other than I was tired of people. Inside the house, another complicated relationship no doubt waited to be dealt with. Gus, probably, or Shannon demanding information on her grandfathers.

The truth is, meeting never-before-met parents takes a lot of emotion. Less than halfway through the process and I felt drained. Fried. Since then I've learned large cities have support groups for people who thought they knew who they were, then one afternoon a stranger knocks on the door and says *Mother. Dad. Whatever.* I don't know what they call the support groups—Switched At Birth Anonymous, maybe—but I know they exist. One sent me a newsletter.

I found Gus dribbling used coffee grounds into the garbage disposal. The moment she saw me, her index finger crossed her lips in the international sign for *Shhh.*

"San Francisco by fourteen," she said. "Bet on it."

"I don't know any bookies."

"Your loss."

I opened the refrigerator for a Dr Pepper. Dr Pepper is my one remaining degenerative addiction. "Gus, I've read everything I can find on mystic, ju-ju bwana fortune-telling methods, and no legitimate psychic in the country reads the future in coffee grounds put down the garbage disposal."

She shut one thick eyelid and cocked her head over the drain. "My mama taught me, her mama taught her. The spirit ear goes way back to Africa."

"How many generations in your family owned garbage disposals?"

Gus didn't care to answer that one. "Going to be war," she said.

"Me and Wanda?"

Her closed eye popped open. "United States of America."

"I have enough problems this week without a war."

Both eyes closed as Gus concentrated. "Against black people. The brothers and sisters going to fight men disguised as plants."

She obviously meant camouflage suits and I was supposed to go "Wow," but I was too worn out to pretend amazement. So I sat at the kitchen table and drank my Dr Pepper.

"You're just like my friend Hank Elkrunner," I said. "He thinks because he's Blackfeet he has to say *Great Spirit* and bond with birds and stuff. You didn't practice any of this voodoo jive till 'Roots' was on TV."

Gus straightened and turned off the disposal. She glared down at me from on high, doing something with her eyes that increased the intimidation factor beyond the normal housekeeper-boss relationship.

"Shannon tells me pretty soon you be listening to Elmore James yourself."

"You think I might really be black like you, Gus?"

"Not like me. I been black all my life."

Throughout my junior high and high school years a rumor floated around GroVont that my father had been black. I don't know how the rumor got started. It may have been because in 1963 I was the only person in northwest Wyoming who used the term *Afro-American*. Or maybe after Lydia took up with Hank Elkrunner townfolk decided cross-racial sex turned her on.

I must admit, I didn't deny the rumor. At times—around girls—I even hinted that it might be true. This was partly to pique curiosity, but more than mere seduction, I'd seen the photos in Lydia's panty box and I liked the idea of Sam Callahan: outsider.

I would be the wandering poet, scorned by black and white, shunned by all, except certain women of both races who are drawn to danger like a moth to flame.

"You're in trouble," Gus said.

"The disposal picked a football game, predicted a war, and said I'm in trouble? What brand of coffee are we drinking?"

"The phone call say you're in trouble. Man says get your ass over to Starmount Country Club. He says now."

"He say his name?"

"Was a horse's name—Scout."

"Skip."

"How do you know? I'm the one talked to him."

I hate being ordered around by men. Women, I can live with. A woman says *Now*, there's generally a reason. Women deserve consideration bordering on servitude, but bossy men piss me off.

"I hope my father is the black halfback," I said. "These white guys are turning out dips."

"All white guys turn out dips."

"Except me."

She blew air out her nose. "You got no room to brag."

I fixed myself an avocado-and-cream-cheese sandwich because it was well after noon and Gus wouldn't make lunch for anyone who wasn't home at noon on the dot. She was strict with mealtimes—breakfast at eight-thirty, lunch at noon, and supper at six—and I was careless when it came to clocks, so I often had to fix my own meals while my cook stood in the kitchen and glared at me.

Growing up in the Manor House, we had a succession of fifteen or so cooks who represented the vast spectrum of female domestic help. Young, old, and indeterminate, white, black, and mixed vintage, the only thing they had in common was not one got along with Caspar and Lydia. A few managed hatred. The only cook I recall as standing out from the group was a red-haired Irish girl who bathed me when the other grown-ups weren't home.

"Where's Shannon?" I asked.

Gus sat across from me, reading *The New York Times*. I consider anyone not from New York City who reads *The New York Times* ostentatious. Gus and I argue about it weekly.

"Her and Eugene drove up the Blue Ridges to buy a pumpkin."

"Long way to go for vegetables."

"What difference it make to them. They're young."

I can remember being young enough to drive 130 miles, one way, for an ice-cream cone. Maurey and I did that fairly regularly with Shannon back in high school.

"What'd they want with a pumpkin?"

She lowered her paper and gave me the you-idiot look. "Halloween. The one night white folks believe in magic."

"Do you believe in magic, Gus?"

She went back to reading the paper. "Says here porpoises can open those little plastic bags in produce sections at the grocery market. If so, they're smarter than me."

"I saw a boy in a space-man suit today. I wondered why he was dressed like that."

Gus turned the page. "The tramp called on the telephone."

"Is Wanda coming home?"

"You fool."

"What'd she want, then?"

"Money."

"She can't have any. What did you tell her?"

"I couldn't lie. I told her you was comatose."

When a male says *Now*, my tendency is to slow down. I suppose I inherited the trait from Lydia. She's the oldest person I ever met who still falls for the child psychology trick where you say "Don't do such-and-so" when you really want her to do such-and-so. Lydia would jump off a cliff if a man in authority told her not to.

First, I got together a six-pack of canned Dr Peppers, four clamps, and three clothes hangers. I poured the Dr Pepper on the lawn, straightened the hangers, and pulled the busted muffler out of my trunk. Hank Elkrunner taught me this trick. You cut the cans into pipe joints, rig up the muffler with the wire hangers, clamp it all down, and hit the road. Sometimes, I'm almost grateful to Caspar for banishing us to Wyoming. Rural competency comes in handy on Sunday afternoons when you can't solve a problem by throwing cash at it.

After more or less fixing the muffler situation, I drove to a flower shop and ordered flowers for all the women I liked but didn't want to sleep with—six arrangements for the three women who run Callahan Magic Carts, and Gus, Shannon, and Lydia. I sent them rubrum lilies and hydrangea, tulips and gladiolus. Basically cleaned out the place of everything with big blossoms.

I couldn't decide on Maurey. A big part of why our next-of-kin-type relationship works so well is because we got the disgusting things over with early and now we can be open and above sexual tension. That's what she thinks anyway.

Me, I don't know. Most of the time, I buy the buddies deal, and I would never hint at thoughts of lustful affection on my part, but every now and then, late at night, I remembered how sweet she had been and how emotional I felt when I touched her. Maurey was the first. And best. She was the one woman I'd slept with I still loved years later.

When it came to the bottom line, in a nerve-racking moment of self-honesty, I didn't send Maurey flowers. I hoped she wouldn't catch the significance.

Don't you just hate kids who work in country club pro shops? *Hate* may be too strong a word, but they're such elitist slimeballs. American pro shops are nothing but a breeding ground for politicians.

"Skip and Cameron around?"

"Mr. Prescott and Mr. Saunders are on the driving range." He arched an eyebrow and stared down his nose at me. "I doubt if the gentlemen wish to be disturbed."

"Doesn't matter to me what the gentlemen wish."

"Are you a member?"

"Are you kidding?"

I watched for a few minutes from the relative safety of the putting green. The two represented more combative possibilities than Billy or Babe had. For one thing, I'd lost the advantage of surprise. Even the most urbane of men can be knocked off balance by "Hi, I'm the son you never heard of." By breaking the news to their wives, I'd given Skip and Cameron time to work up a stance.

The very tall man swinging an iron would be number 56, Cameron Saunders. He wore rubber cleats, madras slacks, a dark blue windbreaker, and a cap that read DUKE. He also had a grayish-black beard. Hardly any of these country-club-cracker, good-ol'-boy types grow beards. Superiority begets a clean image.

Skip Prescott had a sparrow hawk face. He wore steel cleats and tight tennis shorts over remarkably hairy legs. Rather than addressing the ball, he attacked it, blasting low bullets that shot off a hundred yards or so before slicing into a nearby duck pond. With every chop of his club, Skip grunted *Ugh!*

I walked down to the Bull Run cart that held their golf bags. May as well start the relationships on an upbeat note.

"Hi, Pops."

They stopped in mid–back swing to turn and stare at me. Cameron stooped and picked up his ball, then he walked over and stood next to Skip, whose face was blotchy red.

Skip set the conversational tone. "I ought to wrap this club around your neck."

I spoke to Cameron. "Is he always like this?"

Cameron calmly unbuttoned the golf glove on his right hand. A right-handed golf glove meant a left-handed golfer. His voice was soft, purrlike. "If he feels threatened."

"I'm not threatening anyone."

Skip was bouncing up and down on his toes. "We castrate blackmailers in these parts," he said.

"I'm not blackmailing anyone."

We observed a moment of silence. That's what males do in a power struggle. They've been taught the strong, silent type wins, so they practice competitive silence. I put on Hank Elkrunner's blank face that he says only Indians and people who have been in prison can do. Skip's eyes popped and sizzled in a mad-as-hell mode, but Cameron's were blue ice cubes. Was like facing down a pit bull and a rattlesnake.

"Tell us what you want from us, then I shall bring my resources to bear and crush you," Cameron said quietly.

Skip couldn't wait that long. "Let's crush the punk now. Who cares what he wants."

This wasn't what I expected at all. How could they be so angry? They created me; I never did squat to them.

"What do you want?" Cameron repeated. He was the slick member of the team. The hit man. He looked like a politician. Skip was nothing but aggression and leg hair.

"I only wanted to say hey to my daddies. Get a close-up look at you, give you a close-up look at me."

Cameron crossed his arms over his chest, cradling the iron under his left elbow. "My position is to deny all charges. I told Mimi you are a damned liar, and if you spread this libelous tale to the media or any of our peer group, I shall sue you for every dime you shall ever have."

I said, "I appreciate your position, but it's horse manure."

Skip more or less snarled. "He'll never have a dime. Look at how he's dressed, like a rag picker. Katrina says he drives a piece of junk. This punk ain't nothing."

I leaned one hand against the Bull Run and considered telling them what the Callahan Magic Cart decal on the right front panel stood for—I could have bought their silly sporting goods store and turned it into a 7-Eleven—but I decided that was none of their affair. These guys were totally blowing fatherhood.

"All day long I've been driving around town meeting your peer group," I said, "and Skip, you must be the most unpopular man in the South. None of your friends can stand you. Babe Carnisek is ready to break your neck on sight."

"Babe Carnisek is a loser."

"Your own wife called you a pinhead."

"Don't you dare slander my wife."

I gave up on Skip and returned to Cameron. "This pinhead is your business partner?"

Cameron seemed vaguely amused. "I cannot allow you to frighten my family."

"Look what you did to my family."

Skip produced a checkbook and a Bic. "Let's talk your language, pal."

"I'm not your pal; I'm your son."

"How much to change your story?"

"I hate to be disrespectful, but stick your money in your ear." See how controlled I was, a lesser person would have said *ass*.

"I have associates who could hurt you real bad," Skip said.

With each exchange, our voices grew louder. It had been a while since I'd dealt with a male long enough to argue. The feeling was like I'd separated from myself, as if I were watching TV and in the program at the same time.

"What's the matter with you?" I asked. "You do an awful thing to a little girl thirty-whatever years ago and now you have the scrotums to act like the injured parties."

That shut everyone up for a while. I think Skip was figuring out what *scrotums* meant in this context. Cameron put both hands in the pockets of his windbreaker. He seemed to be figuring repercussions. What I noticed was how pretty the day was—silver-blue sky setting off the sienna red of post oaks lining the fairways. That's my pattern during heightened emotional states—I focus on irrelevant details.

"Would you mind taking off your cap?" I asked Cameron.

He considered refusal, then gave a what-the-hell shrug and took off his DUKE cap.

Just as I suspected. "You're bald," I said. "You're left-handed and edging into fat." I left out tall. "You probably aren't the sperm father anyway."

I couldn't believe the coldness of his eyes. The man could out-Indian Hank Elkrunner. I tried staring him down but lost and had to cover my loss with talk. "But just because you aren't the genetic culprit doesn't mean you aren't morally responsible for what you boys did to Lydia."

Skip blew up. "What *we* did to Lydia. Your mother was a whore."

Time for the dramatic gesture. Lydia didn't teach me much, but she was the queen of the dramatic gesture. I moved up within six inches of Skip's face. "To hell with your associates, Mr. Prescott"—if you say *Prescott* right, spit sprays on the *P*—"either hurt me now or shut your ugly beak."

Skip's blotches spread down his cheeks to his neck and he blinked like a strobe light. I expected him to belt me and us to roll around the driving range grass like grade school ruffians. But Katrina was right—he was a wimp. Thank God.

I snatched the club from his hands, spun around, and walked back to the golf cart. "Here's how we test our steering wheels," I said, and I showed him a trick my sales manager, Ambrosia, taught me. I stuck the club handle through the wheel and wedged it under the instrument panel. Then I bent Skip's golf club into a U.

Skip's eyes went wide at the sacrilege. Cameron smiled.

Time for the tough-guy exit. I threw the ruined club in Skip's direction. "Next time it's your spine, Pops."

Pretty effective. I wish a woman had been there to watch.

8

Gilia Saunders was waiting at my car. She stood, blond in the sunlight, holding a purse-like gym bag on her right arm, wearing a jeans skirt and a short-sleeved shirt with no collar and an alligator over her left breast.

"Men piss me off," I said. "Anything they can't control is a threat."

"You've been talking to Dad," Gilia said.

"Do you think I'm dressed like a rag picker? What the hell is a rag picker?"

She studied me with that non-judgmental look on her face. She had the cheekbones and neck of an Indian. I was real aware that she was an inch or so taller than me, which put her around five eight, tall for a girl. She also had considerably better posture.

"You are dressed casually," she said.

I had on a Wyoming Cowboys T-shirt and button-fly Wranglers. The T-shirt—jeans, too, for that matter—had seen better days. But I was raised to think men who care about what they wear are vain.

She did this shrug thing with her shoulders that made the alligator jump out at me. "I don't mind. I like a man with the confidence to look like a slob at the country club."

Mixed signals here. Was she implying she likes me or I'm a slob? Or both?

"How was your swim?" I asked.

"Two miles of backstroke. Then I came here for lunch, hoping I would run into you."

Holy shit, I was having a non-typical day. "How did you know I was here?"

"Mom told me the men sent you a summons."

"And you were hoping to run into me?"

She nodded, but didn't explain why she was hoping to run into me. She leaned the bag on one hip and stood with her shoulders square to the Dodge. She seemed to expect me to talk, only I couldn't know what to say until I knew why she was here.

To move the conversation along, I said, "Gilia's a flower."

"You got it."

She put a hand on the chrome trim on top of the Dart. Her fingers were long and large boned, like her hips and knees. Four fingernails were shiny perfect—Mary Kay showpieces—but the index finger fingernail was torn short and ragged.

"Could we go somewhere and talk?" she asked. "Dad might see us here. He wouldn't like it."

"You want to talk to me?"

"Why not?"

We got in the car and I drove us to a city park. It was only a block-long grassy place astride a stagnant creek filtering down a weedy ditch. On the far end a couple of unattended children played on a wooden merry-go-round. I parked where we could watch the children but not be expected to run rescue on a skinned knee.

Gilia scooted away and leaned against the far door. "Do you ever feel like you're the only one left speaking the language you speak?" she said. "Everybody in the world knows words you don't know."

I could tell this woman wasn't into small talk. "Sometimes I can't process waitresses or store clerks."

She nodded eagerly. "Exactly. It's like the syllables are jumbled and I've lost the decoder ring."

"I don't understand the relationship here. Am I supposed to treat you like a woman I would enjoy talking to, or a possible sister?"

"Don't you talk to your sister?"

"I never had a sister, although my mom was more a sister than mother."

"I have two brothers."

"Actually, she was more a bad baby-sitter than a sister or mother."

"One of my brothers is Southern macho and the other's a brat."

"I met the brat. He thought I was Jehovah's Witness."

"That's Bob. Ryan is the Southern macho. He lifts weights and watches TV sports and says 'Bitchin' when Mom isn't around. I don't understand how I'm your possible sister. Katrina Prescott didn't explain and Mom wouldn't stop crying, but it seems like either my dad is your dad or he isn't."

"Is your mother Skip Prescott's sister?"

"How'd you know?"

I ran a relationship chart in my head. "That means you might be my sister, but it's just as likely you're my cousin."

"Out with it. What's the deal here?"

I told her the story of Christmas Eve 1949—how Paw Paw Callahan promised he would come home but didn't, so Lydia called her friend Mimi's brother and the boys came over and Skip injected oranges with vodka from a syringe. When I came to the rape, Gilia got real still. Before that, her eyes had been moving, watching the children on the merry-go-round, keeping track of street traffic. At the word *rape* she looked directly at me. I had to meet her eyes or lose credibility.

"Dad pissed on her?"

"That's what Lydia says."

We were quiet a long time after that. She looked down at the floorboards. I could see her jaw, clenching and unclenching beneath the skin. Her hair was very blond, right up to the scalp.

"I don't know Dad well," she said. "They shipped me off to boarding school in the eighth grade. Then I was accepted at Georgetown.

The last four months is the first time I've lived with him since I was a little girl."

"You went to prep school?"

"Boarding school."

"You tied sweaters around your neck and wore shorts with baggy pockets for tennis balls? You played field hockey and compared boys of the Ivy League?"

Gilia almost smiled. "The cheap preppie label comes off after your first divorce."

"You're too young to be divorced."

"There's no such thing as too young to be divorced."

She told me about the art history professor at Georgetown who could order off a French menu and recite Shakespearean sonnets, substituting his own feelings for the final couplet.

"I'd never dated a boy over twenty-one. Jeremy was so forceful when he said Salvador Dali was a no-talent bum."

"You married the guy because he trashed Salvador Dali?"

Gilia's face was amazingly expressive. Watching her was like reading a newspaper; everywhere I looked was a story.

"I guess so. And he was good in bed. I'd never slept with an experienced man before."

I almost told her about Maurey training me to get the girls off every time, but I still wasn't certain of our genetic relationship. It'd been so long since I'd met someone I had anything in common with, the tendency was to suspect shared parentage.

"Why did you get divorced?" I asked.

She gave the shrug I was already fond of. "He was a humanist who believed in situational fidelity. I talked myself into not seeing it until the night he got me in bed with him and a coed bimbo. After that I had to leave."

"But you went through with it the once?"

She shrugged again.

"How did group sex make you feel?" I asked.

"Suicidal."

"No sex is worth suicide."

"To save myself, I stopped thinking and feeling and I slithered

65

home to Mommy and Daddy. Now I shop, swim, and watch network television. Far as I see, that's considered normal here. Everyone in my family stopped thinking and feeling years ago."

A woman in a red Volkswagen bus pulled up at the other end of the park and hollered something at the children on the merry-go-round. They pretended not to hear her. The little boy fell off, picked himself up, and ran to the teeter-totter. He ran up one end of the teeter-totter and made it a couple steps onto the high side before his weight brought it down with a bang. The woman came out of the Volkswagen with her hands on her hips.

"So I went through the motions of behaving the way I was expected to behave," Gilia said. "Recently, I've come to the conclusion that I have nothing in common with anyone I know or will ever know."

"That's a good way to get depressed."

"Tell me about it, Jack. Then one morning when I'm in the depths of numbness, a funny-looking man walks into the family room and announces my solid-to-the-point-of-nauseating father once gang-banged a girl and this funny-looking man may be my brother."

"Funny looking?"

"In a cute way."

"I'm funny looking in a cute way?"

Gilia leaned toward me. "Don't you understand, Sam. You're my wake-up call."

Some people, especially women, put tremendous stock in eye contact. These people, especially women, have the strange notion that by locking their eyes to yours and staring deep into your soul via the cornea and pupil they can detect a mistruth. Or even the smallest hint of insincerity.

Personally, I don't buy the gig. It may work on amateurs and children, but the pros are well aware of the eyeball-to-eyeball test. When she bullshits, Lydia is the queen of sincerity. She'll get up breath-smelling close, gaze solemnly into the sucker's eyes, sometimes even touch his hand with hers, and lie like a dog. Conversely, honesty makes her so uncomfortable that she disguises it behind glib patter. I learned at an early age to distrust her when she tries to tell the truth and believe her when she doesn't.

Hank Elkrunner says the Blackfeet consider it rude to look at a person you are speaking to or a person who is speaking to you. Beyond rude, it just isn't done. I asked him if all Indians practice this custom and received a short but direct diatribe on the white's stupid belief that all Indian tribes are the same.

"I don't know anyone but Blackfeet," Hank said. "You want Apache taboos, call Hollywood."

Gilia obviously did not follow Blackfeet tradition. Her blue eyes bored into me with the intensity of a lunch whistle. Made my stomach flutter and my brain feel like I was inhaling pure oxygen from a tank. She had a way of cocking her head to one side, as if to give herself a new angle on the truth. Suddenly it became very important that she not find me wanting.

When Gilia finally looked away and I was once again able to see the world around us, the two children had disappeared along with the woman in the red Volkswagen bus. A healthy couple rode down the street on bicycles. An older woman in a tweed sweater walked a cat on a leash. It seemed like a long time had passed since Gilia got into my car. I imagined the autumn leaves were redder than they'd been before we locked eyes.

"Why choose today to start popping in on your possible fathers?" she asked.

Why choose today? It'd been twenty years since I learned they existed. I couldn't recall why I hadn't acted earlier.

"My wife left me last week. She ran off with the pool man."

"I'm sorry to hear that."

I shrugged, keeping up a brave front. "I don't handle grief well, so my daughter stole these old yearbook photos Lydia cut out of the boys who did her."

"Your mother knew who raped her?"

"She never told me. Shannon—that's my daughter—went to the library and researched the names and addresses. She thought I would cope better if I had something to do."

Gilia's mouth opened slightly and her pink tongue pressed against her upper front teeth in one of those gestures people do when they're thinking. She said, "You're turning the lives of five men and their families upside down because your daughter thinks you need something to do?"

"That's a harsh way to put it."

"How would you put it?"

I didn't answer. The truth was I hadn't given much thought to the men or their families. I hadn't given much thought to anything. The search for an unknown father seems to be a primal drive. An instinct.

"How do the men react when you appear on their front porch dredging up old sins and claiming to be a son?"

"Billy Gaines wants to do lunch."

"Billy Gaines works for Dad. It's hard to picture him raping a flea."

"Babe Carnisek denies the possibility."

Her head did the cock thing again. "He denies what he did to your mother?"

"No, Babe seems kind of proud of that, which is odd. What he denies is that anyone who looks like me could possibly be related to him. Says I'm too scrawny for his son."

I paused in case Gilia wanted to disagree with *scrawny*. "Your father threatened legal action and Skip Prescott is ready to hire a hit man."

"Why?"

I shrugged again. "They think I want something from them."

"Do you?"

"No."

The woman walking the cat came back from wherever they'd been. She—the woman—was duck toed and wore white sneakers with the kind of hose that only cover the ankles. The cat on the leash was mostly white with black markings. Three feet were white and one black. Like all cats, she reminded me of Alice, which put me dangerously close to depression.

To fight the depression, I looked back at Gilia's face. There was a small freckle or birthmark in that little dimple between the inside of her right eye and the bridge of her nose. I had an almost irresistible urge to touch it. Often I get irresistible urges to commit inappropriate acts, and if I don't mount resistance, the urge can lead to a terrible social blunder.

"You said five guys," Gilia said.

"The fifth was a black halfback named Jake. I haven't spoken to him yet."

Gilia stopped leaning against the door and sat up. "Why did you leave the black one for last?"

"I don't know." Why had I left the black one for last? Ever since I was thirteen and learned I had five possible fathers, I'd had the feeling he was the one. I suppose it came from some romantic notion that I was special—that the world-famous author with the tortured soul would always be an outsider. Different. Unique. I like to feel unique.

"When are you going to see him?" Gilia asked.

"This afternoon, I guess. Might as well hit them all now as later."

She touched my arm, below the elbow. It was the most surprising thing that had happened all day. "Can I come with you?"

"Why would you want to do that?"

Her tongue showed on her teeth again. She sat staring at me until I thought she'd forgotten the question, then she said, "I want to see the process."

"The process?"

"I want to see you when you tell it."

That brought up so many questions I couldn't ask any of them. There was nothing to do but drive the car.

9

The drawback of living in the same place throughout your twenties and early thirties is you can't have a new emotional adventure without being distracted by reminders of past emotional adventures. For example: I once tongue-jobbed an IRS representative on that very wooden merry-go-round where the kids had been playing.

I'd gone into the IRS office to explain why a novelist's entire life should be tax deductible because a novelist's life is the raw material by which he creates his product, and isn't that the definition of a tax-deductible expense? Made sense to me. But this semi-skinny GS-7 with diamond post earrings went bureaucrat on me. She sniffled, shuffled papers, and said in a smarty pants tone that even though Bucky and Samantha hit a movie on their trip to the Matterhorn, I still couldn't deduct all the movies I'd paid for last year.

"I'll just bet you have a sexual fantasy you've never told anyone," I said.

Which is how I ended up on a whirling merry-go-round with my nose between the thighs of an IRS agent. Part of her fantasy was the merry-go-round had to be spinning real fast, so I was pushing like a maniac with my feet on the ground and my face in an awkward position. Her labia were neon purple and the left lip was lots bigger than the right, kind of like a banked turn on a bobsled chute. She tasted like peanut butter. To this day, I get that taste in my mouth whenever I pay income tax.

I drove us across Lee to Freeman Mill Road, past Battery Warehouse, Bill Bailey Tires, Madame Xenia the personal psychic, two Oriental massage parlors with discreet parking in the rear, and Chick's Private Investigations on the second floor above an AME Zion Church. Gilia didn't say anything until we came even with Gillespie Golf Course, which is where Greensboro's black people play.

Most of the black golfers out that day carried their own clubs, although I did see two men smoking cigars in a Gettysburg. The men had on the same ugly-colored pants as the golfers up at Starmount Forest. I have a theory that when stereotypical styles jump from one racial, sexual, or generational group to another, it's the ugly stuff that jumps first.

"Rape is the most terrible crime there is," Gilia said.

I nodded. "Sometimes I can imagine conditions where murder or stealing might be fair, but I can't come up with a justifiable rape."

She crossed her arms under her breasts. "This destroys the father-daughter relationship."

"I'm sorry."

To fill space, I explained how Western civilization sprang from the ancient Roman Empire and the origin of the Roman Empire is dated from the rape of the Sabine women. Therefore our Western civilization was founded on slime and is doomed to rot.

Gilia said, "I can't forgive him."

The block Jake Williams lived on was made up of small off-white houses with mostly green-shingled roofs and unpainted porches. Many of the yards contained flat-tired cars that appeared more as growths from the dirt than modes of movement. A couple of houses had window unit air conditioners. Jake's house was neater than the

71

rest—kept-up lawn and uncracked framing. A glider sat on one end of the porch.

The woman who answered my knock looked from me to Gilia and back. She didn't seem hostile or anything, but if we were salesmen, she definitely didn't want any.

I told her my name and said, "We're looking for Jake Williams."

Her eyes snapped. "What for?"

I glanced over at Gilia who had gone noncommittal. "I'd just like to see him for a minute," I said, "if he's home."

"What are you two up to?" Gus has what you'd call a black accent. When she talks, her voice is husky the way you think of when you think of Billie Holiday. This woman didn't have any of that in her voice. She sounded like a schoolteacher.

"I was hoping to speak to Mr. Williams a moment on personal business."

The woman studied my face, I suppose searching for clues that a swindle was being played. I tried to look innocent.

Finally, she blinked once and spoke. "Mr. Williams passed away."

My stomach felt sick. I looked over at Gilia again. A lock of blond hair had fallen across her cheek; otherwise she hadn't moved.

"I'm sorry to hear that," I said. "When . . ."

Her hand clenched the doorknob. "Thirty years ago last January sixteenth."

"I'm sorry." All that time growing up I might have been an orphan, or half orphan, and I didn't even know it. The woman offered no details, and it didn't seem appropriate to ask.

"I guess we'll be leaving now," I said.

"Wait a minute, you can't do that." Her hand came off the doorknob. "Why did you want to see my Jake?"

I turned toward Gilia. "It's not important. We won't disturb you further."

"Disturb me? You come waltzing up to my door asking to see my husband who's been dead thirty years, and you don't want to disturb me?"

"I'm sorry," I said for the fourth time in as many minutes.

"You are not leaving here until you tell me what this is about."

I looked back at her. "You don't want to know, it would cause you pain."

Her chin lifted. "Well, it's too late for that now, isn't it?"

Gilia finally spoke. "May we come in?"

Inside, the house was dark furniture and soft lighting behind lamp shades. The couch and chairs had lace doilies over the arms. A glass bowl of candy corn sat on the coffee table. The woman crossed to an RCA radio and cut off the classical music that had been so low you could hardly hear it anyway.

Sure enough, she was a schoolteacher. Students' papers lay stacked in graded and ungraded piles on the stained pine dining room table, the graded pile veined by red pencil marks. Jake looked at me from framed photographs atop the piano. Like a campfire in the dark, he drew Gilia and me across the room.

The woman said, "He was killed in Korea."

I picked up a picture of Jake in his army uniform. He was grinning and firing an imaginary tommy gun at someone off to the side of the picture. He looked about fourteen years old with big ears and a short haircut. He wasn't any blacker than Maurey after a summer in the sun.

"Is this the one your mother had?" Gilia touched the frame around Jake's yearbook photo. Number twenty, gray jerscy, leather helmet.

"Yeah."

There was also a wedding picture of both of them dressed up, looking shy and happy and wholesome. The girl held a corsage in her hands. Jake smiled at her, protectively. Knowing Jake would soon die and the girl would be alone made it the saddest picture I'd ever seen.

I turned to look at her. "Would it be personal if I asked your name?"

Her eyes were on Jake. "Atalanta Williams."

I pronounced it like the city the first time and she had to correct me. Then I got it right.

"Atalanta," I said. "That's pretty."

Gilia glanced from the photographs to me. Jake's eyes were different from mine. And the nose. Heck, I don't know if we looked alike. I've always made it a point to avoid mirrors.

"So talk," Atalanta said.

"I'd rather not."

"I didn't ask what you'd rather do."

"You owe it to her," Gilia said.

This wasn't what I wanted. When Shannon had said wreak vengence by destroying their wives, it had sounded good in theory, but the reality sucked.

"Jake may have been my father," I said.

Atalanta took it well. She didn't speak or anything. Just stared at the pictures on the piano. I followed her line of sight to see which one she was staring at. I think it was a five-by-seven head-and-shoulders shot of Jake wearing a coat and tie.

"Five boys had sex with Mom and she got pregnant," I said.

"Was she white?"

"Yes, ma'am."

"What do you mean, 'had sex'?"

I looked at Gilia but she gave no answers. "They raped her."

"It's a lie," Atalanta said.

"I don't think so."

All the years I'd lived in North Carolina, I'd never seen a black woman cry. She made no sound. Nothing but tears and sharp intakes of breath. I looked down between my hands at Jake, wishing he hadn't been there that night. Wishing he wasn't dead and I wasn't born.

"Get out of my home."

"That's fair."

"And put down my picture. You can't touch him."

I put down the picture.

"You are a lying little white boy. How dare you come into my home desecrating the memory of my husband."

"I didn't want to."

"You are trash."

"Yes."

10

T hat house was nothing but one big shrine," Gilia said. "I'll bet you anything Jake left for the army about a month after he married her, when life was still perfect and she hadn't had time to stop worshiping him. It's love cut off at the peak that cripples people, not the long, ugly divorces."

I had been highly confused when we left Atalanta Williams's house, so I drove south a while, then east, then back north, not really aware of where I was going. Having pain is nothing—you live through it and go on—but causing someone else pain is totally unacceptable. I can't stand hurting people. Won't stand hurting people. And, yet—guess what?—I'd just trashed a perfectly nice woman.

Gilia was cool. She seemed to know that movement eases turmoil. After an hour or so of silently circling Greensboro, she suddenly got talkative. Mostly she talked about college days and the busted marriage with Jeremy. She had a story about a roommate sleeping with her boyfriend that was pretty good. Usually when a woman tells the roommate/best friend/sister-slept-with-my-man thing, they're pissed off at the whole female gender. They never seem to blame the guy, but Gilia completely left out the self-pity part of the story.

"Those two sluts deserve each other," she said. "Their biggest problem was who got to face the mirror when they did it."

My fathers didn't come up until Bojangles chicken, where we stopped for a bucket of wings. We sat in the car, chewing bones and sucking grease off our fingers while she gave me the love-cut-off-at-the-peak theory.

"Jesus," I said.

"What?" Gilia had a dribble of barbecue sauce off the left corner of her lips.

"Or Elvis Presley. Or Marilyn Monroe. If any of that bunch had lived past fifty, they'd have been forgotten. Die young if you want worship."

Gilia stuck a wing in her mouth and stripped meat as she pulled out the bone. She ate like a little kid who wants everything at once. I like a woman with an appetite. "So this teacher sat in a dark room for thirty years, mourning her perfect husband, having no life outside his memory, and you come along and smash everything to hell."

"You're the one said I owed her the truth."

"By then it was too late." She took a slug of Mr. Pibb. "You'd said too much to leave her alone with her imagination."

"But the truth was worse than anything she could have imagined."

Gilia sucked her thumb, then examined the nail. "Don't you see, knowing for certain is better than imagining, even when what you know is awful. Imagining makes you doubt your sanity. At least when you know the person you love is a pig, you can get on with the grief process."

"You're talking about Jeremy."

"He had me believing I was clinically paranoid. I'm at the school counselor whining 'I know he's a good man and it's all in my mind' when the jerk is screwing every bimbo on campus, including the school counselor."

I thought about Wanda. Would it have been better to suspect she was a slut but not know, or to know? To tell the truth, I hadn't even suspected. The first I heard about her migratory snatch was when she said I didn't meet her needs and I'd driven her into the arms of another.

"One thing I do know," I said, "is I'm done with fathers. I don't plan on seeing another male relative again. Ever."

"What if they aren't done with you?"

I dipped a corner of my napkin into my 7Up and reached across to blot the barbecue off Gilia's chin. "I am no longer involved."

Fat chance. While we'd been circling the streets of Greensboro, pockets of people affected by my actions had been choosing up attitudes. Not near as many chose passivity as I'd hoped.

The first mistake was not taking Gilia back where I found her. Since the Saunderses lived a half block from the eighteenth fairway, she'd walked to the club, and, in our innocence, it made sense to drop her at home.

Before I even turned off the key, angry hands reached in both doors and yanked us into the open.

"Sonny!" Gilia yelled.

Then, "Ryan, you let go of him!"

A lot of people were shouting at once. The sucker pinning me against my own Dodge ordered Gilia into the house. This had to be the macho brother.

"Let go of him, you little shit!"

I agreed with the shit part, but Ryan wasn't little. Sons of linemen grow up big.

He breathed beer in my face. "Stay away from my sister."

"She's my sister too, jerk."

That set him back a moment. Meanwhile, the goon Gilia had called Sonny came charging around to our side of the action. One look told me here was the spawn of Skippy. Sons of quarterbacks grow up compact and sneaky.

Sonny even had Skip's snarl. "You, mister, are going to take back every lie you said about my dad."

"Forcing me to call the truth a lie won't make it less the truth." Let them work their way through that logic.

Didn't take long. Ryan came back with the tough guys' universal retort. *"Oh, yeah."*

Beyond Ryan's fat shoulder I could see Skip Prescott standing on his own porch. With a drink in his right hand and his left hand sunk in his tennis shorts' pocket, he came off as the slightly amused massah who'd ordered the whipping of a bumptious slave.

"Still afraid to fight your own fights, huh, Daddy?" I called out, which got me a frown from Skip and a jerk forward, hard shove back against the car from Ryan. Behind us, I could hear Gilia begging Cameron to call off the dogs.

Ryan had a jaw big enough to club cattle. "What were you doing with my sister?"

"Communicating."

He didn't like that. The kid wasn't stupid—just big and Southern.

Sonny played cheerleader. "Wipe the pavement with the bastard. Show him never to mess with real men."

I decided to go like-father, like-son. Ryan was calm, yet dangerous; I should turn my attention to Sonny the rat terrier.

"You're no better than your dad," I said. "Our dad. You make threats, then find someone else to carry them out."

"I'll break your neck."

"Either hurt me now or shut your fat face."

Sonny hit me in the gut. As I doubled over, Ryan let go of my shoulders, then teed off on my chin. Gilia screamed. I remember that detail—Gilia screaming.

I made it to the pavement, went fetal, and rode out the pounding. All in all, it was pretty typical of two guys beating the snot out of one guy while a woman goes ballistic in the background. I'd written the scene several times for Young Adult sports fiction, so it was as if I'd been there before.

Lying with my forehead stuck to concrete, part of me disengaged from reality and sat on the hood of the Dodge, taking notes: Sonny goes for the face, Ryan for the kidneys, someone is dragging Gilia into the house. There was more lower back pain and less blood than in the versions I wrote. Otherwise, I'd pretty much nailed the sensation.

Katrina Prescott stood in the middle of the street, less than a block from what I've come to call Sam's Massacre. It's a wonder I didn't run her down, what with being slumped over the steering wheel with blood dribbling in my eyes.

I braked hard and avoided killing her, but Katrina didn't seem to notice the brush with death. Instead, she hopped in the passenger seat and started talking.

"Skip is cruel and abusive. I'm so glad you're driving him nuts; it's a wonderful turn of events."

"Mrs. Prescott, I've had a hard day. I'd just as soon go on home now."

"He forced me to take tennis lessons."

"That is cruel."

"Against my will, he made me get a breast enhancement—silicone. Are you going to drive or not?"

I tried not to look, but, heck, women get silicone implants so you will look. Why is it whenever a woman tells you she's had an implant, she's offended if you look down there?

I shifted into first and moved on up the street. "Couldn't we talk another time, Mrs. Prescott. I have a headache."

"You look awful."

"There's a reason for that."

Katrina didn't want to hear it. "Skip diddles his secretary, he diddles Cameron's secretary, he diddles the jailbait in the shoe department. The one time I had a lover, Skip planted dope in Sean's trailer and called the police."

"I saw that story on 'Dallas.' "

"Before that, Skip gave me syphilis and to this day he accuses me of giving it to him."

"All men do that."

"I hate Skip."

"Everybody hates Skip, Mrs. Prescott. Can I please go home now?"

"Do you believe in phrenology?"

It seemed like I'd passed out and missed a transitional statement. "Telling the future by bumps on someone's head?"

"Phrenology is not fortune-telling. It's the science of character analysis through the study of skull structure."

"My housekeeper hears the future from coffee grounds in the garbage disposal."

Katrina pulled her legs up under herself and sat facing me. "Listen, the skull is made up of twenty-six round enclosures with vacant interspaces. Each enclosure corresponds to a trait, and the larger the enclosure, the more prevalent the trait."

"I'll give you a hundred dollars to get out of my car."

"May I feel your head?"

"Do you have to?"

Katrina clamped her hand on my forehead and let her fingers slowly drift to my eyebrows. She touched the side of my head in what on TV they call the Vulcan death grip. Meanwhile, I turned right twice, trying not to roam too far from Starmount Forest.

"Poor self-esteem," she said. "A disfigured parental love, unconventional sex preferences, no wit whatsoever."

"Don't touch my ears, Mrs. Prescott."

"The benevolence node is prominent. You must be very kind."

"The node wasn't prominent until your son hit me."

"Shush."

I think boredom causes insanity. Look at rich people. Or Southern California where the weather never changes so people go crazy from nothing else to do. Katrina went into a kind of spell with her fingers on my head. Her eyes took on that glaze professional women get when you eat them.

"Now, you feel my head," she said.

"I'd rather not, Mrs. Prescott."

"I felt yours."

Another right turn past a Presbyterian church. "Frankly, whenever I've touched a woman on the head, sooner or later, I go to bed with her, and I don't think that would be a good idea for us."

I glanced over to see how she took this. Many women don't like it if you say you don't want to go to bed with them, even if they don't want to go to bed with you. Sure enough, her lower lip trembled.

"What's the matter?" I asked.

"You don't want to feel my head, you think I'm repulsive."

"I want very much to feel your head, Mrs. Prescott, but your husband may be my father and your son just kicked me in the face. I don't think feeling your head would be appropriate."

Tears leaked. "I am a desperately unhappy woman and all I want is for you to feel my head."

Ask anyone I'm related to and they'll tell you my tragic flaw is the inability to say *No* to a woman. I felt the top where she'd found my self-esteem, then down to sexual preferences and on to wit. She did have a lump over sexual preferences, but other than that, all I felt was hair on a head. Katrina leaned forward so I could rub the muscles at the top of her neck.

"Now, tell me all the details," she said.

I touched her about a second longer than I had to, and that made me feel guilty. Gilia might not understand.

"Which details?"

"The details about Skip and your mother. He said she was a whore."

"Lydia is no whore. Skip and the guys raped her."

"Oh, my God. You know, when we were freshmen in college, I think he date-raped me. I was never certain."

"Can I go home now? Can't you see I've been beat up?"

Katrina pouted. She was a woman who controlled men with her lower lip. "Not until you promise to tell me everything."

"I promise—but only if you let me go."

"Tomorrow."

I drove back toward the Prescott-Saunders houses while she gave directions to some private club she belonged to where I was supposed to show up at eleven the next day. I didn't pay much attention because I had no intention of showing up.

I stopped the car at the spot where I'd almost flattened her. Katrina opened the door but didn't get out.

"If you don't show up tomorrow, I'll come to your house."

"You don't know where I live."

"Don't be silly. Skip has a private detective on retainer. By dark we'll know every single detail of your life."

"Oh."

"Don't stand me up now." She kissed air and left.

~

It was almost dark when Katrina went her way, which meant Skip would soon know every single detail of my life. I wondered what that meant. I guess we're all curious as to what a thorough investigation of ourselves would turn up. Would Skip hear about my interest in clitoral manipulation and general distaste for men, or would he receive a Dunn and Bradstreet on the health of Callahan Magic Carts? And which of these was me?

I hoped he didn't try the plant-the-dope, call-the-cops trick. I'd long since traded in my amyl nitrate for beta carotene, but there would always be a certain fragrance of unresolved college karma wafting on the breeze, waiting for a chance to haunt.

As I drove home through the deepening dusk, the only thing I knew for certain was this had been the longest day in history. Between Gilia, Atalanta Williams, and Ryan's fists, my body and brain were pulp on a stick. I swore never to look up my ancestors again. Shannon could deal with them from now on. She was young.

I parked the Dodge in front of the garage and, remembering threats, locked the doors. Shannon's Mustang was nowhere in sight, which meant she was probably out being loose with the psych major. One more nail in my already hammered back. On the edge of the lawn, I bent forward with my hands on my knees, trying to ease the kidney pain, when a figure in black charged.

Moonlight glinted off the blade of a knife—just like in a book—and I yelled.

"Clark. Stop!"

He stopped. Consider it a miracle.

"What the hell are you doing?"

Clark's face was dead pale and wrinkled.

"Never hold a knife up high like that. Didn't your father teach you anything." I raised my left forearm to his right wrist. "Look how easily you can be stopped." The boy seemed to be in a trance.

"Give me the knife." Gently, I pried it from his frozen fingers. It was a serrated kitchen deal, the kind used to cut tomatoes. "Hold the knife at elbow level with the blade up. See, the victim can't block without getting cut."

"I'm going to kill you."

"Not until you learn how to handle a knife. Here, you try." I stuck the knife back into Clark's hand, where it dangled uselessly.

"You have dishonored my father."

"Actually, your father dishonored my mother."

"My father has never committed an un-Christian act in his life. That's what I hate about him."

The kid had an incomprehensible viewpoint toward parents. I could relate to that.

"Billy can't help who he is," I said.

Clark passed the back of his hand over his face, then his eyes seemed to focus and he saw my condition. "Did I cut you?"

"The blood's from another father's son. Listen, you want to come inside? We could talk about this love-'em, hate-'em problem people get with moms and dads."

I started limping toward the door, but Clark stayed put. He said, "She must have been a total sleaze."

I stopped. "Lydia is not a sleaze. Not total, anyway."

"Only a sleazy woman would seduce five boys at once."

"She was fourteen and they raped her."

At the word *rape* Clark began to shake. "Saint Billy would never."

"You were hiding behind the door, did you hear him deny it?"

"I'll kill myself." He held the knife across his wrist.

"You've been looking for an excuse all day."

His eyes jerked toward me. "I'm not kidding. I am going to kill myself."

"At least do it right. Don't you read books?"

"I know more about suicide than anyone in my class."

"Cut yourself that way and you'll be two days bleeding to death." I grabbed his wrist and twisted the knife ninety degrees. "Slice up the vein from the bottom to top. Lay it open and you'll squirt like a stuck pig."

I felt Clark's wrist tighten, then he touched blade to blue vein. Nothing happened. I didn't stop him and he didn't go on.

His breath smelled of horehound drops. "You're not taking me seriously, Mr. Callahan."

"No, I'm not." I released his wrist. "I'm sorry, Clark. I know I should but I'm too beat to humor a sad teenager. Come by in the morning and I'll sincerely tell you why life is better than death. It is, you know. Took years, but I finally figured the thing out. Right now, I need sleep."

"For my father's honor, one of us has to die."

"Can't we forget the whole thing?"

He pointed the knife at me. "One of us has to die."

My body was fast running out of gas. Even riding the bike a hundred miles had never worn me out this thoroughly. Bike fatigue was merely physical torture, and physical torture sometimes clears the mind. It sure helps you forget your other troubles. But the walk from Clark to my front door was a hike through the La Brea tar pits. Deathbed flu. The boy was beat.

How many people had I brought to tears today? How many threatened me with violence, compared to how many turned violent? And don't forget Gilia Saunders. I didn't even know the questions to ask on that one.

I dealt with the doorknob and thought, guess we'll have to start locking soon, then I stumbled into the shelter of the family foyer and fell over a pumpkin. Landed on my hip on another pumpkin, which started a pumpkin avalanche. When the slide finally stopped, I lay on my back surrounded by mountains of pumpkins, oceans of pumpkins. The entry hallway was belly deep in orange.

I did not care. I did not give a hoot. I was not affected. Nothing and no one mattered except crawling up the staircase and into bed.

11

I dreamt of clitorides. Squadrons of clitorides marching in formation like mushrooms in *Fantasia*. High clitorides, flat clitorides, hard clitorides, squishy clitorides. Amber waves of clitorides.

My dreams used to center on the entire vertical ravine, from furry outgrowth to the hillock atop the twin cliffs—major and minor—leading into the black swamp from which all life arises but no man returns. Of late, my dreams had forsaken the chasm in general to focus on the pleasure button perched on high. Women try to keep pleasure caused by the pleasure button secret from men, because men are limited to the pressure cooker squirt, and the male gender would probably quit having sex if they found out women are having more fun than men are. Yet—the big yet—modern women demand that we know exactly where the button is and how it is operated.

The days when Henry Miller could write in *Tropic of Cancer* "A cunt came into the room," "She was a cute cunt," "Only a rich cunt can save me now" are long dead. And good riddance. Today, clitorides walk into rooms.

~

When I awoke, the weight of gravity had tripled overnight. A psychic anvil balanced on my forehead and my internal organs felt calcified. We're talking symptoms of oncoming depression. Depression is paralyzed spirit. If they ever invent a pill that cures depression, I'll take it. Even if the price is impotency, I'll pop that pill in a heartbeat.

The only hope is to go through the motions. Shower, shave, brush the teeth—wonder how many years till they fall out. Maurey Pierce told me if you act normal long enough someday you'll become normal. This was when I was fifteen and dressing like Scott Fitzgerald and wondering why girls wouldn't go out with me. Maurey said if I brushed my teeth twice a day and read *TV Guide* cover to cover every issue pretty soon I would stop being strange and girls would begin to make eye contact.

Downstairs, I found Gus, Shannon, and the male Eugene sprawled around the kitchen table, drinking coffee over the local morning paper. To my complete disgust, Shannon and Eugene both wore bathrobes.

"Have you no shame!"

"C'mon, Dad. You and Mom were living together at thirteen."

"That's because your mother was pregnant."

Eugene grinned. The chump sat there in *my* bathrobe—a blue terry-cloth number that safety-pinned together because a woman named Linda used the belt to tie me up and somehow it'd gotten lost.

The import of my last words made me nauseous. "You're not?"

Shannon broke into laughter, joined by Eugene and Gus. They laughed at me for trying to be a traditional father.

"Of course not," Shannon said.

Since no one jumped to pour my coffee, I poured it myself. One thing Gus can do is make good coffee. "That's not something to say 'of course' about," I said. "Pregnancy is an accident."

Shannon held her cup out to me. I refilled her but ignored Eugene's similar silent plea.

"After the olden days when you and Mom were active, the scientists invented something called birth control," Shannon said. I hate tacky kids.

Eugene said, "Shannon has a diaphragm."

"You went to a doctor and told him you were planning ahead to have sex?"

"Daddy, this is the eighties. Times have changed since you were young."

"I'm still young."

Gus did her nostril exhale blast that says it all. "I got a grandpa acts younger than you and he's in a rest home."

Eugene smirked into his empty cup. He had no call to come off young and vital; his hairline was already in full retreat. By the time Eugene made thirty he was going to pass for Friar Tuck. I may not have much, but at least I've kept my hair.

Gus pushed herself up from the table. "Eat your beans, you'll feel better."

"I am not in the mood for red beans."

"Your father's pouting again," Gus said to Shannon.

"I am not pouting, I'm just tired of red beans for breakfast. Why can't we have biscuits and ham like other rich families with black cooks?"

Gus said, "Racist cracker."

"Did you meet your fathers?" Shannon asked.

"Why are there two hundred pumpkins in the foyer?"

"Three hundred fifty," Eugene said. He was eating beans. He seemed perfectly happy to sit at my table in my bathrobe eating my beans. After sleeping in my daughter's bed. Goldilocks incarnate.

"Did you meet your fathers or not?" Shannon asked.

"Yes, I met them."

"All five?"

"One's dead."

"Which one?" Eugene asked.

"The black guy."

"Figures," Gus said.

"And?" Shannon was impatient. I didn't know what to tell her. The fathers were good, bad, and ugly, like everyone else. They had families and jobs. None were in the CIA or professional baseball, and, so far as I could tell, none had made a career out of rape.

Shannon stared at me. "Did you figure out who's the real father?"

"Yesterday was the worst day of my life, including the day Wanda left. Confronting the fathers was stupid. Idiotic. I did it because you two made me and now it's over and buried and I demand to know why there's three hundred fifty fucking pumpkins in the foyer!"

"Daddy. That's no way to talk in front of guests."

Another morning at Tex and Shirley's. I hadn't eaten a meal cooked by my cook in three days. The waitress with JUDY on her name tag recognized me from the day before—asked if I wanted cheese blintzes again. I said, "Sure thing," without thinking because I was still going over what I should have said during the conversation back home. Us writer types aren't good at live conversation. It takes eight drafts for me to sound spontaneous.

What happened was the kids had gone philanthropic at a pumpkin stand on the Blue Ridge Parkway.

"The little ragamuffin behind the counter wasn't even wearing shoes," Eugene said. "We had to nurture her somehow."

"Shannon hardly ever wore shoes when she was a little ragamuffin."

"We witnessed classic poverty in America. The girl obviously had a vitamin deficiency, and I don't doubt she'd been physically abused. The vast majority of women in her socio-economic class are physically abused, statistically speaking."

So Shannon rented a U-Haul trailer and bought out the pumpkin stand.

"Your daughter has a heart of gold," Eugene said.

Young men speak in clichés; old men live them. "Why not give the girl all your money and let her keep the pumpkins to sell to someone else?" I asked. "Lord knows we don't need more than one pumpkin."

"Categorical impoverishment disdains charity," Eugene said. Shannon wasn't speaking to me. She does that whenever I won't cooperate.

"I've found people you think won't accept charity generally will when you word it right."

Eugene sent me a look like I'm simple and he's not. "These pumpkin sellers are endemic of the old Appalachian value system which ascribes nobility to poverty, but only in the context of the self-contained family unit, much like John Boy and the Waltons. Charity is viewed as debasement."

Gus snorted and spoke to Shannon. "Does he talk that way in bed?" I left before Shannon answered.

At first I thought the waitress looked like the woman who walked her cat on a leash, then I realized she was the woman who walked her cat on a leash.

When she brought my blintzes, I asked, "Why walk a tied-up cat?"

She looked at me suspiciously, which is nothing new. Waitresses often look at me suspiciously. "Have you been spying on me?"

"I saw your cat yesterday and wondered why you walk her on a leash."

"You ever try walking a cat without a leash?"

"My cat Alice went outside on her own."

The waitress put her hand in her uniform pocket, then took it out again. She touched her ear and blinked quickly. "I can't risk that with Judy."

I looked at her name tag. "You're Judy."

She continued to move her hands nervously. I could tell this was a touchy subject. "Mr. Angusen named Judy after me. Mr. Angusen was my husband, before he caught the emphysema and said he'd rather die than quit Kent cigarettes. He was so crazy about our kitten that he named her after me."

"My friend Maurey named a horse after her father."

"Judy is all that's left. I can't risk losing her too."

Made sense to me. "I used to be emotionally dependent on a cat. You reach a point where something outside yourself has to hold you together because you can't do it on your own anymore, and a pet is the only choice."

The waitress had sad eyes I hadn't noticed the day before when I was busy fingering Linda Ronstadt. "What happened to your cat?" she asked.

"Alice got old and died."

"How did you handle losing her?"

"I got married."

I would never have married Wanda if Alice had lived. Alice was my cat who stuck with me while a score of women didn't. Alice didn't care for my women. She made a habit of peeing on panties left on the bedroom floor. I'm convinced several of my one-night stands would have lasted several more nights if the women involved had awoken to dry underwear. Alice was eighteen when her kidneys started to fail, and, for seven months, I injected her twice a day with fifty cc's of electrolyte fluid. At the end I hand fed her ice for a week as she died. I doubt if I'll ever get so close to an animal or person again. Intimacy on that deep a level takes too much out of you. After I lost Alice, I wallowed in fuck-and-suck avoidance for a month until Wanda came along, and, in a gush of relief that someone might actually take me for the long run, six weeks after I met Wanda I married her.

Then, ten days less than a year later—game four of the '83 World Series—Wanda scrammed. She calculated the timing to inflict the highest amount of pain possible; of that I am certain. No woman just happens to leave her husband during the World Series.

My first marriage—the one we don't talk about at family gatherings—lasted eight weeks. I was twenty-five, Leigh was thirty-seven and had just been divorced by her husband of fifteen years, who dumped her for Tammy Faye Bakker's publicist. He left Leigh with a shattered personality, which I helped her glue back together piece by piece until she was whole enough to leave me for an underwater welder.

She said hurting me "balanced the books." I asked her why she married me in the first place and she said, "To prove to myself someone still wanted me."

12

Lydia publishes feminist literature, Maurey runs the ranch, I write Young Adult sports fiction, but what keeps all our noses above water is golf carts, an irony not lost on anyone, except possibly Lydia. In some circles I'm known as the golf cart czar. Actually, only one circle, but the people in it pull a lot of weight at country clubs across America.

The Callahan family used to be known as carbon paper czars. Caspar Callahan Carbon Paper once stood as a veritable giant in the world of record keeping. But then Caspar died and a couple months later I happened to be in the Wachovia Bank wrangling the red tape it takes to get yourself into a dead relative's safe deposit box, when the Xerox van delivered a 2400 series copier to the back door.

You've never seen such ecstatic secretaries. No more hassles with lining up three sheets of paper. No more smudgy fingers.

I sold out lickety-split. Take that, Minnesota Mining. Absorb another competitor, I'll just drive down to Atlanta to a baseball game. The San Francisco Giants were playing the Braves—Juan Marichal against Phil Niekro. Willie McCovey led off the eighth by drilling a Niekro screwball through Chief Nokahoma's tipi—a stand-up triple. Lum Harris chewed and spit and waved in a left-handed reliever.

That's when the family fortune zipped into the modern era. A big healthy girl in a Braves cap and hot pants rolled through the bullpen in a motorized baseball on wheels, picked up Hoyt Wilhelm, and whisked him, silently, electrically, to the mound. I knew right then, in mid–Cracker Jack bite, that I had to own a motorized baseball.

So, I sank the carbon paper profits into golf carts.

To be honest, which God knows is what I'm striving for here, I didn't immediately recognize the motorized baseball as a plastic shell mounted on a golf cart. I hated golf then—although not as much as I hate golf now—and I simply didn't think in terms of market.

Golf isn't really a sport. It's fancy pants networking; rich white guys in spiffy outfits, cruising the lawn in one of my carts, comparing financial tidbits and sexual exploitation fantasies. Golf is for doctors and bankers and all those career guys who, being a writer, I consider myself superior to.

We owned one of each Callahan Magic Cart Company model. The garage was so packed that sometimes I had to park my 240Z in the driveway, back when I had a 240Z. Shannon organized cart polo matches over at the junior high football field. Cart polo is an outgrowth of cart croquet. Both games use beach balls, golf carts, and croquet mallets. Cart polo is a lot of fun—you can drink and play simultaneously—and I wish it would catch on with the college kids so I wouldn't have to feel guilty about making a fortune off a non-sport I find disgusting, boring, and morally offensive.

"You didn't have to come in," Shirley said. "Everything's flowing smooth as peaches, so we don't have any use for you."

"I thought it was time I stop moping around the house and get back to work."

"Moping around the house is what you did best before you married the Queen, and practically all you did while she ruled the roost. I fail to fathom what this 'get back' to work refers to."

Shirley is my bookkeeper and one of the three women who each thinks she runs the Callahan empire. I have Gaylene in production and Ambrosia in sales. All three have copped a the-owner-is-harebrained attitude toward me, forgetting I'm the one who created this nifty system of delegated authority. I hired them all years ago at salaries considerably higher than what's paid men in similar jobs. Back then, Carolina women didn't even have similar jobs. Shirley, Gaylene, and Ambrosia came from positions where they mostly fetched refreshments, ran personal errands, and covered the boss's butt when he screwed up—with raises directly contingent on attitude.

Ambrosia, who has the thickest accent in the South, explained to me what *attitude* means in upper-level management lingo. "A good attitude is when you'll suck off the boss and a bad attitude is when you won't. I had a bad attitude."

My gang was so thrilled to be chosen for real jobs that they worked twice as hard as men would have and netted me a couple million a year, after taxes. If that makes me a harebrain, the world is full of well-to-do rabbits.

"Pretend I'm your employer, Shirley. Give me tidbits of accounts receivable."

"Accounts receivable is none of your concern."

"I've already begged my daughter to behave even vaguely like a daughter today. Don't make me degrade myself to you too."

Shirley gave me one of those looks I imagine ept sergeants give inept generals. She spoke quickly. "Ambrosia got drunk with some CEO from North Dakota last night and sold his country club a hundred ten Shilohs." Naming our cart models after Civil War battles gives the line a thematic unity.

"How about Gaylene?"

"Gaylene paid the union steward a kickback. We're covered through the winter. Anything else you need to know to make believe you're a vital cog in this here well-oiled machine?"

Shirley has a grandson Shannon's age. Can you believe a woman that old would treat me with such disrespect? "That'll be enough."

She turned back to her office, which is larger than mine. "The Coke machine is out of Fresca again. You want to do something worthwhile, call Dixie Distributing and make some threats."

"Can you get me their number?"

"You've got eyes and fingers. Look it up yourself."

I sat at my desk with my hands folded in my lap, waiting for something to happen to change my dull ache of a life. The desk was completely clean except for a Smith-Corona typewriter in the dead center and a small, framed photograph, facedown, in the left-hand upper corner. The facedown face on my laminated desk belonged to Wanda the wife. I'd put her facedown when I discovered I couldn't write Young Adult sports fiction with her staring at me in disappointment because I wasn't Saul Bellow.

I'd never promised to be Saul Bellow, never even hinted that I might write something more literary than tales of right and wrong set in the metaphorical world of the baseball diamond. Sports is today's battleground between good and evil. The goals of sports are honest and understandable—if you play by the rules using your mind and body to the best of your abilities, you win. Athletes with character flaws lose.

Cowboy-and-Indian fiction used to be good versus evil, until public perception of who were the real-life good guys in that one switched. Real life has nothing to do with good versus evil.

I opened my top drawer and pulled out the manuscript I'd been working on for over two years. *Bucky on Half Dome.* In the first draft of *Bucky Climbs the Matterhorn*, Bucky had been Becky. Becky wore braces on her teeth and had a will of iron. She could hang off the rock by the fingers of one hand and live on bushes and berries for a week. Becky was the stuff of legends.

The sex change was performed at my editor's insistence. She said Young Adults would not accept a female lead, except in the genre of horse books. Teenage girls eat up bonding-with-animals stories, but I refuse to write horse books.

She did allow me to give the boy Bucky a female sidekick, as long as things stayed just pals—non-romantic and for God's sake, non-sexual. So, I created Samantha Lindell. Bucky and Sam's relationship is modeled on what I have with Maurey Pierce. It's not in the books, and none of my teen fans know, but the reason the need for physical release doesn't cause Bucky and Sam tension is the kids got that one out of the way years ago, before puberty.

"Life is much like the self-locking carabiner," Bucky Brooks said as he fit himself into his harness and prepared to rappel off the Blacktail Butte shield.

Samantha Lindell's blue eyes sparkled in the mountain sunlight. "Bucky, you pick the oddest moments to turn philosophical."

"Think about it," Bucky said, then he took the two loops of rope in his rough, yet sensitive, hands, leaned back over two hundred feet of air, and jumped.

Not the first lines of *Tale of Two Cities*, I admit, but books have been opened on less. Somewhere around page ten, I met Wanda, and now, a year later, Bucky and Sam were mired on page sixty-four, still nowhere near base camp, much less the mountain. Bucky had been asked to guide the President's spoiled-rotten son on a five-day climb up Half Dome in Yosemite Park, and one of the three bodyguards who were supposed to accompany the party had been revealed to the readers as a KGB agent with assassination on his mind. The President's son had been rude to Sam—called her a "chick," said "Chicks can't climb with men"—and that was as far as I got.

The five years before I met Wanda I produced five books; one was even mentioned in *The New York Times Book Review*'s annual juvenile fiction roundup. Then, fifty pages in a year. Nothing in the last four months. Some would take this as a sign I was better off without her, but I don't know. There had been no way to maintain writing momentum and hold my marriage together at the same time.

Wanda had crises. I'd put out two pages, then she'd have an anxiety attack over personal fulfillment or President Reagan or something. Kafka himself couldn't have written the week before Wanda started her period.

Maybe it's better to work on a marriage than write sports books for teenagers. People say, "Gee, weren't Dostoevsky and van Gogh admirable for all the sacrifices they made to create their masterpieces," but I say the true artistic hero is the guy who gives up everything to produce something crappy. Anybody can lose a wife to win a Nobel Prize. Try losing a wife for *Bucky on Half Dome.*

I flipped through the manuscript, finding a phrase I liked here and there, sometimes an entire sentence. The scenes had been written weeks or even months apart, so the thing lacked consistency. The President's son had red hair on one page and blond hair three pages later.

It wasn't all tripe. A paragraph on page thirty-five gave me an idea for later in the book—Bucky could save the KGB agent's life, even knowing he meant to kill the President's son. I got to thinking about the President's son and what it would feel like to be constantly coddled and resented. Would the boy stay a jerk or grow to learn tolerance of others and respect for nature?

This was interesting. For the first time in months I looked at my own writing as a source of potential. Maybe the book could be saved and I would be more than a bank account for one group of women and a climax-producing object for another group. Living your dreams through what you can do for women isn't truly satisfying. Not like creating a novel.

I finished the last page and turned it over onto the pile. The question was: Carry on or trash it? Would a teenager someday pick up my book and be improved by it? Most teenagers are so unhappy, a book doesn't have to change their life, just help them forget it for a few hours.

Wanda said my Bucky stories would inspire some pimply book-worm to take up mountain climbing and he'd fall off a cliff and get killed and it would be my fault. She first slept with me because I was a writer, but she couldn't stand me when I actually wrote.

After six rings I decided the company had no one in charge of answering phones. Maybe she was at lunch, or maybe she didn't exist. I pictured women all over the building muttering to themselves. "Not in my job description."

"I need some money."

"Wanda, how did you know where to find me?"

"That Nazi maid of yours told me where you were."

"Her name is Gus." Gus must have told her the place I'd least likely be and accidentally gotten it right.

"This separation isn't working out," Wanda said.

"Does that mean you want to come home?"

Her laugh dripped with derision. "I need some of our money. Paul says his needs are not being met."

Paul? "You left me for a kid named Manny."

"Okay, Manny, then. Have it your way. I don't want to argue, I just want cash. I held your sensitive little psyche together for a full year. Believe me, I earned my half."

I wondered if Shirley was listening in. "Nobody's disputing that you earned your half, Wanda. I only want you to come home. I love you."

Her sigh winged across the telephone lines. "I know you do, Sam. Don't grovel."

"I didn't mean to grovel."

"I must face the fact that I don't love you and I never loved you. Can't you understand how humiliating this is for me. I gave my marriage everything and now I must admit defeat."

"You don't sound humiliated."

"I am truly devastated by your failure as a husband, Sam."

I stood up behind my desk. "I'm not the one who humped the pool man."

"How dare you throw that in my face. Your neediness made me hump the pool man and all the others. I didn't want to cheapen myself but you forced me to and I will never forgive you."

All the others? The conversation led where it had to from the start. "I'm sorry, Wanda."

"Just send me the money. Twenty thousand for the first payment." Wanda gave me an address in High Point. She ended with, "You should prepare yourself. Paul and I are thinking of moving back into the house."

"But it's my house."

"I have as much right to live there as you."

~

I chose to flush the manuscript down the toilet, but anyone who has faced an open commode with sixty-four pages in hand knows the futility of that idea. No symbolic act should require a plumber. Instead, I closed both lids and removed the top of the tank. Then I slid Bucky and Sam into the tank water and carefully set the top back into position.

13

Katrina Prescott's health club had once been an office building for upscale orthodontists and Realtors and such, but the owners went Chapter Eleven and the new people kicked the young professionals out, tore down most of the internal walls, and hired a bunch of personal trainers from California. I'd been offered a piece of the club, but investments have never been my thing. I'm loyal to golf carts.

The extremely healthy-looking surfer at the front desk seemed to know who I was. She said, "You're late."

"I'm not supposed to be here."

"Mrs. Prescott is waiting in the private sauna. Just follow the hall to the end and turn left."

I found Katrina Prescott sitting on a wooden bench in a very hot room. She had one towel wrapped around her head and another towel around her body.

She said, "You're late."

"Couldn't we go somewhere where it's not so hot?"

"Take off your clothes, darlin', you'll be fine."

"I'd rather not do that, Mrs. Prescott." I looked for a place to sit, but the only choice was a wooden bench lower than the one Katrina sat on, which would afford me an uncluttered view up her towel. Better to remain standing.

Katrina's skin sparkled from a film of perspiration. She said, "You really stuck a bee in Skip's jockey shorts."

"Can't we go somewhere else? I don't enjoy hot, confining spaces."

Katrina lowered her body towel. "Do you like my breasts?"

I was afraid this would happen. "The nipples are cantaloupe colored."

"They cost Skip six grand apiece. How about my stomach. Do you like my stomach?"

"Don't go any lower."

Katrina unwrapped her head towel and handed it to me. She shook out her hair while I blotted my wet face and wondered what she used to hold the false eyelashes in place. Leaning to one side, she regarded me as an object of curiosity.

"Skip learned a lot about you last night, and there's more coming in today."

"The hairs in my nose are scorched."

"Mostly money matters which bore me to death, but some of the information was interesting."

Sweat dripped off my earlobes. That had never happened before.

"You're thirty-three but you have a daughter who is nineteen," Katrina said.

"Leave my daughter out of this."

She arched an eyebrow. "Your wife of eleven months left you recently. Before her you had a checkered personal life of short-term relationships—including one former marriage—going back about twelve years. Before that you couldn't get a woman with a stick."

"Who did this detective talk to?"

"How many women have you slept with?"

I couldn't see a breast enhancement line, but maybe it was hidden in the fold.

"That depends on your definition of 'slept with.' "

"Had sex with."

100

"I'm not clear on that definition either."

Katrina made a sound of impatience. "How many women have you stuck your pistol in?"

"Not that many. I generally keep my pistol out of sex."

She frowned. "A hundred."

"I don't think so, I'm not that kind of boy."

"If you got laid every other month for a dozen years, you'd have had seventy women."

"Gentlemen don't keep score, Mrs. Prescott. And I object to the word *had* when it comes to this subject."

"You prefer *diddled*?"

"I prefer we talk about what you asked me to come here and talk about—my mother's rape."

Katrina continued to study me. Sweat trickled down my rib cage and the inside of my thighs. I wanted to take off my shirt but felt she might misinterpret my actions.

"How does my body compare to the average woman?"

Her legs beneath the towel were quite tight, for an older, short woman, and her stomach muscles were good. The shoulders rode higher on the neck than I generally liked. "You have a very compact body, but there's no such thing as an average woman."

"I want you to make love to me now."

Okay, perverts, I admit it. The thought had crossed my mind. "The temperature's a hundred and fifty degrees in here, Mrs. Prescott. We can't make love."

She threw aside her body towel. "Skip is afraid of you. I can't begin to say how excited that makes me."

"Would you like me if Skip didn't hate me?"

"Of course not, you dress like domestic help."

"Then it's not me you want, but a way to hurt Skip."

Katrina stood up. "What's wrong with that, darlin', do you want me or not?" Drops of sweat clung to the ends of her pubic hair. From deep in the forest, a clitoris called my name.

S a m.

"Yes, I want you. I want every woman, but I only want them for the right reasons, and hurting my father is not an appropriate reason to have sex."

She touched my cheek with pampered fingernails, then ran her hand down my neck to my chest. "Any reason for doing it is the right reason."

"I disagree with that attitude, Mrs. Prescott."

Fingers fluttered across my stomach. "You're trying to tell me you loved all seventy women you screwed."

"I never said seventy, but however many it was, yes, I wanted to be closer to each one as an individual. I wanted to bring them joy."

Her eyes snapped. "Bring me joy, Goddammit."

I yelped. "You don't want joy, you want revenge."

"Revenge would bring me great joy."

"It's not the same thing. Let go of my crotch, Mrs. Prescott."

She kneaded. "What's my name?"

"Katrina."

"I want to see it." With her free hand she started digging at my jeans' button and zipper.

"No. I don't want to have sex with you."

Suddenly, the fire left her. Katrina released me and slumped back onto the bench. She sniffled. "Why do you hate me so?"

"I don't hate you, Katrina."

"You've slept with seventy floozies in Carolina and you won't sleep with me."

"Some of them weren't floozies."

"Am I that ugly?"

I stepped toward her. "You aren't ugly at all, you're compact and pert, but the truth is I look at you as something of a mother figure. After all, you are married to my possible father."

She was probably faking, but what with all the sweat, I couldn't tell real tears from manipulation. "Skip will be so happy when he finds out you rejected me."

"He doesn't have to find out."

"Skippy finds out everything. I'll never matter to him because no one will ever again want me."

She was a lot more appealing pretending to be vulnerable than she had been pretending to be invulnerable. The poor woman was one artificial layer over another all the way down to the core, where I imagined a little lost fetus the shape of that rubber thing in the center of a golf ball.

"Tell you what, Katrina. I really don't want traditional sex with you, but maybe there's another way to bring you joy."

Her face lit. "How, honey?"

"Lean back against the wall."

Katrina fingered the bumps on my head while I went to work. First impressions had been right; she talked through the entire orgasm.

After Katrina's final yelp I drove down to the interstate and checked into the Ramada Inn to take a shower. Signed myself in as F. S. Fitzgerald. When you carry cash you can do that kind of stuff. I stretched my shirt, jeans, and boxers on the air-conditioning/heating vents and turned the fan to HIGH. My clothes might smell, but at least they'd be dry and that was the best I could do. Shannon and Gus would notice if I bought a shirt and came home wearing something I didn't go out in. The instinct to notice changes gives women a tremendous advantage over men.

After the shower I lay on the bed and watched Phil Donahue interview a Type A personality in a suit. Even with the sound off, I didn't like the man. I rolled onto my back, covered my face with a pillow, and considered Katrina. Like most fireballs, she was insecure, and what she wanted wasn't that hard to give—in fact, it was fun to give—but the relationship was deeply flawed: She didn't like me and I didn't particularly like her. So why should I go crawling around between her thighs when only yesterday I'd met someone good who could make a difference?

I'm sorry to say, Katrina wasn't the first married woman who'd asked me to save her. My one God-given talent, besides Young Adult sports novels, is that I can meet any woman and tell precisely what she needs—lover, listener, friend, father, mentor, a lifelong commitment, a servant, meaningless orgasms, a confidante, or nothing whatsoever—but my God-given weakness is I feel a compulsion to fill needs wherever I find them, regardless of consequences.

Filling each need you come upon causes conflict. You can't commit for life to every woman who needs a lifelong commitment in order to be whole. There's too many of them; besides, when I tried with Wanda, it didn't work. And you sure as hell shouldn't give meaningless orgasms to one woman while hoping to be all of the above with another.

So—bottom line—Katrina had to go. No more sauna sex. She could cry about her low self-image till doomsday, I wasn't going to build her up at the risk of losing something I wanted. For a change.

I checked out two hours after checking in. The desk clerk gave me a look, but I didn't care. I had resolve.

14

A yellow Ford EXP with District of Columbia plates was parked next to the garage. It was probably Eugene the balding boy's and I hadn't noticed it when I left that morning. Sometimes I notice everything and other times I notice nothing at all. Lately the notice-nothing periods had been throwing off my balance.

Shannon, Eugene, and Gilia were sprawled in various postures around the parlor, hacking at the pumpkin mountain. Everyone seemed so cheerful and comfortable that at first I didn't realize what was wrong with the picture.

I said, "Gilia."

She looked up from carving molars in a jack-o'-lantern. "Hi, Sam." She'd done the nose sidesaddle to look like Richard Nixon, or maybe it was the orange jowls. Something made the pumpkin a spitting image.

"Grab a knife and dig in," Shannon said.

I dropped next to Gilia on a couch cushion they'd pulled onto the floor. Gilia smiled and handed me a pencil-thin X-Acto knife. "I like your family."

"Have you been introduced?"

"We're all buddies on this bus," Eugene said. It rankled me some to think a stranger would consider Eugene part of my family. He sat in Caspar's Lincoln rocker, which I'd never had the gall to sit in, slicing the tops off a pile of pumpkins on the coffee table. The kids had quite the efficient operation. Eugene circumcised and eviscerated, so to speak, and the girls created pumpkin personalities. The vegetable art was easy to separate. Gilia was into cubism—triangle eyes, rectangle mouths with squared-off teeth—while Shannon was sloppier. Her guys had noses all over heck and the eyes of a Picasso. Everybody was fast. Maybe a hundred heads crowded around the legs of Me Maw's baby grand, with another fifty topped and scooped, waiting for surgery. A gross four-foot mound of slime and seeds rose from newspapers spread across my oak floor.

"The detective says you're an immoral scumbag," Shannon said.

I stabbed my pumpkin in its future eye hole. Slicing down, I tried to remember if Gilia mentioned the detective yesterday, or that information came from Katrina only.

"What detective?"

Gilia was watching me. "The one who showed up at Skip's house last night and again this morning. They made me read his report because I rode around with you and everyone is afraid I'll pick the wrong side. Ryan says he'll box my ears if I ever speak to you again."

Shannon was outraged. "Box your ears? Where did this guy find his word choice?"

"Nineteen fifty-two. When they showed me how terrible you are, I had to come and see myself."

I stabbed a nose. "I don't think I'm terrible."

"Repeat that affirmation several times daily and soon your superego will recover from its recent humiliation," Eugene said. He flipped a wad of orange snot on the goop pile.

"Did you really eat LSD in college?" Gilia asked.

"Who told Skip?"

"And you were arrested for having sex on a Ferris wheel."

"Alicia couldn't get off in bed. I had to get her off."

Shannon pointed her knife at me with much better form than Clark had shown the night before. "Daddy, why was it okay for you to have sex and do drugs but not okay for me?"

"Double standard," Eugene said.

"It is not a double standard. In those days we believed in peace and love. Kids now do sex and drugs for all the wrong reasons."

"He knocked up a thirteen-year-old girl," Gilia said.

Shannon frowned. "She was my mother."

"Did Skip tell you I was thirteen too? And Maurey seduced me. I wasn't given a choice."

"It doesn't say anything about your age in the ad," Gilia said. "Just that you impregnated a thirteen-year-old."

A bad feeling crept into my stomach. "Ad?"

"Skip's buying a full-page ad in the *Greensboro Record* so he can expose your sleazy past."

"The newspaper won't print it."

"I told him that, but Skip says they will or he'll pull the Dixieland Sporting Goods account."

"They still won't. Except for politicians, ads like that are illegal."

"Then he'll have flyers printed."

Advertising seemed like overkill. I'd never done anything that even vaguely compared to the nastiness of rape, and you didn't see me printing up handbills on Skip and the gang.

"What traitorous hell bitch gave him this dirt?"

"Your wife."

Gus brought in a tray with a bowl of toasted pumpkin seeds and brandy snifters all around. Seemed a bit early in the day to be drinking with my underage daughter, but I didn't want Gilia thinking I was structured, so I kept my mouth shut and flew with the flow, or whatever they call good sports these days. We held our snifters aloft while Shannon recited the poem about teeth and gums, look out stomach here she comes. Gus and I downed moderate sips, but the three young people chugged the load. When Gus saw this, she glanced at me and tossed the rest of her brandy down her throat. I followed suit. Tasted like NyQuil.

107

Hands on hips, Gus studied my artwork. "What you making there? Looks like a sicko paper doll."

I turned the pumpkin face out. "Isn't it obvious?"

"Van Gogh's self-portrait," Gilia said. "The later one."

"Right."

Shannon hummed a riff from the "Twilight Zone" theme, then said, "Warped minds think alike."

Eugene grinned as if he knew all the answers. "Sympatico." This from a man with drippy arms the color of a hepatitis victim.

I was secretly pleased and alarmed at the same time. While I'd always wanted to meet a woman who thinks like me, this parallel brains jive might be more genetic overlap than compatibility. I'd reached the point where I really hoped Gilia wasn't my sister. Or cousin.

"Anyone with class can recognize van Gogh," I said. I decided a giant ear hole would be the magic clue.

Gus snorted. "I got class and I thought it was an electrocuted cat."

Gilia touched my sculpture, the other side away from where I was cutting. "I like it. No one who sees van Gogh in a squash could be an immoral scumbag." She and I made meaningful eye contact across the pumpkin.

Shannon jumped in to wreck the mood. "My daddy can. Don't let his sensitivity line fool you, I'll bet cash he's been woofing it up on a married woman all morning."

The X-Acto knife slipped through pumpkin meat and stabbed me in the palm. I dropped the knife and sucked my hand a moment to compose myself. They were all looking at me.

"I was only kidding," Shannon said.

I put on my innocent face. "Some people's kids are too precocious for their own good."

She blushed a Cabernet color. Maybe she was chastised, but, more likely, she realized she'd accidentally nailed me. Shannon sees through my innocent face the way I see through Lydia's pretending to lie whenever she tells the truth. Contrary to what we've been told, children can detect deceit in parents much easier than parents can detect deceit in children.

~

To cover the awkwardness of the moment, or possibly out of disgust at me, Shannon dipped her right hand into the pumpkin pulp mound, came out with a hefty wad of slime, leaned across Gilia's latest jack-o'-lantern, and pasted me right between the eyes. *Splat!* Juice and stringy, mucus-like stuff trickled down my cheeks and the bridge of my nose. I sealed my left nostril by covering it with a finger and sneezed, rocketing a seed out of my right nostril through van Gogh's ear hole.

Shannon went back to work on a pumpkin. Gilia stared at me, and Eugene stared at Shannon. Gus helped herself to toasted seeds. Dignity seemed important. Maintaining a rigid decorum, I got to my feet and walked behind the girls toward the bathroom. As I passed Shannon, I leaned over and scooped up a handful of orange slime and dumped it down the back of her shirt—my shirt, actually, as she'd recently taken to stealing my dress Van Heusens.

Shannon's spine snapped upright, but she made no noise. Her hand flipped up as if she were throwing salt over her shoulder, only instead of salt, my face caught pulp. The pumpkin slime in my mouth gave me another metaphor for the taste and consistency of a turned-on woman, which I needed. There's a limit to how often you can compare something to raw oysters.

I cupped my hands together for a double load of what felt like alfalfa-fed cow poop. Lifting my hands high, I brought the whole load down on her head. Take that, trollop.

Shannon turned to face me. The only sound was the gentle crunch of Gus chewing seeds. I glanced over at Gilia. She hadn't decided if this was family horseplay or an all-out fight. I hadn't either. Shannon was just like her mother in that I couldn't tell squat about what she was thinking until she decided to tell me. At the moment, for instance, as she pulled my belt toward her and dumped a pint of goo down my boxers, was she angry as hell or amused no end? My next move should have been dictated by attitude, but not knowing attitude, I answered her shorts shot with cleavage filler.

Shannon's mouth and eyes went rigid. She looked so much like Maurey I wanted to apologize. I wanted to hand her a handkerchief and say, "Whoops, let's forget the ugly incident. We'll pretend it was a recurring dream."

Fat chance.

She started to circle, which made me nervous. I'd expected more goop and was prepared to take my medicine, but this empty-handed circling threw me off. We rotated like the Earth keeping track of a pissed-off moon. What was the moon up to? She had a glop of pumpkin on her forehead and a seed stuck in her right eyebrow.

Then Shannon stopped. "It's not nice to slime your daughter," she said.

"You slimed me first."

She shook her head. "You'll never learn, will you?"

"What's that supposed to mean?"

Her eyes were bulletproof glass—space age plastic. Ten thousand howling Zulus firing spears at helpless Redcoats. Unable to meet such fierceness head on, I looked away, first at Eugene, whose face revealed an intellectual interest in father-daughter dynamics, then at Gus, who was chewing and watching something behind and below me.

Maybe I heard her, or maybe I simply felt Gilia's presence. Whatever the cause, I glanced between my legs just as Shannon charged.

Splat! The classic Three Stooges kneel-behind-the-knees-and-push maneuver. What the Bowery Boys called a number seven. I landed neck deep in slop.

I read in one of Wanda's *Cosmo* magazines that men often express a desire to crawl into women they copulate with. *Cosmo* took this as a return-to-the-womb neediness. I, personally, have never had any desire to return to Lydia's womb. The fact I was once that close to my mother is appalling, and I have no wish to be inside a woman again. However, for those men who fantasize about crawling up the crotch of an excited woman, I suggest they first try bathing in pumpkin pulp. A lesson might be learned.

Shannon and Gilia thought my predicament was a hoot. Cause for belly laughs all around. Eugene had fallen on the floor, struck down by hilarity. Even Gus chuckled.

I sat up, grabbed Gilia by the arm, and yanked her into the pile—where her intense laughter turned into a shriek. Shannon put out a Blackfeet war cry—taught to her by Maurey, who learned it from Hank Elkrunner—and dived on both of us.

15

S hannon apologized to me the next morning, an event worthy of "Ripley's Believe It or Not."

"I'm sorry I said you were woofing it up on a married woman yesterday," Shannon said. "You're such an easy target, sometimes I forget you have feelings."

I hung my head and stirred my red beans. "You cut me to the quick."

"I realized that afterwards. You got so pale."

Was she being ironic? Lydia and Maurey taught me long ago never to take a woman's word at face value. I decided the proper course was silent yet wounded. Lies of omission are easier to cover than the out-loud kind.

Shannon brought her coffee and sat down opposite me. "Gilia is amazingly nice—I can't remember the last time a nice woman liked you—but you know how it is when a daughter's father gets a new girlfriend. There's a moment of jealousy."

"Gilia isn't my girlfriend."

"Daddy, don't be a fool. Of course she's your new girlfriend. I think she'll make a wonderful mom."

As a responsible parent, my job was to disagree. "She's only five years older than you are."

"If the shoe fits, don't ask how old it is."

"Who told you that?"

"You did, the night you went off with Jimmy Otake's grand-mother."

Why don't children ever forget? Shannon had been seven when I went off with Jimmy Otake's grandmother.

"But Gilia's a blonde," I said. "I don't care much for blondes."

Shannon's laugh was effervescent. "Daddy, you want any woman who wants you. This time you lucked out and found a good one, so don't blow it. Here, she left me her phone number. It's a personal line into her room, so you don't have to deal with the family."

I looked at the slip of paper in my hand. Gilia was a high-quality woman, which was the last thing I needed coming off the hard rebound from Wanda. Gilia was young, good-looking, and ener-getic—all that potential and long legs too—and she would break my heart. No, now was not the time to mingle with lovable women.

"I'm not going to call her," I said.

"Give me one semi-rational reason why not."

"To start with, Gilia might be my sister."

"Gilia told me her father is left-handed. You're right-handed, therefore her father isn't your father."

"Gilia's right-handed."

"Perfect. He's not her father either."

Gus stood in the parlor with her arms crossed over her chest. Or-ange slop hung from the piano, the chairs, the table, the William and Mary desk and bookcase, a Matisse print, and a Schenk origi-nal. I tried to remember the difference between stalagmites and sta-lactites.

"It's drying hard," Gus said.

"I don't suppose you'd—"

"In a pig's eye. I'd quit and go work for Jesse Helms before I'd clean this room."

I'd suspected as much. Spontaneous messiness always brings backlash.

"Call Manpower and have them send over a team of winos. Tell them I'll pay double."

"You'll pay triple."

Gilia answered on the seventh ring. "What took you so long?" she said. "I thought you'd never call."

"I planned to never call, but I thought I should explain why I can't call you."

"Are you going to Tex and Shirley's for breakfast? Skip's detective says that's what you usually do about now."

"Two days in a row. I hate it when you do something two days in a row and people start calling it a rut. That detective is damn presumptuous."

"He's only been on the job a day and a half."

"I refuse to be predictable."

"I only asked because I'm thinking I might join you there."

"At Tex and Shirley's?"

"We could talk."

"What about?"

"Sam, didn't you ever meet someone for breakfast? You sit and drink coffee and shoot the shit."

"I'm real bad at shooting shit."

"I'll teach you, Sam. Hanging out is one of my talents."

Blues music came from Gilia's end of the line. She must have been listening to it when I called, but if so, why take seven rings to answer?

"Won't the detective tell Skip, who'll tell Cameron, and Ryan will box your ears?"

"I'm twenty-four years old, they can't control me with threats."

"They can me."

Gilia's laugh was clear water bubbling down the side of a mountain.

~

So, Gilia and I started meeting each morning at Tex and Shirley's Pancake House. It'd been so long since I'd talked to anybody about anything, that, at first, I felt exposed. I kept expecting her to get bored, like the two mental therapists I'd been dragged to over the years did. Lydia seduced the first one, and the second one, in college, told me to grow up.

"The prom's over," he said. "Stop your whining."

But Gilia never acted bored or impatient. She listened while I rambled on about life with an airhead mother, and metaphors in baseball, and the transcendence of Young Adult sports fiction. The trick to seducing women is to shut up and listen to them—no one's probably done that before and they'll generally sleep with you out of gratitude—but with Gilia, I didn't want to seduce her so much as get to know her real well. And that meant allowing her to know me.

This is revolutionary stuff here.

She mostly talked about prep school and college and the strange men and women who live in Washington, D.C. I'd been raised rich, at least until Caspar cut us off there for a few years, but I'd missed the prepster-debutante-networking thing. I guess Lydia wanted me to grow up normal.

Gilia was very passionate about art history. She had real opinions on movements and periods and all that stuff that most people only fake having opinions about. Her favorite American painter was an Impressionist named Lilla Cabot Perry. Once Gilia got started on Lilla Cabot Perry, she would go all morning if I didn't jump in when my turn came to talk.

Gilia won Judy over that first Monday.

"His wife treated him poorly," Judy said as she poured my coffee.

"She must have had bad tastes," Gilia said.

"It was because his kitty passed on and he was vulnerable."

Both women looked at me with obvious sympathy. I ate it up.

"When did your kitty die?" Gilia asked.

"Two years ago, the last weekend of March."

"You must have really loved her."

"My cat's name is Judy," Judy said. "We're very close." Gilia didn't ask why a waitress named Judy had a cat named Judy. Instead, she went into what kind, how old, what do you feed her, don't you just love it when she lies on your neck and purrs.

"You must have a cat yourself," Judy said to Gilia.

"I have a Siamese named Beaux, but he thinks he has me."

In no time flat Judy was bringing extra strawberries for the strawberry pancakes and not charging for coffee. "This one won't get jealous of a passed-on cat and leave you," Judy said.

"She'll find another excuse," I said, and they laughed as if I were kidding.

When it came time to go, Gilia waved to a man who sat a couple tables over, reading a *Sporting News*.

"Mike, there's someone I'd like you to meet," Gilia said. Mike was a little guy with muscles and a narrow mustache.

"Mike Newberry, meet Sam Callahan. Mike's the detective who's been researching your life."

He held out his hand, but I hesitated a moment, unsure if it's proper form to shake with the man who's tailing you. Were we supposed to be adversaries or just two people trying to get by? In the end, I decided it didn't matter and shook his hand anyway.

He pretended not to notice my hesitation. "I've heard so much about you, I feel like we've already met," Mike said.

"How is Wanda?"

His mustache crinkled into a frown. "Angry."

"Is she taking care of her health?"

"She was drinking like a fish, but I couldn't see as it bothered her health."

"What is she doing?"

Mike folded the paper under his arm. "Mostly she bad-mouths you. She thinks you did something terrible to her."

I looked at Gilia. "I was monogamous, I swear."

"You've got me convinced," Gilia said.

"I never did her any disservice."

Mike cleared his throat—a male habit that has always irked me. "She thinks you were holier-than-thou."

You can't win with a righteous woman. You either mess up and give them cause for hatred, or you don't mess up and they call you a goody-two-shoed wimp.

"Listen, Mike," I said, "it would be nice if you didn't mention Gilia in your report to Skip. Her family might not understand."

"*Shit bricks* are the words," Gilia said.

Mike smiled, showing slick teeth. We were playing on a field he understood. "I think that can be arranged."

"In fact, how would it be if I pay the same fee Skip is paying, then, instead of wasting your time following me, you could stay home and watch television, and every evening I'll telephone a report of my day?"

He rubbed his chin, as if he'd once had a beard. "You'll report everything? Not hold back the dirt Mr. Prescott wants to hear?"

I gave him the innocent face, which works a lot better on strangers than daughters. "Why would I hide anything?"

"Except me," Gilia said.

"This way you collect from Skip, you collect from me, and your time is free to take on more clients."

"Sounds reasonable," Mike said.

"Quite reasonable," Gilia said.

"How much do you want for the down payment?"

"Drink like a fish" is one of those expressions that won't stand up to close scrutiny, along the lines of "work like a dog" or "sweat like a pig." Obvious questions come to mind. A more exact wording might be "Wanda's psyche is immersed in fluid, much like a fish is immersed in water."

Drinking like a fish wasn't a habit Wanda picked up after leaving the manor. She specialized in sticky liqueurs—flavored schnapps, Grand Marnier, that sort of thing. When we first met she used to drink herself comatose and pass out with my penis clutched tightly in her fists—or fist if I wasn't hard. If I tried to roll over or, God forbid, get up to take a leak, she would squeeze like vise grips on a hose. At the time, I took this as a sign of love, but five hundred miles of pedaling the Exercycle 6000 brought me an insight: Wanda is afraid of being alone. The sticky liqueur and tight penis hold combine to give the illusion of beating back the void.

117

Maurey Pierce drank like a fish throughout college and that farcical marriage to Dothan Talbot. After her dad was killed by her horse she wallowed in the bottle until social services took her other child, Auburn, away from her and she reached that crossroads where you either lose everything that matters and die or you go to meetings in church basements the rest of your life. Maurey chose meetings.

At Auburn's custody hearing Maurey and Dothan each paraded out a Goddamn plethora of witnesses to show the other was an immoral, unethical, unfit sleazeball. Maurey flashed her clear blue eyes at the judge and convinced him she was a cleaned-up sleazeball, or recovering sleazeball, as she put it, so she won custody of Auburn, and in the parking lot outside the courthouse Dothan slapped her in the ear and Lydia decked him with a Sage Graphite II fly rod case. A baseball bat couldn't have knocked him any flatter.

Except for a month-long backslide when her mother died, she's kept to the clean liver program ever since. The bender at Annabel's death surprised me some because Maurey and her mother never got along that well, even more so than the average parents and children who don't get along. Basically, the thing came down to they were both in love with the same man, Maurey's father, and they never worked out the jive you're supposed to work out about that.

The summer Maurey was pregnant by me, Annabel fell off the deep end, mental hygienically speaking, and she never quite came back. She lived a foggy, scattered existence more or less held together by pharmaceuticals and Maurey's little brother, Pete. Six years ago Annabel buffed her Thorazine with too much Halcion and tried to fly off the Snake River bridge. Maurey got drunk and disappeared, then a few days later Pud Talbot disappeared, and before I made the connection, they reappeared together.

I turned jealous jerk and gave her grief over noodling another Talbot and we went eight months without speaking before we had an emotional best-friends-in-spite-of-you-being-an-idiot reunion where we hugged and cried and pledged eternal trust. Eternal trust or not, Maurey still hasn't told me what happened during the missing month. Sometimes I daydream that I was the one who went after her instead of Pud.

~

Trolling town looking for someone to talk to. Manic-depressives have all the luck; they soar between crashes. The best us regular depressives can do is battle our way up to normal every now and then. Talking about Alice had left me bummed and flat, and while you'd think the new friendship with Gilia would pep me up, I was in one of those states where even when something good happens you dwell on the fact that it can't last. After bitter experience, I'd found the black states can be lightened somewhat by massive exercise, being around cheerful strangers, or seeing *I Was a Male War Bride*, starring Cary Grant and Ann Sheridan.

Which is why I trolled Battleground to the Baskin-Robbins corner in search of the happy, pregnant girls. My hope was they went for ice cream about the same time every day and their giggles would improve my outlook.

Fat chance.

Babs sat alone on the bench, tears dripping from her pink chin onto a rocky road sugar cone. She whimpered, "I'm never telling my baby his father's name."

I wished she'd said that earlier. "Why?"

Babs made an effort to smile, but failed, which only made me sadder. "Guess what?" she said, "Lynette run off with Rory Paseneaux."

"Your husband?"

"I'm gonna get him annulled. He took my best friend and my grandmother's afghan and run off to Charlotte. Says he's gonna drive stock cars."

"Let me get you a napkin."

I went inside to find a napkin and collect myself. I hate it when people other than me get hurt. Somehow, pain is worse for happy people and puppies because they don't expect it; they're not mentally prepared.

Back outside, I asked, "When did this happen?"

"Last night Rory ordered pizza and him and Lynette went to pick it up on account of my feet being swollen. They knew my feet would be swollen, they planned it all out."

"They leave a note?"

Babs cried with one hand on her belly and the other holding the cone. Her eye makeup left a single black trail down her face. She nodded to my question. "In the refrigerator, but I knew before that they'd snuck off. Lynette's overnight case was gone. She don't need a toothbrush to pick up a pizza."

When Wanda left me she didn't sneak off at all. She announced her plans during "The Yellow Rose," when I was in the midst of a tremendous Cybill Shepherd fantasy involving an electric piano and yards of Saran Wrap.

Wanda stepped between me and the TV and said, "You have driven away the only good thing that will ever happen in your life."

I said, "What's that?"

She had me carry her baggage out to the 240Z, where Manny the pool boy sat with the engine running. Knowing Wanda's convoluted sense of honor, sneaking off would have been dishonest. Sleeping with the neighborhood was allowed, but sneaking away wasn't.

Babs sniffled. "Me and Lynette have been best friends since second grade. If we have girls, we was going to name them Babs and Lynette, after each other."

Even though friendship is more important than romance, there's no depths to what friends can do to each other in the name of romantic love. "Maybe she'll come back," I said.

"I wouldn't speak to her if she did. She stole my Rory." Babs dropped the ice cream; her chest shook like she was hyperventilating. I put my arm over her shoulders and rocked her gently while she pressed her wet face against my shirt.

"What am I gonna do now?" she asked.

"Have your baby."

"Rory took our half of the rent. The other half is Lynette's and she's gone too. And I was on his insurance at the plant, only now he don't have a job. Who'll pay the doctor?"

"Don't worry about the money," I said. "I'll take care of that. You just take care of your baby."

16

Most of my heroes committed suicide. That thought came to me late Monday night when I should have been asleep, but, as usual, wasn't. I'd ridden the Exercycle 6000 twenty miles at high tension, but stopped because I couldn't concentrate on Wanda. Gilia's face kept getting in the way.

I lay in the bed with three pillows next to me for the arm and leg that had to be draped over someone before I felt okay enough to sleep. No help. I didn't feel okay and I wasn't asleep. Buttons in the mattress poked into my ribs. Why do mattresses have buttons? I got to thinking about Alan Watts and his views on sleep, which led to a local poet named Randall Jarrell, then Sylvia Plath and Marilyn Monroe, who Maurey says slept naked, and it dawned on me that these four people had two things in common: They were all my role models and they all killed themselves. And my heroes who didn't kill themselves on purpose—Gram Parsons and Hank Williams—killed themselves accidentally. Were these people I wanted to model my life after?

Baseball heroes don't commit suicide. Sandy Koufax, Moose Skowron, Vin Scully, I could think of a dozen admirable baseball people who hadn't killed themselves, but let's face it, at thirty-three, you can't sign on as disciple to a baseball player.

The door cracked open and a form slithered into the room. My first thought was, Skip's hired a hit man.

"Who's there?"

"Who do you think, darlin'?"

"Oh, shit."

"You don't sound happy to see me. I can't believe it, you must be covering up your true delight at my arrival so I won't become over-confident." She was wearing a nightgown, a filmy, flowing number with ruffles. She floated through the dim moonlight like a short ghost.

"Katrina, this isn't a good time. I have someone with me."

"No, you don't."

I sat up in bed. "How can you tell?"

"Those're pillows. Anybody can tell the difference between pillows and women, 'cept maybe a horny man." Katrina slid across the room. "I was lying there next to old Skippy, tingling from head to toe on account of what you did this morning."

"You don't have to thank me."

She sat on the edge of the bed. Her fingertips brushed my arm. "I decided once wasn't enough."

"Katrina, that's not fair. I do you a favor and now you want more. How did you get in, anyway? The door's locked."

"The side door isn't." She ran her fingernails up and down the inside of my elbow. I swear, she purred like Alice.

"We don't have a side door."

"Behind the weeping willow."

"That's the servants' entrance. Nobody's used that door in twenty years."

She leaned so close her lips grazed my ear and said, "It still works."

"Am I wrong or did you pick up a French accent since this morning?"

Her tongue flicked in and out of my ear. In my experience, women who are into tongue flicking all read Danielle Steel.

"My grandmama was French. It comes out whenever I'm crazed

with lust." She lifted the sheet and slipped under. I slipped right out the other side—stood there feeling foolish in plaid boxer shorts.

"Sam." Katrina blinked seductively. "If you reject me there will be repercussions."

Veiled threats are a sure sign that a relationship is fixing to wash down the tubes.

"I'm not rejecting you, Katrina. I just can't have sex in my own home. What if my daughter hears us?"

Katrina giggled. "Does your daughter sleep three doors that way?"

I nodded, not liking the giggle.

"She should be worried about you hearing them, not the other way around."

"Them?"

Katrina made her face into a pout and talked baby talk. "Uh-ho, Sammy's wittle baby is making diddle-widdle wight under Sammy's nose."

I hate women who talk baby talk. It's all I can do to sleep with them.

"Don't go away," I said. "I'll be right back."

"Honey, I wouldn't think of leaving."

I'm a spy in my own home. I stood outside Shannon's door, barefoot in boxer shorts, listening to the sounds of passion. The bed rocked a steady rhythm, *chunka chunka chunk*. I bought that bed for Shannon at the High Point furniture mart. She chose it because she liked the ironwork design on the headboard. In my mind, I could see her hands intertwined in the iron design while Eugene's sweat dribbled into her pores. You try to be both mother and father, you try to set a good example, you want to lock them up so they'll never be hurt, but the books and magazines all say "Set her free, let her go." And look what happens. A balding male who can't even talk right charms his sleazy way into her body. God, I hate men.

What to do? Call the police? Ignore the atrocity? In the olden days a man would have smashed down the door with a shotgun and forced Eugene to marry her, but times have changed. Marriage is the last thing I want for a daughter of mine.

123

Shannon made a low gasp followed by a series of *peeps*. I'd heard those *peeps* before. In the throes of sex, each woman emits a unique sound. I've been with screamers, cursers, huff-and-puffers, and women silent as stone until that sudden shriek. One woman actually shouted "Bingo!" The tones, rhythms, even the words are like snowflakes, similar from afar but up close no two are the same.

Yet Shannon was pretty darn close to someone I'd heard before. My mind raced back through the years and bodies until it suddenly struck me—Maurey. Her mother. At thirteen Maurey had sung the *gasp, gasp,* then five *peeps* in a row. The *peeps* had been like a two-minute warning.

Sickened yet fascinated, I listened to Shannon build toward climax. I was amazed. The sound of passion is genetic. A woman echoing her mother couldn't be learned behavior, has to be heredity. Maybe it goes clear back to the moment of conception, in which case impregnation must be accompanied by orgasm or the song is not passed on.

I watched Mom have sex in our living room once and her sounds were completely different from Shannon's and Maurey's, which means the gene isn't passed through the male side. Lydia sounded like a kid having an asthma attack. That night I saw her doing it, the guy came and quit before she got off—an immoral act, if you ask me—so I didn't hear my mother's orgasm. Probably for the best.

The emotions you feel watching your mother get laid don't even compare to how you feel when it's your daughter. That was my baby in there with a penis crammed inside her. The little girl I raised through kindergarten birthday parties, mumps, first bike, driving lessons, first zit. I wanted to throw up. What if Eugene was a pervert? A bondage freak with a French tickler.

What if he toyed with her heartstrings and left? Wam, bam, thank you, Sam. Even worse, what if he stayed? They might fall in love and become life mates, and I would have to be gracious. I refuse to be gracious to anyone noodling my daughter.

I doubled up my fist and rapped on the door. The sounds suddenly stopped.

Shannon shouted: "What?"

"Are you practicing proper birth control?"

Short silence, then: "Daddy, go away!"

Back in my own bedroom, Katrina had tossed her nightgown aside. She sat naked on the bed, rubbing Wanda's vitamin E oil into her thighs under the sheets.

She looked up at me and said, "I chap easy."

I leaned back against the closed door. "My baby is having sex."

"Good for her."

"I shall never have an erection again. The penis is a blind and cruel animal without conscience or mercy."

"You talk like there's one big schlong out there that ravages little girls."

"There is. All schlongs are one schlong and the one schlong is soiling Shannon."

Katrina stared at my boxers. "You really can't get a stiffie?"

"I'm limp with outrage."

She threw back the sheets, revealing her tight little body. "You've still got a tongue."

17

For a few days life reached a pattern of some sort. Breakfast pancakes with Gilia, oral perversions with Katrina, miles and miles on the Exercycle 6000. At night I telephoned Mike Newberry to fill him in on the day's activities: dry cleaners, the Magic Cart office, a drive over to Winston-Salem to see if Rainbow News and Novels still stocked *Jump Shot to Glory*, egg sandwich for supper. Mike accused me of holding out the juicy stuff, but there wasn't any juicy stuff, outside of Katrina's taco, so I made some up.

A novelist can't stand to tell a boring story. I invented a Chinese brothel in Siler City where I wiled away the afternoon. I told him I lost ten thousand dollars betting on cockfights.

Tuesday noon I had a remarkably close call at Katrina's health club. Turned out to be the same health club where Gilia swam. I ended up hiding in the women's shower, then escaping down a laundry chute and out a fire exit. After that I insisted Katrina meet me at the Ramada Inn. She took out a room with a weekly rate.

At breakfast Wednesday, Gilia was indignant about the invasion of Grenada.

"Seven thousand crack marines against two hundred Cuban construction workers," she said, "and Reagan's behaving like we whipped the Kaiser."

"Are Grenadians black?"

Gilia's hair was in a ponytail, which excited me for some reason. She looked clean and wholesome, like untracked snow. I guess no boy can resist putting tracks in untracked snow.

"Spanish, I think," she said, "but maybe black. Jamaicans are black and Grenada is somewhere near Jamaica."

"My garbage disposal predicted a war against black people."

"That's interesting."

"Actually, my housekeeper, Gus, predicted the war against black people, but she heard it from the garbage disposal."

"Seven thousand marines against construction workers could hardly be called a war."

I went on to explain Gus, which is no easy trick. She's six feet two inches tall, and twenty-five years ago she played basketball for North Carolina A & T, back when girls' teams had six on the floor instead of five the way they do now. Gus reads *The New York Times* every day and dabbles in the stock exchange, but she believes there's a sign that migrates around the body, putting hexes on various organs. She won't eat cranberries or tuna and she once punched out a UPS driver who called her Aunt Jemima. She's saving her money for a personal home computer.

"We had a black maid but Mama accused her of wasting toilet paper. Now she won't hire anyone but Quakers," Gilia said.

"I saw a black woman at Skip's. She wouldn't speak to me even though I asked politely if anyone was home."

Gilia slid the check to her side of the table. "That's Phadron. Skip hires illegal aliens who don't speak English. Ryan says Skip threatens them with deportation if they don't sleep with him and Katrina can't do anything to stop it."

"Sounds like a sad situation." I made a grab for the check but she snatched it away. A traditional Southern woman would have protested delicately, but still let me win.

She said, "I suspect Katrina does her share to balance Skippy's sins. She's been awfully chipper the last few days."

"Chipper?"

"Mama suspects the tennis pro."

That afternoon a thin man in an extremely cheap suit showed up on my doorstep. I'll wear a sports jacket now and then, but I stopped wearing suits after Lydia told me the neck tie is a phallic symbol. I'm not ashamed of having a phallus, but I sure as heck don't brag about it.

The man called me Mr. Callahan.

"My name is Sam. I don't like being called mister; it's too male."

"Here, Sam." He handed me some official papers.

"This is a legal document," I said.

"You think fast," the thin man said.

The papers were from Wanda by way of a lawyer and signed by a judge.

"What's your name?" I asked.

"Vernon Scharp."

"Do you enjoy process serving?"

He looked at me to see if I was condescending or interested. He must have decided I was interested. "I could tell you stories would straighten your hair," he said.

"I imagine you run into a lot of shoot-the-messenger mentality."

"Shoot, knife, and beat with a baseball bat."

"I'm asking because I own a golf cart manufacturing company, and I'm certain we could find a job for you at the plant." I gave him the address and told him to speak to Gaylene. "Work for us and you won't have to wear that suit."

"What's wrong with my suit?"

The papers said I was not to dispose of any assets; piddly amounts were okay, but big ticket items were out of the question. I read the papers carefully, then filed them in a jack-o'-lantern.

Thursday, I did lunch with Billy Gaines. We met at Tijuana Fats where he asked if I had any plans for the future and was I seeing anybody—Dad kind of stuff. I was touched that at least he tried. He even wrote my birth date and shirt size in his pocket calendar.

I didn't tell him about the two death threats I'd received in the mail. They were written in purple ink on the title pages of *L'Idiot de la Famille* by Jean-Paul Sartre and *Cancer Ward* by Aleksandr Solzhenitsyn. If I had Clark for a son, I would probably take my supposititious heir to lunch myself.

Supposititious is my new word of the month. Say it slowly—*supposititious*. It means a person you've never seen before who shows up out of nowhere, claiming to be your child. Imagine: a special word for people in my situation. *Supposititious* comes from the same word as *suppository*. Don't ask me why.

Bastard is another special word for people in my situation. Fatherless. Born of an unwed mother.

The disgrace of being a bastard never bothered me much, growing up. For a long time, I didn't know it meant anything specific. Bastard was simply another insult, like squirrel or douche bag, that children yelled at each other. Dothan Talbot was the one who taunted me with *bastard* most. He was the one who explained in detail exactly what the term meant and exactly why I was one. I didn't care. I had impregnated Dothan Talbot's girlfriend and everyone knew calling me names was nothing but lame sour grapes.

The single practical skill Lydia taught me as a boy was not to give a hoot what anyone thought of us. That's a rare attribute in junior high, but with the town character for a mother and a daughter by the eighth grade, I'd have been in big trouble without it.

I telephoned Lydia to see how the poison chew toy saga came out.

"Wire me five thousand dollars," she said. "I need it today, tomorrow may be too late."

"For bail or lawyers?"

"The *Politics of Pudenda* is the most important treatise written in

129

this country since *Female Eunuch*. It will change the very foundation of society."

"I'm more interested in whether you murdered the President's dog."

She made the exhaled sound of impatience. "Hank did one of his chants and buried an antelope liver next to the warm springs. FedEx lost the package."

"Is this cause and effect?"

"Sam. Listen when I talk. We're in a bidding war with Simon and Schuster, I must have five thousand dollars today. This afternoon."

"Oothoon Press is in a bidding war with Simon and Schuster?"

"Are you so pussy-whipped by the harlot you can no longer fathom the English language?"

"Are radical feminists allowed to say *pussy-whipped*?"

"In *Politics of Pudenda* Muriel Blackwell has a plan to end all wars and injustice. She calls for an international ban on the male gender owning private property. Once the greed motive is removed from men, women can stabilize society."

"Her theory sounds fascinating, Lydia, but I can't send any cash right now."

"*Sam.*" Her voice was loud, on the edge of frantic. "Oothoon can't change society without that money."

Oothoon Press got its name from a poem by William Blake. Blake's Oothoon is raped—"Bromion rent her with his thunders"—then her husband accuses her of asking for it; says she enjoyed being raped. So he seals her in a cave. Lydia calls this the Every-Woman story.

"Don't most publishers make a profit on books and use that to buy more books?"

"Spoken like a true anal-aggressive. Where would the world be if Virginia Woolf's publisher thought about profits?"

"My life wouldn't be any different."

There was a moment of silence. "Wire the money, Sam."

"Wanda slapped a temporary restraining order on my assets."

"So?"

"So if I give you five thousand dollars they might put me in jail."

"I am not giving up *Politics of Pudenda* for that cow. You can just go to jail for your mama; my work is more important that yours anyway."

Interesting leap of logic. I decided to change the subject. "How's Maurey?"

"Here's an idea. Transfer all the family funds into my name. That way Wanda can't rob you blind and I'll send out whatever you need to get by, just like you do for me."

I didn't say anything. The only way to handle a conversation with Lydia is to shut up and frustrate her. Hank Elkrunner learned that long ago, but I never quite caught on.

Lydia said, "Pete drug in this week. Hank says there's something wrong with him."

"There's always been something wrong with Pete."

"I can't believe I raised a homophobe."

"What's wrong with Pete has nothing to do with him being gay. He was a weird kid years before he turned to men for comfort."

"Pete brought his lover home with him. Chet is a polite boy who supports my campaign to re-educate America."

"Shannon moved a man into her room."

"Good for Shannon."

"They pant and grunt all night and he sits in Caspar's rocker."

"You should have burned that chair when the old goat died."

"Things aren't going well here, Lydia. I could use some motherly compassion."

"For five grand I'll ship you all the compassion I've got to spare."

I looked pudenda up in my *Webster's Ninth New Collegiate Dictionary*. It's the plural of pudendum—the external sexual organs of a woman, which is roughly what I had figured. *Pudenda* is Latin for *something to be ashamed of*. Chew on that fact awhile.

18

I wrapped a towel around my waist and stepped from the bathroom of room 247 at the Ramada Inn to find Katrina Prescott
sitting on the edge of the bed in her bra and panties, crying.

"What's the matter?"

"You don't love me."

I blinked twice. "Am I supposed to?"

"My husband doesn't love me." Her voice was fragile. "My son
doesn't love me. You'd think at the very least, my lover would love
me."

I didn't know what to say. Maybe it's because of the early years
with Lydia and Maurey, but I've always saved love for family and
friends. Lovers were something different.

Katrina's hands twitched in her lap as she whispered. "Nobody
loves me."

I wanted to deny that, but when it came time to say what she
needed to hear, I failed.

"Katrina, you threatened me with repercussions if I refused you sex. It's hard to love someone who holds you with threats."

"I love Skip."

I sat down. "Jesus."

She said, "Christ."

Wanda telephoned.

"You have a beautiful voice, Wanda."

"Where's the money I was promised?"

"Have you thought long and hard about coming home? I want you to consider saving our marriage as an option."

"You've broken every promise you ever made me. I don't know why I dreamed this time would be any different."

"I haven't broken every promise."

"Name one."

"I was nice to your mother."

"Mom thinks you're a sleazy bastard."

"I was monogamous, like the vows said we both should be."

"Go ahead, rub my face in it."

"Most women like a man who's monogamous."

"Sam, you are lousy in bed."

"Let's shoot for a second opinion."

"No wonder you're obsessed with your tongue. It's bigger than your dick."

"No one's ever complained."

"Your daughter is a slut."

I was silent awhile, thinking. "Wanda, I changed my mind. I don't want you to come back after all."

"Sensitive, aren't we?"

"Have a nice day."

I hung up.

When the phone rang, I was standing crucified halfway up the climbing wall. I'd positioned a two-inch lip to stand on and Katrina had strapped each outstretched arm to pitons wedged into plaster artificial cracks. Back to the wall, literally and metaphorically, my major fear was falling off the lip and ripping out both shoulder sockets.

What happened was I had made the mistake of using the old "I'll bet you have fantasies you've never told anyone" line. Katrina's fantasies are considerably more complicated than your average woman's fantasies—nothing as tame as lick-the-anchovy on a merry-go-round.

According to Katrina, all her life—from puberty anyway, which to hear her tell it came at six—she had dreamed of decking herself out in a cheerleader uniform and dancing for Jesus on the Cross. Don't ask me; I think it had something to do with being raised Catholic. All those years of kneeling before a nearly nude longhair twisted her sense of desire. She said each night after she said her prayers and before she went to sleep, she would reach up and touch the man hanging over her and wish he were real.

Saturday afternoon after my household had left for the day, Katrina showed up in the Page High red sweater and white pleated skirt and her hair in pigtails. She did warm-up cheers while I hung naked on the wall.

> *Two bits*
> *Four bits*
> *Six bits*
> *A dollar*
> *All for the Pirates*
> *Stand up and holler*

Then she jumped high, squealed, and came down in splits. Twenty-five years out of high school, yet the woman had the flexibility of a teenage gymnast. She hung a pom-pom on my penis and pranced around the room, doing kicks over her head and shouting *"Go, team!"*

Playing Jesus was okay; I'd always had a crucifixion complex. Also, I was exactly the same age as Christ when they nailed him.

What I didn't like was hanging from a climbing wall with a pom-pom on my dick. I'd never even climbed the climbing wall, which was actually a bunch of Matolius Simulators bolted to oak. I only bought it for Shannon because a few years ago she decided she had to go out to Wyoming and climb the Grand Teton. That summer, she did—zipped right up the sucker. She came home all jazzed for rock climbing, but by Christmas she was into mountain biking and had abandoned the climbing wall, never to touch it again. I'd forgotten we even owned the thing until Katrina realized the possibilities of suspending Jesus six feet off the floor.

So, the phone rang and Katrina brought it over on the long cord, and she stood on top of a Nautilus bench press bench to prop the phone between my shoulder and ear.

"Cowboy, your life is about to take a turn for the worse."

"Is this Skippy?"

Katrina dropped down a couple steps and commenced to suck.

"I recently purchased a seven-millimeter Mauser with your name etched on the stock."

"Skip, I fail to see why you are angry with me."

"Consider this a last warning."

"I've never done anything to you." I looked down at the part in Katrina's hair. Her scalp was a concrete-colored furrow aimed at my belly. She was working amazingly hard, for a married woman.

"Tomorrow your *S* is going to hit my *F*."

I've always had mixed feelings about the blow job. It feels terrific, but over the years men have taken a superior attitude toward women who give oral pleasure. Appreciation gives way to power, which leads to the cocksucker charge.

"What exactly do you want me to do?" I asked.

"Buy time on every radio station in town."

"Ouch, not so rough."

"Go on the air and announce you are an illegitimate bastard with no notion of paternal lineage. Hell, say the whore gave virgin birth if you want, just put a stop to rumors of my involvement."

"I haven't heard any rumors of your involvement."

"I'm faced with snickering at the club. Even my wife has started to doubt my innocence."

Skip's wife switched her attention from the head to the ball sac.

"You should have thought of that thirty-four years ago."

"Last warning, hear. Tomorrow, your name is mud."

After Skip hung up I couldn't lift my head and release the phone for fear of cold-cocking Katrina. I simply hung there with a twisted neck while she mangled my privates.

When Katrina came up for air, she asked, "What'd Skipper want?"

"The usual."

"Let's trade places."

That's when Gus walked in.

"You got that nice Gilia girl fooled into thinking you're all right. Why you want to go sticking your pork where it don't belong?"

Gus was baking pumpkin pies—dozens of pumpkin pies. She'd taken one look at me spread-eagle on the wall and marched straight into the kitchen where she banged pans together until Katrina gathered up her pom-poms and went home.

I stuck my finger into a cooling pie. Gus swatted at me. "That's not for you."

"Twenty-five pies and I don't get a bite?"

"You don't deserve a bite. Get out of my way."

"She asked me to do it."

All my women can be fierce when they decide I'm stupid, but Gus can look bigger and meaner than any of them. "Ever' time a woman ask you to do something, you have to do it?"

"I can't very well say no."

"What you can't do is pork any woman that lets you pork her."

"Why not?"

"God*damn*, you're a fool." Gus stalked to the oven, thrust her hands into mitts, and began shuttling pies in and out.

Throughout adulthood, I have been promiscuous as hell when I'm single and monogamous as hell when I'm not single. No exceptions; no compromises. Should Gilia and I ever formalize the connection, I would be true and blue for however long we stuck together, right up to death do us part. But in the meantime, according to my take on right and wrong, it was perfectly fair to relax with Katrina. I was in the right.

Of course, this nifty rationale blew to smithereens at the thought of Gus telling Gilia what Katrina and I had done on the climbing wall.

"What'd you come back so soon for?" I asked. "I thought you were gone for the afternoon."

Gus straightened. "I got home and found your letter in my apron. Figured you better read it."

"Someone sent me a letter?"

"Black woman. A black woman writes a letter it must be important. Black woman isn't going to send you chitchat."

"You opened my letter?"

" 'Course not. I've got morals, unlike others in this room."

What I needed was coffee. Unfinished blow jobs always make me crave coffee. For some reason I can't explain, I've had a number of unfinished blow jobs in my life. It's like the women get down there and start making lists of places they'd rather be.

"You need these grounds, Gus? I want to make a new pot."

"Don't you go throwing out my grounds."

"That's why I asked. I never throw out old coffee grounds without permission." I spread a *New York Times Book Review* on the counter and dumped out this morning's grounds.

"So, if you didn't open my letter, how do you know it's from a black woman?"

Gus went into her apron pocket and sailed the letter across the room. "Handwriting's a black woman's."

The address was in blue ink—large letters with big loops and carefully dotted *i*'s. There was no return address.

"You can tell a person's race and gender by their handwriting?"

Gus slammed a pie onto the counter so hard the other pies jumped. "I should get paid extra for working with a handicapped boss."

"Just wondering."

" 'Course I can tell black from white and man from woman. I'm not blind."

I turned the letter over. A Christmas Seal picture of a tiny angel and star held down the back flap. "Is my handwriting black?"

"No."

"Part black?"

"Your handwriting's Chinese."

137

~

Mr. Callahan,

I wish to speak with you regarding the matter you broached at my home Saturday afternoon last. If it is convenient, would you meet me after Sunday services at the Mt. Zion Baptist Church on Benbow Ave. I shall be on the front lawn around 11 a.m.

Mrs. Atalanta Williams

19

The trouble—besides guilt over Atalanta Williams, anxiety over Gilia, confusion over sex with Katrina, and the perpetual sorrow of being alive because my mother was group raped—was sleep. I couldn't do it. Or, I couldn't fall asleep until dawn, but once there, I couldn't wake up until it was time to go to sleep again.

The entire week I stumbled around with swamp water on my brain; trance movements from home to Tex and Shirley's to work to the Ramada to the Exercycle 6000, and then, more exhausted than I thought humanly survivable, I lay in my bed and ZING—the swamp turned into a beehive. My skin itched. Someone else's rock video lit up the backs of my eyelids and I thought of everything that had ever happened or would happen anywhere in the universe. I dickered with God.

Sunday morning, twenty minutes after I drifted into the blessed relief of sleep, Ivan Idervitch leaned on my front porch doorbell. Ivan

Idervitch is the nine-year-old from across the street and down a couple, and when you first see Ivan what you notice is his horn-rimmed glasses. They make his eyes big as Ping-Pong balls, but for some reason I don't notice the eyes, just the glasses. I always try to be nice to Ivan because his parents make him wear suspenders. My mother made me wear dickies in Wyoming when none of the other boys wore dickies, so I know how it can be.

Ivan Idervitch rang the doorbell for like ten minutes before I managed to pull on a bathrobe and stumble down the stairs. Shannon and Eugene were still doing whatever disgusting thing they did, and Gus was nowhere near. She only takes one day off a week and she chooses which day based on whenever she feels the urge.

"Here." Ivan thrust a pink paper at me.

"What's this?"

"Stuff about you. The man's paying me two cents apiece to give them away to every house in the neighborhood."

"Everyone in the neighborhood will see this?"

"All the neighborhoods. My whole Cub Scout pack signed up. It's our weekend project."

"I'll give you a dime apiece for what you've got there."

Twin lights went on behind the glasses. The boy was a born MBA. "Fifteen cents."

"Twelve. And if you go back for more, I'll buy those too."

"How about the other kids?"

I wondered how many fliers had been printed compared to how much my reputation was worth. "Okay, twelve cents, but the man can't find out where his fliers are going."

Ivan blinked behind his glasses. "Ten cents for the other kids and I get a two-cent fee for bringing them in."

"When you grow up, come see me and I'll give you a job."

"No, thanks, Mr. Callahan, I'm going into the insurance field."

The flier was about what you'd expect. A Xeroxed photo of me sat in the upper right hand corner. I don't know when Mike Newberry took my picture, but the graininess made me look like a man who robbed gas stations.

The left side had a big headline that read PROTECT YOUR CHIL-DREN FROM THE NEIGHBORHOOD PERVERT and under that, in slightly smaller letters: SAM CALLAHAN ON A RAMPAGE AGAINST GOD, DECENCY, AND SOUTHERN VALUES.

Then it listed twelve major social blunders:

- Impregnated a 13-year-old girl
- Arrested for copulation on a carnival ride
- Writer of pornographic children's books
- Had simultaneous sex with twins
- Frequent drug user including LSD and Double Humpies
- Contributor to left-wing radical organizations
- Gambles on cockfights
- Frequents Oriental brothels
- Commits perversions involving oral sex and food
- While married, carried on an adulterous relationship with his colored maid
- Tells slanderous lies concerning his parentage
- Spat on the Confederate flag

At the bottom of the page it said: If you love your family, you will rise up and drive this blasphemous sex fiend from your midst. Then it gave my address and phone number.

Gus wasn't going to like number ten. Any problems Skip and Wanda thought they had with me were diddly compared to what would happen if they pissed off Gus.

And the sex with twins charge wasn't true. I'd fed that one to Mike Newberry Friday night. I once had sex with a twin, but I didn't know whether she was Melissa or Melinda. They were always switching clothes and personalities to fool people. I wanted sex with the other twin but I was afraid to give it a shot because I didn't know which one I'd already been with.

The left-wing radical group and spitting on the Confederate flag incident happened at a Charlie Daniels concert in Georgia. I paid a girl wearing an EARTH FIRST! T-shirt five dollars for what she said was genuine Macon County moonshine but was actually Coleman fuel and mint leaves. I spewed on the biker in front of us, whose leather jacket had you-know-what sewed on the back. He would have beat the crap out of me if the EARTH FIRST! girl hadn't lit a match and torched him. In the ensuing confusion, we ran and hid in her van.

Ivan brought in 3,500 fliers before ten-thirty. When I left to meet Atalanta Williams, Shannon was at the kitchen table, passing out money to a steady stream of Cub Scouts. Eugene sat on a stool, reading the flier over and over and asking questions that began with "Did you really . . ." I think I'd finally impressed the dork.

I waited in the park across from Atalanta's church, watching the weather, the traffic, and squirrels. The weather was mixed, puffy clouds and cool. Traffic was light to none. "The Battle Hymn of the Republic" wafted from the red brick church, across the neat lawn and juniper hedge, and past the Signs on Wheels sign that read HAVE GOD, WILL TRAVEL.

I was more than a little uneasy about this meeting with Atalanta. I'd hurt her unnecessarily and deserved any scathing accusations she wanted to hurl. But, sitting in the Sunday morning quiet of the park, I was even more uneasy about the direction my life was headed.

People who mattered—Maurey, Shannon, Gilia—were being shortchanged, emotionally speaking, while people who didn't mat-ter—Katrina, the fathers, Wanda—were taking control.

I've had this recurring dream ever since college, where I'm in the backseat of a speeding car with no driver. I fight to reach the wheel as the car careens through crowded streets, killing people and ani-mals. It flips children up onto the front hood where their faces flatten against the windshield and I can see their mouths open to scream. Real life was beginning to ache like that dream.

The double doors opened and people began coming out of the church—men in dark suits and women in shiny dresses. The wor-shipers were all black except two older women who seemed to be dressed alike. They had on blue hats and white gloves. A lot of people lit cigarettes. That's one of the big differences between North Caro-lina and Wyoming. Most everyone in North Carolina—black and white—smokes cigarettes. Not many white people in Wyoming smoke, and there aren't enough black people to tell what most of them do.

Atalanta Williams was one of the last ones out of the church. As she made her way through the groups of people, the thing I noticed was her posture. I imagine Eleanor Roosevelt had posture like Atalanta's. Nearly everyone she passed smiled and said something to her. Atalanta said something back, but she didn't smile.

I met her on the edge of the church parking lot. She held her white leather Bible in both hands. The red ribbon marked a place toward the back of the book, one of St. Paul's letters or Revelations or something.

Atalanta looked toward the church. "I have to apologize for the way I behaved toward you and the young woman last week. It was inhospitable and un-Christian."

"I'm the one who should apologize, Mrs. Williams. Had I known about your husband, I would never have come to your house."

"Let's find a bench."

Atalanta didn't speak again as we crossed the street back into the park and sat on a wooden bench next to a sumac. The amazingly bright leaves gave off a shimmery bonfire effect.

"The fall of our junior year, Jake played in a Guilford County all-star game," Atalanta said. She sat very straight with her eyes not focused on anything present. "Jake had played against white boys before, but that was the only time he ever played on the same team with them. He thought it was a great opportunity, even though the Negroes had to come to the game already in uniform because they weren't allowed in the white boys' locker room."

I decided not to say anything. My personal apology had been lame enough, without trying to apologize for the entire white race.

"After the game, Jake started spending time with some of the white football players. I didn't like it much, and I must admit we had words. Jake seemed to think it was modern or hip or something. He bragged about introducing the white boys to John Lee Hooker.

"That Christmas I spent with my grandmother in Asheboro. The entire family went down and I had a fight with Papa over inviting Jake. Papa didn't approve of Jake."

143

"Fathers never like their daughters' boyfriends."

Atalanta didn't comment, but you could see the past playing through her mind like a home movie. The fight with her father. The trip to Asheboro. I've had long periods of living in memories and it's hard. Too many booby traps.

"When I came home, Jake had changed. He no longer spent time with the white boys, but he didn't say why. I always thought they hurt him somehow—treated him like a human one minute and an animal the next. Those things happened quite often back then."

She lapsed into another memory. I tried not to look at her for fear of intruding on her privacy. "We never talked about it and in a few months Jake was back to normal."

A squirrel hopped toward us through the fallen leaves. He stopped about five feet away, cocked his head at an angle, and watched us through his left eye. The last of the cars pulled away from the church. The only car left in the parking lot was a gray-and-green Chevrolet that must have belonged to Atalanta.

Her eyes shifted from the past to her hands holding the Bible in her lap. "I think I could accept it if he'd only had sex with her." Her right hand started to shake. "But I cannot bring myself to forgive him for rape."

Atalanta's hands were small, like Maurey's. The left hand clutched at the right to stop it from shaking; I couldn't conceive of her making a fist.

"I'm sorry, Mrs. Williams."

"It changes everything."

"I'm sure Jake was a fine man. He just made a mistake. Maybe the white boys called him chicken if he didn't do what they were doing."

Atalanta raised a hand to brush against her eyes, then lowered it onto the Bible again. "There is no excuse."

"When you want to be accepted, you'll do almost anything."

"No." She turned to look at me and I had to meet her eyes. "If you are Jake's son, I want to know. You would be part of him and I cherish any part he may have left behind."

"Do you think I am his son?"

She studied me a long time. "I don't know."

"I'd hoped someone would recognize something in me."

She shook her head slowly. "I've held on as hard as I could, but after thirty years I mostly see him as he is in the photographs."

She leaned forward a little bit and stared intently into my eyes. I didn't look away or blink. After messing up so many lives, hers more than anyone's, it seemed important to come to some conclusion, to discover who was my father so I could set the other four families free.

But Atalanta gave it up. She looked back across the street at the church and her eyes almost, but not quite, relaxed. "You could do worse than having Jake Williams for a father."

"Of the five, he's the one I'm hoping for."

"If you find out, yes or no, will you tell me?"

"Yes, ma'am."

"I miss Jake every day."

20

Gilia was the worst driver I've ever ridden with as a passenger, not that I've been a passenger too often. Her idea of merging lanes was to roll down the window, stick her hand out, and wave fingers at whoever she was cutting off, as if people don't mind you barging in so long as you're friendly about it.

"D.C. drivers are mythologically terrible," she said. "Politicians and bureaucrats refuse to recognize the authority of the red light. I think that says something about our government."

"The middle lane is for turning left." She'd just pulled an illegal maneuver that caused a moving van to lock its brakes and honk and my testicles to leap skyward.

"I don't make decisions that far in advance."

We were driving to High Point in her Ford EXP in hopes of finding and stealing my Datsun 240Z.

"Why did you let Wanda take your car in the first place?" Gilia asked.

"She wanted it."

"You always give women what they want?"

The answer seemed too obvious to say out loud. Besides, I thought one of us should concentrate on the upcoming intersection.

"Women must take constant advantage of you," Gilia said. "I like that."

We parked across the street from the address Wanda had given me several times as the place to send money.

"Kind of run-down, isn't it," Gilia said.

"I should save her from this dump."

"She must have wanted to leave you real bad to move here."

No 240Z or any other car was in front and the house looked dark and empty. Beyond empty, it looked uninhabited. There were no curtains or shades, no clutter on the porch that sagged vaguely southeast. Several windows were cracked or broken.

"Maybe she doesn't live here but uses the address as a mail drop," I said. "She was accustomed to a privileged way of life."

"Only one way to find out."

"You stay here while I check things out."

"Don't be silly, I'm with you."

"If she comes home while I'm inside, things could get ugly."

"I like other people's ugly scenes. All that intense emotion, words spoken without thought, domestic violence—it's neat if I'm not taking part."

"But what if she expects you to take part?"

"I'll slap her upside the head."

I looked at Gilia in the late afternoon light. Her eyes sparkled, but I couldn't tell if it was from resolve or amusement. She was either being supportive in my time of tension or making sport of my personal problems. Either way, it would be nice not to face Wanda alone.

As we walked toward the house, I said, "Sometimes I wish I believed in firearm ownership."

She buddy-punched my shoulder. "Yeah, right, Wyatt Earp. In a showdown you're more likely to pull out a credit card than a gun."

~

The front door was locked and I was ready to give it up and head back to Greensboro, but Gilia reached through a broken window pane and flipped the bolt.

"You've got spine to spare dealing with my father and Skip, why turn into a whuss when it's your wife?"

"Wanda's meaner than your father and Skip."

The living room wasn't as bad as I'd expected—bare floor, single mattress up against the wall, overflowing ashtrays, pizza boxes with the one-two Domino's logo. I'd expected rotting trash and human feces; this was no worse than the average freshman dorm. On one wall someone had painted a Harley-Davidson that was fairly good.

Gilia wrinkled her nose at the smell. "So what's Grandma's jewelry stored in?"

"A box covered with green felt; at least that's what the stuff was in when Wanda took it. Desperate as she's been for cash, I doubt we'll find much."

Gilia bent down and turned over a couch pillow next to the mattress. "This it?" She held up Me Maw's jewelry box.

I nodded. "I don't suppose—"

"Nope."

I wandered down the hall and into the kitchen, where my baseball cards lay stacked on a linoleum-topped table. They were a mess. She'd mixed American League with National League and relief pitchers with starters. A sticky bottle of Log Cabin syrup was balanced on 1968. I guess she hadn't had time to figure out how much the collection was worth or where to sell it. She'd only stolen it to hurt me anyway; I told her a long time ago it wasn't worth huge amounts on account of Caspar burned all the pre-August 1963 cards, including a 1954 Alvin Dark that was the pride of my youth.

Don Drysdale, '65, fell on the floor, and when I bent to get him I discovered one table leg was propped up by *The Shortstop Kid*. I dropped to my knees and pulled it out from under the leg, which caused the table to tip and more cards to fall. *The Shortstop Kid* had been my first published novel. The day my carton of books arrived, I'd been so proud I took a picture of the mailman.

The cover was a boy in a home uniform, tagging second and making the throw to first. The kid on the cover was right-handed and my kid was left-handed, but even that didn't spoil the moment. I opened to the title page and read the inscription: For Wanda, My love for you shall never fade nor falter. You are my purpose. Yours, Sam.

"Sam, come here," Gilia called.

"Just a sec. I found the cards."

"Now would be better."

I followed Gilia's voice down the hall and into a bedroom, where I found Wanda passed out in a bed with two men—kids really. She was in the middle, on her back with her mouth open, naked. Wanda's breasts were so small she looked like a little girl. Her pubic hair had grown out some since I'd last seen it, and she had a bruise, or a hickie, I don't know which, on her thigh.

"Are they alive?" I asked.

Gilia stood against the wall. "I think so. They all seem to be breathing."

The guys had long hair. One wore an ankle bracelet made of leather and the other had a dark blue tattoo on his shoulder that said HOG. Both of them were touching Wanda.

"They're making a movie," Gilia said. She nodded toward a Panasonic videocamera on a tripod. It was aimed at the bed. A red light on the side blinked slowly.

I looked from Wanda to the book in my hand, and back to Wanda. Memory was hard to connect to reality.

Gilia stepped toward me and touched my arm. She said, "I can't picture you married to her."

"Would you gather up the cards? They're on the kitchen table."

"What are you going to do?"

"I'd like to stay here and watch her for a while."

Gilia glanced in the rearview mirror, then over at me. "Did you steal the videotape?"

"How did you know I wanted to?"

Her face crinkled into a smile. "I'm starting to see how that misguided mind of yours works."

Everybody thinks they know how I think but me.

"You look at watching your wife's porno flick as a duty," Gilia said, "as if you owe it to the experience of losing her."

Those weren't the exact words I'd used, but close enough. *Punishment deserved* was what I'd thought. The moral person does not avoid punishment deserved. But then at the last moment, in a giant spiritual step either forward or backward, I chose to skip the heartache.

"Besides," Gilia went on, "that tape in the hands of a lawyer would put an end to Wanda's hopes of taking your money."

"I guess I couldn't do that."

"Or we could mail the tape to her parents. It might actually help Wanda in the long run."

"I'm not good at hurting people in the short run to help them in the long run."

Gilia made a right-hand turn that left rubber on the curb next to my driveway. Her mind seemed to drift, which left her braking foot unattended until almost too late to save my garage. Only by stiff-arming the glove compartment did I avoid seat belt burns.

"You always drive like this?" I asked.

She looked at her hands on the steering wheel. "I was thinking about seeing Jeremy in bed with another woman. They were ignoring me so I got up and sat in a chair at my vanity table and watched him on top of her. She lifted her feet high and sweat ran down her neck. Jeremy's eyes were open in that foggy look I'd always thought was love. It was like a dream where you want to scream, but can't."

"Wanda must have been a low-quality person when I married her. I wonder why I didn't notice?"

"You see what you want to see and hear what you want to hear."

"Is that a quote? Sounds like Shakespeare or Woody Allen."

"It's me."

"Oh." We sat looking at the garage, the yard, and my big old house. I didn't want to go inside. I wanted to sit next to Gilia and feel clean.

"Did you love Jeremy?" I asked.

"A lot. Did you love Wanda?"

I saw Wanda on our wedding day. She'd worn a beige dress and smiled at me. "I thought I could save her."

"That's not the same as love."

I leaned across and kissed Gilia. Her lips didn't respond. She didn't flinch or fight, but it was definitely a one-sided kiss.

After about four seconds, she pulled back and said, "I'm sorry."

"Is it because you might be my sister?"

The eye contact was intense. "The rebound is too hard right now. I trusted a man and he slept with others, and no matter how nice it feels with you, I know it felt just as nice once with Jeremy. I can't ever go through that again."

"My wife sleeps with others and I don't see it as a reflection on the female gender."

Gilia's eyelids were so vulnerable they were translucent. "I'm not ready to trust yet."

Pursuing Gilia went against the choose-women-who-can't-hurt-you rule. A tramp's exit had knocked me into emotional chaos; the mind shuddered to think what would happen if I got attached to, then lost, Gilia. A good relationship might be more risk than I was willing to take.

"When do you think you may be ready?"

She shrugged. "I have no idea. Maybe never."

"I'll hang around a while and see what happens."

"I'd like that."

Gilia covered my hand with hers. It was more intimate than any sex I've had. She said, "Breakfast tomorrow?"

I said, "Cheese blintzes at nine."

Gilia drove away, and as I carried the grocery sack full of baseball cards, Me Maw's jewelry box, and *The Shortstop Kid* across the yard, I was forced to face the question of ethics. If you're planning, or hoping, to have an exclusive involvement with someone in the future, should comfort sex be cut out now? I wanted to pursue the friendship and more with Gilia, but because she had been hurt by an untrue man she was particularly sensitive to adultery, even more so than your average woman. I had as much as told Gilia that unlike her sleazeball husband, she could trust me; therefore it did not seem proper to do what I had been doing with her Aunt Katrina.

On the other hand, it's not like Gilia and I were going steady. We weren't even dating yet. There'd been a few conversations over breakfast and one unrequited kiss. At what point does a commitment begin? Normally you'd think the line was clear-cut, but I've run into problems during that fringe period at the outset when one person thinks you have an unspoken understanding and the other person is oblivious. Those unspoken understandings can wreak havoc.

Something heavy hit the garage wall from the inside—*Thonk*. My heart fired off a monumental beat and my legs went limp. Setting the bag on the grass, I moved closer to listen. A low buzz came from the wall itself, or maybe from something pressed against the wall. Thoughts ran to Mike Newberry or Ryan and Sonny, the vengeance boys. Shannon and Eugene could be in there committing a strange new sex ritual. So many ways of being perverse had come along in the last few years that I'd lost track.

A new sound, like a soft hum, filled in under the buzz. As I reached for the door, there was another *Thonk*. Sudden sounds where sounds aren't supposed to be means a surprise is coming, and nineteen out of twenty surprises are bad news. I did the Indian stealth walk around to a scrap pile on the back side of the garage and picked out a solid two-by-four. Wouldn't stop bullets or Ryan Saunders, but it was enough to slow down pretty much anyone else. At the door, I slowly turned the knob in my left hand and raised the two-by-four in my right hand to ear level, then I pushed with my shoulder.

Nothing happened. It was stuck. I leaned back, slammed into the door with my shoulder, it flew open, and I blew into the garage like a Laurel and Hardy routine—splat onto the floor.

The light blinded me, which was weird because I hadn't seen any light from outside. A rubber wheel passed within inches of my face. As my eyes adjusted, I realized golf carts were moving about the room. Two carts—Bull Run and Antietam—made tight circles, while Vicksburg, the Wilderness, Shiloh, and Appomattox Courthouse had all hit a wall—causing *Thonks*—where they buzzed as their tires spun on concrete.

When the Bull Run passed by a second time, I jumped in. A brick had been placed on the accelerator. I turned off the key and coasted to a stop beside the worktable next to the tool rack.

That's where I found Clark. He was lying on his back on the table, eyes closed and hands cupped on his sternum, like a laid-out corpse.

"Clark."

"Let me die."

"Not in my garage."

He didn't open his eyes or move his hands. He simply repeated, "Let me die, let me die."

I climbed out of the Bull Run and walked around the garage, turning off golf carts. He'd sealed both doors with masking tape, which is why the one I came through had been stuck and no light had been visible from outside. After collecting all the bricks, I walked over and sat back down in the Bull Run.

"Clark, you screwed up."

His eyes flew open. "That's no way to speak to a suicide. You might push me over the edge." For some reason, he'd taken off his shoes and socks, which only made the black outfit look sillier than ever.

"You're already over the edge. Look at this golf cart."

Clark sat up and studied the Bull Run. "So."

"Do you see an exhaust pipe?"

His forehead rippled in thought.

"An exhaust pipe, Clark. Even an idiot knows you can't kill yourself by sucking exhaust off an electric golf cart."

He blinked several times. "Why not?"

"Jesus." I spoke slowly and distinctly. "Electric motors have no exhaust. No exhaust, no carbon monoxide; no carbon monoxide, no death."

His entire body sagged as failure washed over his face. I've never seen anyone so disappointed at not being dead.

He said, "Now I'm back to killing you."

21

I mount the Exercycle 6000, crank up the tension, and ride. Straight into the Charlie Russell print, I pump until sweat pops onto my forehead like water drops on a hot griddle. Intense energy expended for the purpose of going nowhere—my mind is too blank to dwell on the metaphor.

For that is the goal, to blank my mind. To forget those I'm hurting and those I've lost. To forget how many people lose loved ones every day. To beat back depression.

Fat chance. Muscles break down before the brain. Three A.M. found me in bed, reading *Varieties of Religious Experience* by William James.

"It is with no small amount of trepidation that I take my place behind this desk, and face this learned audience."

Literary Valium. If James didn't put me out I was doomed.

I was reading his dismissal of medical materialism—which treats pining for spiritual veracity as a symptom of a disordered colon—when the phone rang.

"Mr. Callahan, you're a father."

My mouth went metallic. "Well, yes, that's true."

"This is Babs." There was a pause. "Babs Paseneaux."

"The pregnant Babs?"

"Not anymore." Giggles bubbled in the background.

"All right. You did it!"

"Three hours ago. The little booger hurt like the dickens."

"I'm proud of you, Babs. You gave birth." I was genuinely happy; felt better than I had in a year.

"Guess who's here?" Babs asked.

"Your husband realized his mistake and came home in time for the baby."

"Shoot no. I'll never talk to that low-life again. It's Lynette. She's right here." More giggles broke out as the girls carried on a whispered conference away from the phone.

Babs came back. "Lynette wants to talk to you."

"I want to talk to Lynette."

Sounds of scuffling and laughter came from their end. The only other woman I'd been around soon after she gave birth was Maurey, and I don't recall her being in such a cheery mood. Upbeat, yes, but not cheery.

"Remember me, Mr. Callahan? Lynette."

"I'm glad you turned around and came back, Lynette. Best friends should never break up over a man."

"*Puh.* Rory Paseneaux is no man. He's a rat. I broke water in the front seat of his precious Chevy and he ditched me. Took off while I was in the Texaco restroom trying to clean up."

"Sounds like Rory is afraid of responsibility," I said.

"Rory is afraid of stained upholstery." Lynette lapsed into a few seconds of silence. Had Rory really abandoned her because she broke water in his car? Southern men are weird about cars, but that was a bit much.

"Babs says you're paying her hospital bills."

"I'll pick up yours too."

She squealed. "I *knew* it. I knew you were the nicest man I ever met. Sammi will grow up to be just like you, only a girl."

"Sammi?"

"Sammi with an *i* and no *e*. She's seven hours older than Sam."

I had a funny feeling. "Who is Sam?"

"Babs's baby, of course. We're going to raise them like twins with different mothers. Sam and Sammi."

This seemed like good news, but I wasn't sure. For certain, it was odd. "Are you girls going to tell the kids who their real fathers are?"

"Are you kidding? Here, Babs wants to talk."

More giggles. More confusion. At least I'd made someone happy. If I have a choice, I'd rather make people happy some way other than giving them money, but I'll take goodwill however it comes.

"You're not mad at us, are you, Mr. Callahan?"

"Why would I be mad? I'm honored you named your babies Sam and Sammi."

"There's more."

"Tell him," Lynette chirped in the background.

"Tell me what?"

"The birth certificate lady said we could write down anyone we wanted as the fathers, so long as he didn't mind."

Uh-oh. "Both of you?"

"We hope you don't mind."

When I walked into Tex and Shirley's Pancake House an embarrassed scarecrow stood beside the PLEASE WAIT TO BE SEATED sign, clutching a stack of menus to her breasts. Behind the cash register, King Kong made change for a postman who didn't seem a bit nonplussed to be receiving money from the paw of a gorilla.

I've been disoriented often enough that I know it doesn't pay to draw attention to the fact. Just keep your head down, pretend everything is normal, and hope that with time the chaos will sort itself out.

"Morning, Mr. Callahan," Judy said as she poured my coffee. Judy wore long whiskers, pointed ears, and a tail. She said, "I'm a cat."

My chronic disorientation is triggered by a daydream mentality. Throughout the drive to Tex and Shirley's, I'd been pretending on their sixteenth birthday Sam and Sammi apply for driver's licenses and spot my name on their birth certificates. They bolt the license

156

bureau and rush to the Manor House, where I embrace my newfound family and give birthday presents.

Maybe the moral thing would be to adopt them, more or less, right now. Take fatherhood seriously, even though it seemed strange to suddenly have two children by teenage girls I hardly knew. Not that I minded, but it was a major commitment to take on without forethought. I'm prone to quick commitments, probably a reaction against Lydia. She's so afraid of commitment that back when I was young and she smoked cigarettes, she wouldn't buy the same brand twice in a row.

I felt sweet breath on my cheek, and when I turned to track down the source, Gilia kissed me. *Smack.* Right on the lips. Her mouth was supple and soft, yet controlled, with a faint taste of Carmex.

"I'm sorry," she said. "I was uptight last night. I have to remind myself there's a difference between being careful and closing up shop completely."

With her face close to mine, the situation clicked. "Today is Halloween. That's why people are in costume," I said.

"Right." She slid into her chair. "So what do you say? Can you handle a relationship where you kiss but don't fuck?"

The suddenness with which Gilia went frank always took me off guard. This wasn't a woman who wasted time saying "Good morning." Judy came by with the coffeepot to take our order—cheese blintzes for me and Swedish pancakes for Gilia. I like a woman who eats real food instead of dry toast and skimmed milk.

After Judy left, I said, "Are there kiss limits?"

Gilia pulled her blond hair into a doughnut-shaped bungee cord sort of thing. I forget what they're called. "Like French?"

"More like necking. Are you talking kiss-hello, kiss-goodbye or a thirty-minute make-out session?"

"I won't set rules. My only request is I'm not ready to make love, so if we ever do neck to the point where I say okay, you have to ignore me and stop."

That's definitely defining parameters. I looked at the hair on her arms and thought of lemon meringue pie. Waking up beside Gilia would be like waking up in a mountain meadow next to a bubbling brook, only without the hay fever.

"I can do that," I said.

"Great."

When Judy brought our food Gilia dug right in with butter and syrup, but I only pretended to eat. What I really did was watch her face. Watching Gilia's face was like watching a time lapse movie of the sky. She registered everything. When I said *father*, her skin tone darkened. *Jack-o'-lantern* caused crinkles to dance. After looking at Gilia a few minutes, I didn't know why I had ever thought Wanda's face was interesting. Wanda had three basic looks—drunk, sober, and PMS. Gilia had hundreds.

I concentrated on the freckle between her nose and right eye. It was like one of those little thermometers that pop out of turkeys when they're done. Gilia's freckle glowed as she approached passion, such as when she raged at Ronald Reagan and the invasion of Grenada. She really cared about current events. Lydia used to be a news junkie, after she stopped drinking and before she went into feminist literature. Now, she's a single-issue newshound. I've never followed the world that closely myself.

"Clark Gaines tried to kill himself in my garage last night," I said.

Her head did the sudden cock to one side thing. "How hard did he try?"

"He made a Polish joke out of it."

The freckle kind of spread toward the eye. That was her introspective look. "Poor kid."

"I think I'll call Billy this afternoon. All Clark wants is attention, but he's liable to slip up and and waste himself trying to get it."

Gilia put both hands around a coffee cup. "I remember Clark from company picnics when I was young. He was the kid the other boys depantsed in the woods."

"I've been that kid. Makes for a tough puberty."

Judy came over to pick up our plates and tell us about the other Judy's pinworms. We listened in interest and Gilia even asked a consistency question. Everyone needs someone who is interested in their problems, especially career waitresses, but I for one was glad I'd finished my blintz.

While I nursed a final cup—my fifth of the day—Gilia stared out

158

the window at the damp Carolina morning. Rain had been threatening all week, and now it looked ready to dump.

"I'm free tonight," Gilia said. "Care for a movie? *Terms of Endearment* is playing at Four Seasons Mall."

It was my turn to pay. "A movie?"

"Like a date, sort of. We'll go Dutch so neither one of us worries about strings attached."

I studied the check closely, making certain Judy added right. "I'd love to, but tonight I can't. There's this CEO in from Nebraska whose country club might buy a hundred ten Shilohs, and I'm stuck with the wining and dining. If it's over early, I'll call."

Gilia cocked her head and studied me a moment. Then she said, "Sounds good. Maybe we'll hit the movie tomorrow night."

22

Okay, I lied. Crucify me. There was no CEO from Nebraska to wine and dine, and if there had been, I sure as heck wouldn't be the winer and diner. Schmoozing was Ambrosia's turf. All I can figure is maybe I was falling in love, because my strictest ethical rule is never, ever lie to a woman. Let them lie to you. Maurey wrote a letter back in college in which she explained honesty, love, and sex. She wrote: "Sam, I've discovered how to seduce anyone I want. If you don't love them, act like you do, and if you do love them, act like you don't."

So, by lying to Gilia, what I actually did was prove my love for her. I only hoped she saw it that way when I got caught.

The direct cause for my lie was Katrina Prescott's birthday. Within minutes after Skip threatened me by phone Saturday, he and Sonny left for the Sport Shoe Trade Show in Atlanta. Every year they spent the first week of November in Atlanta, staying abreast of new developments in footwear—and drink and fornication, according to Katrina—and every year Katrina threw a hissy fit because Halloween was her birthday.

And Friday, in a moment of post-orgasmic pity, I'd promised Katrina she didn't have to spend another birthday alone. The poor woman wanted a spark of out-front, formal celebration—something more traditional than bondage stunts with a stranger in a Ramada Inn motel room. She wanted to dress nice and eat in a public place with civilized lighting and table service. That's not asking so much for a birthday.

She applied pressure and I said *yes*. I haven't said *no* to a woman yet. No reason to think I'd start on a birthday wish.

Gaylene stormed across the Magic Cart Company parking lot, demanding to know who this Vernon Scharp was who'd shown up saying I promised him a job.

"He's a process server."

"And how does serving processes qualify him to build golf carts?"

"I felt sorry for him," I said. "Bringing people bad news must be a sad way to make a living."

Gaylene stared up at me and twitched. She's fifty or so and about four ten, and the plant workers are scared to death of her. Much of my fear of fiery little women stems from Gaylene.

"You plan on hiring every sad case you feel sorry for?" she asked. "Because if you are, I'm going to work for R. J. Reynolds."

I'd hoped to mention Babs and Lynette, but this didn't seem the time. "I won't do it again."

"Write the checks, Sam. Leave running the shop to me."

Mrs. Gaines told me Billy was in Atlanta at the Sport Shoe Trade Show. I'd never met the woman and didn't know if Billy had told her my story, so I felt funny about saying, "I'm your husband's bastard son and your legitimate son tried to kill himself in my garage last night." There'd been enough life-shattering conversations lately; I couldn't handle another one.

"What should I tell Billy this is in reference to?" she asked.

"His name came up as a possible judge in the Coke versus Pepsi competition."

"Billy only drinks root beer. Caffeine makes him irritable."

"I'll make a note of that."

Moses Cone Hospital was only too happy to accept my credit card. I talked to a woman in patient billing and I'm not sure but I thought I heard a smirk behind her voice. The whole staff was probably gossiping about the man who fathered two babies in one day.

She asked my relationship to the patients and I said, "Benefactor."

Next I called the Dyn-o-Mite Novelty Company to cancel the As-God-Is-My-Witness bumper sticker. So much for my anti-monogamy pledge. From now on side sex would be fraught with guilt, which is how it should be, I suppose.

Wanda's voice crackled. "Have you no gratitude?"

"Hi, honey."

"After all I sacrificed for us as a couple, you have the unmitigated gall to break into my home and steal my property."

"My property, actually."

"You did me wrong, Sam, and now you *owe* me."

"I notice you saved the autographed copy of *The Shortstop Kid*. Freud would take that as a sign you still love me."

"The novels are trash, Sam. Only a whore writes genre fiction."

"I saw your little video setup."

Wanda's controlled breathing oozed over the line. "My Art Erotica is none of your business."

"Haul me into court and we'll let the judge decide who's creating art and who's a whore." I couldn't help but wonder how charging Sam's and Sammi's births on my credit card would go over at a divorce hearing. Didn't take a writer's imagination to foresee messiness.

162

"I know you too well, Sam. You don't have the balls to fight me."

"Want to bet?"

She hung up.

Shirley poked her head through my office door.

"A man's roaming the halls, looking for you."

"I'm not here. Send him to whoever I would send him to if I was here."

She scowled as if I'd insulted her intelligence. "I already did. He says he has to meet with you, personally. He looks like a politician."

"Oh, God, it's Cameron Saunders."

"Should I tell him to go away?"

"Hell." My mind raced through the boundless implications. Unlike Skip Prescott, who ran on heat and steam, Cameron wasn't the type you could dodge until he lost interest. "Send him in."

Tall, bald Cameron glided in on Cole-Haan shoes. I own a pair, but I'm not pretentious so I don't wear them. Cameron wore a three-piece suit that fit him perfectly and a tie so tasteful I could spit.

He said, "Mr. Callahan."

I said, "Mr. Saunders."

He stepped forward and spread a deck of Polaroid prints across my desk. I picked up the one on my far left, carefully, by the borders, so as not to smudge the picture of Katrina and me entering room 247 of the Ramada Inn. They all followed the same vein—Katrina and me coming out of room 247 with her hand on my butt, Katrina in her red-and-white cheerleader outfit, walking into the Manor House, a through-the-window shot of Katrina dancing while I hang naked on the wall with a pom-pom on my crotch. In each photo, she was smiling and I wasn't.

"You hired another detective," I said.

Cameron flashed his ice blue smile, smug as a snake on a rat. "Frankly, my man was following Katrina. You came as something of a bonus."

I stood up and moved to the window. From behind a row of pines, a Piedmont Airlines plane lifted off, headed west, where I should have been.

163

Cameron spoke to my back. "My ambition is to run for Congress, for a start."

"I knew you were a politician."

"And I cannot afford a business partner whose wife causes scandals."

"What does Skip think of you spying on his wife?"

"Skip doesn't think."

"He doesn't know." I watched the weather and waited for whatever was coming next. The problem, as I saw it, was I'd let myself fall into the hands of an unethical man who hated me while I loved his daughter. I smiled at my reflection in the window; that was nice, I loved his daughter.

Cameron leaned forward with three fingers forming a tripod on my desk. "Bottom line, buster. You are to leave Greensboro. You are never to speak of the incident in question to anyone. No newspapers. No TV. You better not even tell a priest, because I will find out and I will destroy you."

One last look at the plane disappearing west, then I turned to face him. "Did you think to ask politely? I never intended going on TV."

"This matter cannot be left to a bastard's discretion. Politics is expensive, the party cannot risk you turning wise-ass the week before an election."

"That'll be the Republican Party?"

He said, "I needn't spell out the consequences."

"Spell them out anyway."

"Skip Prescott." Cameron's upper lip glistened with a light film of sweat. I'd seen the same film on Gilia and thought it lovely.

"To tell the truth, Mr. Saunders, I'm not afraid of Skip. What exactly could he do?"

"His money can hire you a gob of grief."

"My money can sue his shorts off."

Cameron strummed his fingers as he studied the photos. His eyes came up to meet mine. "Gilia."

Got me cold. "Why would Gilia care what I do?"

His laugh was bitter. "Nothing in my political career is being left to chance."

"You're spying on your own daughter?" No way could a man this sleazy be my father.

"For some inexplicable reason, she has developed a trust in you. Consider how these photographs will affect that trust."

Since the bald buzzard wasn't Dad, that cleared up the incest problem, at least as far as sister went. She could still be a cousin. None of it would mean squat when Cameron showed her the pictures.

"That's a lousy way to use your daughter."

He shrugged. "I am protecting her."

"If I had proof my daughter's boyfriend was a pervert, I wouldn't blackmail him. I'd tell her."

He smiled again. "That would do away with my leverage, wouldn't it?"

The numbness started in my solar plexus and spread in and up until all the major organs were desensitized. This sort of thing happens when you live by your own private version of right and wrong and say to hell with everyone else's values. I'd justified Katrina on the grounds that I was not yet promised to Gilia, but when it came time for Gilia to know the score, my justification stank.

I made it into the executive bathroom, fully intending to vomit, but as I knelt over the toilet bowl I remembered my novel *Bucky on Half Dome* in the tank. Even though a few pages had curled about the flush mechanism to the point where they disintegrated on touch, most of the manuscript surfaced more or less whole. I cradled the sopping mess in my arms and carefully carried it to my desk, where I cleared a space by tossing Wanda's picture in the trash.

Shirley poked her head back through the door. "What did the politician want?"

"Blackmail."

"I should have thought of that years ago." When I didn't laugh, Shirley went away.

The typewriter ink hadn't smeared, but my handwritten notes in the margins had. I read the page where Bucky assures Samantha's mother that their trip holds no danger. Tension between Samantha and her mother runs through all the Bucky books.

Peeling the sheets apart required concentration—not my strong suit, at the moment. Fifteen minutes' work brought back six legible pages, then I gave it up as a waste of time. Even nauseous, I knew I was only pulling the past out of the toilet because Cameron had mangled the future. And the past itself was shot; the book had gone underwater in the first place after Wanda spoiled my memories. Which left nothing but the present, and right now the present wasn't so all-fired wonderful either.

What I needed was advice from someone simple. Complex people get so distracted by looking four moves ahead that they're frozen when it comes to what to do next. Slow thinkers make faster decisions.

So I headed for the hospital. Not that Babs and Lynette were slow, as in stupid; they just knew the worth of intellect, which doesn't rate too high compared to other functions.

First stop was the viewing window by the nurses' station. Sam and Sammi lay next to each other in clear, Plexiglas bassinets with crib safety instructions on the side. They both wore white knit hats and had rose-petal eyelids. I could tell which was which by the rubber bulb thing the nurses use to clear gunk from babies' noses. Sam's was blue, Sammi's pink. I pretended they were forty-three and called me Dad. I would be seventy-six.

Two doors down the hall, Babs and Lynette sat propped up in bed, wearing billowy purple nightgowns, sucking Coca-Cola through hospital straws and watching *The Bold and the Beautiful* on the wall-mounted TV. When they saw me they both squealed and broke into labor and birth stories.

"Dr. Hayse told me I was the bravest girl he'd ever seen," Lynette said.

Babs flounced on her pillow. "He said the very same thing to me too. I bet he says that to ever'one."

"Be just like a man."

I talked. I hadn't meant to when I walked into the room, and I'm not certain how I got started, all I know is the whole story poured out—from Christmas 1949 to Cameron calling his daughter "Leverage." The first few minutes Lynette split her attention between me and the soap, but by the end I had both girls rapt. It was the longest uninterrupted speech I've ever made to a woman.

When I was done, I sighed once and waited for their verdict. Hearing it aloud made me realize how tawdry I was. The girls could condemn or shun me; they still had time to change Sam's and Sammi's names. Whatever they did, I deserved it.

Lynette sucked air off the bottom of her Coke can. "Shoot," she said. "That happens all the time on TV."

"All the time?" I hate it when my problems aren't unique.

"Not all the time," Babs said. "Not exactly like you told it. But nobody knows who their folks are and someone's all the time threatening to expose someone else."

"So what do people on TV do?"

Babs giggled. "The dumbest thing they can think up."

Lynette nodded. "People on TV are stupid."

"Any geek knows what you should do," Babs said.

I didn't get it. If any geek knew the answer, why didn't I? Novelists are supposed to understand the human plight.

Lynette said, "Dump the woman you don't like and beg forgiveness from the one you do."

Babs added, "Only you better confess before her daddy spills the beans. If he tells, you're in deep doo-doo."

I considered the advice. It had to be good; no one who says *doo-doo* has hidden motives. Besides, nothing I'd tried had worked.

"If you were Gilia and I confessed and begged your forgiveness, would you forgive me?"

Lynette looked at Babs, who thought a moment, then said, "Fat chance."

23

Catharsis comes from the ancient Greek word καζαιρω, which literally translated means "to pass a hard stool." That evening as I stood in my room dressing for the appointment with Katrina, I passed a hard stool. It was inspired by what Lynette said about soap opera characters always doing the stupidest thing possible.

As a kid, I lived for books. I inhaled every book I could lay my hands on, from Nancy Drew to Hemingway and beyond. Books were real; social reality was a bother. Tom Swift and Peter Pan were stronger, faster, smarter, and morally superior to anyone I saw in person; therefore whenever I faced a situation I learned to take the course my heroes would have taken.

Here comes the catharsis: Fictional people don't make logical choices, they go with whatever is most interesting for the story. And stupid mistakes are much more interesting than wise conduct. Which means that when it comes time to decide the future, I—deliberately—am stupid.

Marrying Wanda to save her was interesting, but stupid. Searching for five fathers, eating Katrina, adopting strangers' babies—all interesting but stupid. I'd found a motto. Or better yet, the inscription for my tombstone: Sam Callahan was interesting, but stupid.

Realizing a fatal flaw in your character and fixing that flaw are separate matters. My first choice under the boring-but-right system would be what to wear tonight. Going as a slob would show disrespect for Katrina and her birthday, but dressing upscale might be taken as a sign we're dating. Didn't want to send the wrong message. I finally decided on fairly new Levi's, a button-up, tuck-in Banana Republic shirt, and a sports coat Shannon bought at the Burlington Factory Outlet store. I considered cowboy boots, but that felt like too much. After all, this was a breakup.

I was sitting on the bed, lacing up my Adidas, when Shannon walked in without knocking. She was dressed as a Tahitian belly dancer—grass skirt and breasts covered by plumeria leis.

"I hope you have something on under the flowers," I said.

"Oh, Daddy, where's your Halloween spirit?" She moved across the room and sat in my desk chair, facing me. "You got a hot date tonight?"

"It's business, a CEO from Nebraska wants to see the sights of Greensboro."

Shannon shot me the female don't-jive-me look and said, "Have your little secrets if you want, I don't care." She picked up Maurey's picture that I like to keep behind the typewriter. Maurey is sitting astride her horse Frostbite on a ridge above the TM ranch. Her hair is in braids and she looks like God's own sweetheart. That photo has caused much resentment among my girlfriends. So much resentment that I had to hide it from Wanda.

Shannon studied the picture of her mother and said, "Dad, I need to explain options to you."

"Options?"

"What I'm going to do and what your choices are next."

This didn't sound good. "What are you going to do?"

She touched Maurey's face. Maurey was twenty-six in the picture, so Shannon could have been looking at an age-enhanced picture of herself.

"I'm going to live with Eugene," she said.

All my liberal upbringing flew right out the window. I said, "You're grounded, little lady."

Shannon lifted her eyes and laughed. "Daddy, you can't ground me."

"I can't?"

"I'm a grown-up now. You haven't tried grounding me since high school."

"That was two years ago."

"You haven't grounded me and gotten away with it since junior high."

"You're just like your mother." Shannon could take that about six different ways, but unlike me, she wasn't into endless nuances.

She looked from Maurey to me. "Okay, here are your choices."

"Is breaking Eugene's nose a choice?"

"No. You can fly off the handle, scream and yell and throw me out of the house, and estrange your daughter for life."

"Eugene taught you that, didn't he? To say *estrange* when you mean *piss off.*"

"Choice two: I live with Eugene in his apartment with the three male roommates."

"I don't like that one."

"Choice three is Eugene moves in here and you treat him like the son you never had."

It didn't take much thought. "I choose number three."

Shannon's face sparkled, making the crap of living around Eugene the child molester worth the trouble. She crossed the gap between us and hugged me. "I knew you'd come through."

"I don't want him downstairs in his underwear."

"Neither do I."

I looked up into her brown eyes. "Shannon, you've been the only consistent, unqualified love in my life. I know you have to leave someday—that's the curse of being a parent—but I'm just not ready to lose you yet."

She smiled and said, "Daddy, you're sweet."

"Promise you won't leave until I'm ready."

"Forget it. You'll never be ready."

Shannon left to find her lover and light pumpkins and I sat in my room with the lights off, looking out at the rain. The steady drizzle matched my mood perfectly. Nothing was absolute anymore. Right, wrong, desirable, and undesirable had all turned on their heads. Amid the uncertainties, the one thing I knew for sure was I had to talk to Maurey.

Her lifesaving voice floated in from Wyoming. "Hello?"

I said, "The deal is falling apart out here."

There was a short pause. "The deal isn't so hot here either."

"What's the matter?"

She sounded flat. Maurey is normally upbeat, or at least interested. I worry when she's down. "I can't talk about it yet," she said. "I'd rather hear your problems."

"Actually, it affects both of us."

"Shannon broke the news."

"She told you first?"

"She asked if I thought you'd boot her out of the house. I said not in a hundred years."

"I raised her but she confides in you."

"Kids never confide in the parent they live with. Are you going to let the boy move in?"

"He's no boy," I said, "and of course he's moving in."

"You did something right for a change."

"If I did, it's the first right move I've made all week."

"Shannon tells me you're on a strange roll."

"Bizarre is more the word." I told Maurey about finding the fathers and what I'd done to Atalanta Williams and Clark Gaines and how I felt about Gilia. That part took a while. Maurey listened and gave the appropriate comments, but her mind seemed to wander.

"What's the girl's father blackmailing you for doing?" she asked.

"Nothing. Well, something. A detective researched my past."

"And?"

"He found stuff."

"Why do I feel like I'm only hearing part of the story?"

In listing the elements making me crazy, I'd left out Katrina and I'd left out Wanda. Ten days ago Wanda had been this thunderhead cloud smothering every thought and action, and now she didn't matter. Eugene might be a pedophilic psych major, but his plan had worked. My mind was off Wanda.

"What's the problem you can't talk about?" I asked.

"I can't talk about it."

"Okay."

"Pete has leukemia."

The rain made falling-star streaks on the window. Beyond the glass, the Georgia hackberries dripped circles of water onto the lawn and the swimming pool speckled like a pond during a mayfly hatch. I tried to remember if leukemia is always fatal or nearly always fatal.

"He's had it two years without telling me," Maurey said. "It's in remission now, but for some reason, he doesn't expect it to stay that way. He and Chet argue positive attitude versus acceptance."

Chet would be the boyfriend Lydia liked. "Is there anything I can do?"

Maurey was silent a few moments. "If he gets worse, I may need you to come home."

I almost cried. Being needed is what I live for. "I'll be there."

"He has no insurance and he's run up thirty-five thousand in tests and treatments—so far."

"Don't worry about the bills."

"Thank you." Maurey's voice broke. "I'm sick of family dying. If I lose Pete, everyone I grew up with will be gone and I'll be the last, which is a first-degree screw job. I don't like it, Sam."

"You still have me and Shannon."

Now, she was fierce. "You better not abandon me too."

24

onaparte's Retreat was a fish and French place way the heck
out Randleman Road, nice enough to qualify as special, but
not so trendy as to make running into Skip's golf buddies
likely. Sea nets hung from the corners of the room with starfish and
dried cod or something hanging from the nets. Lighting came from
candles that must have been cheap because mine strobed. The place
reeked of hand-holding and eye contact by candlelight.

Cool fingers touched the back of my neck. "I can't get enough of
your amativeness nodes," Katrina said.

I tipped my head way back to look up at her. "Do you like Blue
Nun?"

"Your hair is nice too."

"Many people say my hair is my best trait."

Katrina moved around the table to her chair. "Anyone who says
that hasn't felt your amativeness nodes." She was wearing a dark
green jacket over a white knit dress. I guess you'd call it a dress;
when she sat down it covered her crotch and maybe an inch and a

half of thigh. If Shannon wore that dress I would send her to her room.

"What's this?" Katrina asked.

"Blue Nun. I thought you might like some wine."

"I'd like some martinis." She pulled off her jacket, revealing her shoulders and a quarter-moon slice of upper chest. Katrina was actually quite pretty, in a miniature sort of way. Her legs would have looked good on an aging movie star.

"Eat fast," she said. "The orgy starts at eight."

"We have to talk about this orgy," I said.

Katrina smiled. "Later. Right now, I'm starved." She ordered mussels and I had the Surf 'N' Swamp—lobster claws and frog legs. The waiter called me "sir" four times.

Katrina was in a good mood. She made fun of my jacket and told me about a fat girl in her aerobics class who'd blown a knee during the stretch-out.

She said, "I love it when women younger than me fall apart."

I took a deep breath and prepared to take the plunge. When it's time for the kiss-off, I'm much more comfortable with women dumping me than me dumping women. I'm real good at the former—never resorting to angry words or accusations, never making the woman feel guilty. Dumping me is easy. But when it comes to the other way around, I'm a coward.

"It's all over, Katrina."

She glanced up from her salad. "I know."

"This is the last time we can see each other."

"I said I know." Her voice was a bit wistful, but far from heartbreak. "Cameron paid me a visit."

I'd been braced for tears in a public place. I wasn't prepared for Katrina being a good sport.

"What did you think of the pictures?" I asked.

"Did you see the cheerleading shot? My thighs were positively grotesque."

"But what about Cameron?"

"Cameron is a pig."

When the waiter brought our main courses my legs and claws were arranged in an artsy, nouvelle-type design on the plate. He went into that routine where they hover over your food with what looks like a walnut fence post.

"Fresh ground pepper, sir?"

A bare foot plopped in my lap. "No, thank you." Katrina had amazing toe dexterity. Midway through the salad, I felt my Levi's zipper slip.

"If you've seen the pictures, why are you so chipper?" I asked.

"I'm turned on just thinking about my birthday orgy."

"There's not going to be a birthday orgy. This is it. Right now."

Her toes grazed up and down. "Don't be silly. The last diddle before you lose a lover is always so poignant. I love it, better than the first time."

"We've already had our last diddle."

"*Au contraire, chéri.* Eat up, the party kicks off at eight, with or without you."

My first thought was this: Starting tomorrow, I was to begin a God-knows-how-long celibate period while I convinced Gilia I wasn't a promiscuous male. That left tonight.

"Why is the orgy on a time schedule?"

"It's that jerk, Skip." Katrina did strange, probing motions in my boxer shorts. "His Highness ordered me home by eight to tape Monday Night Football."

"Why not program the VCR to turn itself on?"

"You ever meet anybody knows how to work those machines? The directions say it can be done, but it's a dirty, Japanese lie."

She accepted another martini from the waiter. I suspected he knew about the footsie game under the tablecloth, but he was too cloying to comment. Whenever I see a waiter I think about the poor single mother somewhere who's out of a job because this guy is too lazy to work construction.

"Skip said he'll confiscate my car if I don't get his precious ball game—every second—so I have to be there to change the tape after three hours. Football games last longer than videotapes." She gave me the most Southern smile you can imagine. "And you know what we're going to do for those three hours?"

"The Ramada Inn?"

The toe popped through. "Nope. We're going to do it right in old

175

Skippy-pooh's king-size bed. This is the last time and I demand it all. Bondage. Fantasy. S and M. Anal. I'll bet you know stuff I haven't even heard of."

Probably true. "How many times have I explained, sex should be affectionate, not revenge."

"Revenge gives a better orgasm."

Katrina eyed me while I looked down at my empty claw and thought of Gilia. Gilia was wholesome, Katrina was sick. Where did that leave me?

"What about the Saunders?" I asked.

"Mimi can get her own gigolo."

"What if they see the lights?"

"So what if they see the lights?"

"How about Phadron?"

"She asked for a raise and Skip had her deported. I never told you about Phadron, how did you know her name?"

I shrugged and faked innocence. "Heard it somewhere, I guess."

The waiter cleared our plates. I said *no* to dessert and *yes* to an after-dinner Grand Marnier. Katrina had another martini. Her foot grew increasingly aggressive.

"I'll do it," I said, "only at the Ramada. One last time, but this is absolutely it."

She smiled. "You'll do it at my house."

"I think that's a bad idea."

She jabbed her toe. "I don't care what you think. Can't you understand that? I no longer care about you."

"You have a warped attitude toward sex," I said.

Now, she was mad. It always frightens me how quickly a woman can go from a perfectly pleasant mood to all-out fury.

"*I* have a warped attitude? What about you, *Mr. Pussy Eater*? You afraid of honest copulation? Afraid to get our little pee-pee dirty?"

Two tables over, a busboy dropped a glass.

"I need romanticism."

Strong words for a man with a foot in his fly.

Katrina laughed—a harsh sound, not tinkle-like at all. "I'll bet it doesn't work. You lead with your tongue because your pee-pee can't cut the mustard."

"That's right, Katrina. You hit the nail on the head."

"Not yet, buster."

"Skip won't do it with me any way but him on top banging like a rabbit," Katrina said as she drove through the slick streets. My car was back at Bonaparte's because I'd drawn the line at parking in front of her house.

"He plays all kinds of games with his girlfriends and whores, but with me it's old, boring squash-the-boobs." Her voice was sad.

"How do you know he plays games with his girlfriends?"

"They tell me. That slut Tiffany Jane in the shoe department says Skip likes to spread-eagle her on a copier and Xerox the whole thing. I tried getting on top once and Skip called me a 'feminist.' "

Although she couldn't be too athletic and drive at the same time, Katrina still managed to keep my attention with her right hand. Manually speaking, most women go at it like the guy is fourteen years old, holed up in the bathroom with a *Sports Illustrated* swimsuit issue while his sister bangs on the door, shouting, "Hurry up." Katrina was considerably more subtle.

She went on. "He's probably got Tiffany Jane in Atlanta right now. Hell, he takes the entire shoe department. I'm taping his dumb football so he doesn't have to pull out his cock long enough to turn on the TV."

In her driveway, Katrina decided we'd had enough foreplay. She kissed me long and hard while I fumbled with my seat belt. During French kissing, the average girl expects the boy to extend his tongue instead of her extending hers, but Katrina wasn't the average girl.

I backed quickly toward my door. "It's almost eight, we better go inside."

"I can't believe you are so anal retentive. If I'd known you were this conventional I'd have chosen somebody else."

"I'm real conventional, Katrina."

"Not according to your phrenological chart."

I got the door open and myself out of the car without falling on the driveway. Katrina followed me out the passenger side, Frenching all the way.

She said, "Let's do it in the yard."

"It's raining."

"I swear, you have no spontaneity."

"I don't believe in spontaneity when it's raining."

As I started across the lawn toward the door Katrina tackled me from behind and rolled us more or less under a shrubby bush. She sat astraddle me with her knees on my shoulders.

I said, "You're not wearing panties."

"Take me now," she said.

"Do I have to?"

No use fighting fate. It actually wasn't that bad by the bush. The ground under my head was nearly dry, and, except for twigs in my back, it was comfortable—not comfortable enough for a nap or reading a book, but passable for nature sex.

Katrina twisted around, yanked off my shoes and socks, and threw them across the yard. She slid onto the grass and began pulling at my jeans and boxers. I arched my back to make it easier on her. When they finally came off, she whirled them around her head like a lasso and let go. Then, she tore off my shirt. This wasn't my first choice for fun, but I could live with it. Both the Prescott and Saunders houses were dark except for a dim security light over by the Saunders' driveway. A larger hedge blocked the first-floor view from the house on the other side. I wondered if Gilia had gone to the movie without me. Maybe she was with a boy her own age.

"Okay," Katrina said. "Let's rock."

She climbed on board and went at her thing; I lay back and looked up at the bush. Sex is a lot more relaxing with the woman on top. You can admire the light reflecting on her body and pretend she's a movie star having the time of her life. You can think about baseball. Woman-on-top combines the best of involvement with the best of spectating; missionary style takes too much concentration.

Whispers came from the street. I clamped my hand over Katrina's mouth and we listened to a conversation between a boy with two heads, a human fly, and Prince.

"Too dark, ain't nobody home."

"We could try."

"Nobody home and they might have a dog. I'm not going in there."

"Chicken lips."

"Worm breath, you're so brave, you go knock."

"I'm not if you're not."

"We're wasting time, I told you rich neighborhoods suck."

"Colored houses give the best candy."

"Hand me an egg. This'll teach 'em to stay home Halloween."

The boy with two heads cocked his arm and let fly. I didn't see the egg, but a *thok* hit the second story of the house. Beneath my hand, Katrina struggled to shout. I clamped her harder as the three trick-or-treaters disappeared down the street.

I moved my hand from Katrina's mouth. "If those kids had come to your door they'd have seen us. Hell, they'd have tripped over us."

"But they didn't." She closed her eyes and resumed hopping up and down.

I grabbed her hips and squeezed to get her attention. "Others will, Katrina. The next batch might come across the yard."

She exhaled an exasperated *"So?"*

"So we have to go inside."

"I'm happy here."

"I won't have sex in front of children. Get up, we're going indoors."

Katrina considered the alternatives for a few moments. Every now and then she gave an experimental jiggle. That's when I realized she was doing Kegels in there.

"Katrina."

"We'll go in the house, but only one one condition."

"I don't do conditions."

"You can't come out of me."

"What?"

"I won't allow a man to pull out just as it's getting interesting."

"I have to pull out to walk."

"In *Five Easy Pieces* Jack Nicholson gets inside Sally Struthers and runs all over the room, bumping into furniture and walls and everything."

"I remember Sally Struthers' tit."

"And now she's on TV collecting money for Feed the Children, so it must be okay. Sally Struthers is normal."

Why not? The standing position always looked fun in the movies. I sat, then raised up on the soles of my feet. Katrina wrapped her arms around my neck, and, with a grunt—several grunts—I made it upright.

All right. Slight wobble but I'm okay. Felt somewhat like a back-pack on backward—all the weight on the hips and the rest was balance. I got my hands on her lower back and we were mobile. More or less. It's not as romantic or wild as it looks in the movies, but then what is? Given a light woman, it can be done.

"Keys," I said.

"My jacket pocket." She pulled her keys out and stuck them between my teeth. Acrobatic details taken care of, she went back to the general purpose of sex—side-to-side, up-and-down, in-and-out. I stumble-shuffled across the wet lawn, for once glad to be barefoot. The porch steps took a one-leg-at-a-time motion with frequent rests. At the top, I sort of fell forward and propped Katrina against the wall. She, of course, did nothing to help. In fact, from the *"God don't stop"* and *"Oh baby"* sounds, she seemed on the edge of something big.

I got the keys from my mouth and fumbled at the lock for some time before the door swung open. Like a groom carrying his bride across the threshold, I stepped into the Prescott house, amazed that we'd made it across the yard and inside without being seen. Katrina kicked the door closed behind me, plunging us into blackness.

What next, I thought, then an instant later blinding light slammed my eyes and a bunch of voices shouted *"Surprise!"*

2 5

Thirty or so people stood in a rough semicircle around the Prescott living room, blinking in the sudden light and the less sudden knowledge of what they were looking at. A few launched into "Happy Birthday," but the song petered out before the second line. My first impulse, which I followed, was to dump Katrina on the floor. She may have been the last person present to realize we had a major social blunder on our hands.

The party-goers stared at my hard-on aimed at the ceiling: Cameron was already in an I-told-you-so mode; Billy Gaines had yet to understand the anatomy of the situation; for some bizarre reason, Mimi Saunders broke into hysterical laughter; Sonny showed humiliation; Ryan, rage. Skip Prescott, the bantam rooster himself, appeared deep in denial.

I searched the crowd quickly until I found Gilia, the only one staring at my face instead of my penis. Her eyes reflected immeasurable sadness, a disappointment so total as to annihilate hope. If the goal of my life had been to hurt Gilia, I could never have hurt her more. I wanted to scream, to beg, to sacrifice everything for the right to start over. I wanted to give birth to her. I wanted to marry her.

I said, "Gilia."

At her name, she blinked, then the mask of withdrawal slipped over her face and she became the same uninvolved, untouchable girl I'd seen the day we met in her mother's family room.

Skip screeched. "Kill the bastard!"

Sonny made a yelp sound, like a run-over dog, and came at me, followed by the bulk of Ryan.

I ran.

The smart move would have been to stand and take my medicine, on the theory Sonny and Ryan wouldn't kill me in a house full of witnesses. Running off into the dark only upped the chances of manslaughter, but when Skip shouted *"Kill,"* my fight-or-flight instinct kicked in, and I defy you to find a man who will stand and fight when he's butt naked and everyone else in the room isn't.

I snagged my boxers off the lawn; there was no time to search for jeans or shoes. I stopped for a moment at Katrina's car, with the thought of stealing it, but the keys were back in the lock, where Sonny and Ryan were falling over Katrina's body as they came through the doorway. I couldn't see well, but she seemed to be grabbing at their legs. I think Sonny kicked her.

Nothing to do but jump in my shorts and run. What I had done to Gilia had to change me—what I did next and how I looked at details. I could not allow less. In the meantime, however, survival mattered. I ran toward the Saunders' front yard, thinking maybe to circle the house and get on the golf course, where at least running barefoot would be bearable. I'm not one of those guys with tough feet. I put on slippers to use the bathroom at night.

Near the property line, a volleyball net sprang from the dark and I nearly decapitated myself. You know how in an intense physical crisis, time accordions so you can think twenty separate thoughts in the blink of an eye? Falling under the net brought on the eeriest déjà vu deal, which before I even hit the ground I identified as the day in the seventh grade when, chasing a foul ball, I hung myself on a volleyball net and lay on the ground, looking up at Maurey Pierce backlit by the sun. These were her first words to me: "Smooth move, Ex-Lax."

The perfect comment for my current situation.

This time, no teenage girl waited to insult me, then become my lover and friend. This time, I pulled the collapsed net off, bounced up, and was running again, without missing much more than a stride. The volleyball net reminded me of something else I'd seen last weekend during my visit to the Saunders' home—Bobby's Sting-ray bicycle leaning against the porch.

Short frame, fat tires, three speeds, not exactly built for the fast lane, but my entire life—at least since Wanda left—I'd been training for an escape by bicycle. Ryan hurdled the fallen net and ran across the yard. For a giant, he had tremendous quickness, but he'd never catch me when I got up to speed. Linemen can move like bulls on lightning five or ten yards, but a quarter mile kills them.

Right off, I learned a big difference between stationary bike riding and real bike riding—curbs. Street burn. I yanked up the bike, remounted on the run, and took off down a cart path that passed through a fence and onto Starmount Golf Course. If I had to, I could hide in a sand trap or water hazard. Me and the snakes.

Behind me, the fall of footsteps slowed and stopped. I figured Ryan and Sonny had doubled back to the house for instructions. Skip would be out of denial by now and well into vengeance. What could he do? Have me killed? Castrated? I hadn't broken any laws, that I knew of, so he could hardly swear out a warrant. Something would happen though. Skip Prescott came from the strain of men you couldn't steal from without consequences. And *stolen possessions* is the term that strain uses to describe another man stuck in their wives.

Even as I pedaled my heart out, Skip wasn't my major concern. No punishment he extracted would be as awful as what I would give myself for hurting Gilia. Shit. She was the first non-screwed-up woman to like me in a long, long time, and I'd sabotaged us. Lydia and Maurey would say I destroyed her affection on purpose. "You couldn't handle the responsibility of accepting love so you crapped the gig." Maybe they were right.

I followed the cart path across the fairway onto the driving range. Golf balls glowed on the wet grass, like a peculiar sort of molecule model. Kids' bikes are geared so high you have to pump about 120 revolutions a minute to get anywhere, which on a short frame means your knees rush toward your face like pistons. It's remarkably tiring. Barefoot and in boxer shorts, it would be a long ride home in the rain.

I crossed behind the dry pool, pro shop, and restaurant and had just entered the main parking lot when a car came flying down the street and whipping into the driveway. Ryan's beefy arm pointed at me from the passenger side. For an instant I was frozen, a deer in head-lights, then I jerked the bike into a U-turn-on-a-dime and pedaled like a maniac.

The car came forward much quicker than I moved away. I rode close to the restaurant wall, Sonny jumped the curb and kept straight at me, apparently planning to smash me and Bobby's bike against the building. I zipped around the kitchen onto a short driveway leading down, away from the club. At the end of the driveway, two Dempsey Dumpsters sat side by side with maybe a two-foot clearance between them.

A two-foot clearance is what a bicycle has that a car hasn't. Going full pedal, I shot between the Dumpsters and out the other side. From the rear, I heard Sonny's tires squeal around the corner fol-lowed by the spine-tearing sound of stomped brakes and an iron thunderclap when they slammed into the Dumpsters.

26

From a block away, the jack-o'-lanterns flickered orange like Japanese paper lanterns outlining the shadow of a fairy castle—the Beast's castle after Beauty taught him how to love and turned him back handsome. It was difficult to convince myself they were real.

I'd been pedaling for several miles, depressed to the core. What had started out fairly simple—meet my fathers—had spun out of control. A week and a half ago I occupied the moral high ground. The men raped my mother and rapists should be held accountable, but instead of holding evil jerks accountable for their sins, I'd run rampant on the innocent families. The wrong people got screwed. Skip would probably divorce Katrina. Gilia had lost her trust, Clark was disillusioned, and the memory that gave Atalanta Williams the courage to go on had been destroyed. And all for what? So I could call a man "Dad"? Genes come from sperm and knowing where the sperm came from doesn't change who you are. Searching for the source is selfish.

Because I was so absorbed with myself, at first I didn't realize the apparition down the block was the place I lived. I had the sense of an out-of-proportion birthday cake. Eugene and Shannon had lined every rain gutter and balcony. The ledge around the second floor glittered with orange candles. One of every six or seven lanterns had blown out or burned out, but that still left three hundred glowing pumpkins. It was the most beautiful man and woman–made thing I'd ever seen.

A knot of people stood in the street, admiring the Manor House. As I rode closer, details became clear on individual pumpkin faces. They'd done the roof in Gilia's heads with the triangle eyes and diamond noses. Down lower, more visible, Shannon's surrealistic faces gave an unsettling gargoyle look to the house. I searched for my van Gogh, but couldn't see him.

A woman in the crowd said, "What's he doing?"

"I think it's a costume," a man said. "Part of the show."

Up till then I'd been so focused on jack-o'-lanterns I hadn't noticed the figure on the porch. Dressed in black, he seemed to be filling a bucket with water from a hose. As I watched, he put on a black glove and unscrewed the bulb from the porch light, then he pulled off the glove and put it in his jacket pocket.

I said, "Clark, you idiot."

The woman who'd spoken first said, "You know that boy? Is he part of the show?"

I dropped Bobby's bicycle on the grass and walked across the yard toward Clark and the house. Behind me, someone said, "That's not a costume, it's underwear."

Clark peered across the lawn. "Don't come any closer, Mr. Callahan." Since last night's botch job, he'd done some homework. An orange extension cord ran from the plug under the light socket to the bucket, where he'd stripped the last six inches of wire and wrapped it around the handle.

"Clark, what in hell are you doing this time?"

His forehead rippled. "You laughed at me. You said only an idiot tries to kill himself with electricity."

"I meant breathing fumes from an electric motor."

"No one takes me seriously."

"I take you seriously, Clark. So does your father."

186

"No, you don't. You all think I'm a clown."

"You don't have to die to prove your emotions are real."

He balanced a foot on the bucket. "The world is an awful place, Mr. Callahan. I'll never fit in here."

Clark stuck his foot in the water and his finger in the light socket.

I rammed him hard as I could with my shoulder. The momentum broke Clark free from the charge but not before I caught a stiff zap. I landed on my left side on the concrete porch and slid into a column. When I looked back, Clark lay on his face in the spreading water from the dumped bucket.

Clark was dead weight as I rolled him over on his back. His face had gone slack and gray. Both eyes were nearly closed, but not quite—twin egg-white slits showed in the folds. I felt his neck for a pulse but couldn't find one, so I doubled up my fist and belted him in the chest. The body didn't jerk or anything, was like hitting a sack of potatoes. I put my ear to his heart and held my own breath, listening. Nothing.

From the street someone called, "Is he all right?"

I grabbed hair and pulled Clark's head back like they teach you in the artificial respiration films in high school. In the films, the victim's mouth falls open and the savior goes to work, but in my case, Clark's jaw locked. First I tried prying it open with my thumb, then I slapped him hard. No good.

I jumped off the porch and ran to the garage for a screwdriver. All the way across the yard, I rehearsed what my life would be like if I let him die. My life, Billy's life, Clark's mother, who must have been at the Prescott party too—losing a child is the worst thing that can happen to anyone, and being the cause of someone losing a child may be second.

Back at Clark's body I jammed the screwdriver between his molars and twisted. I may have broken his teeth, I don't know, but somehow I got him open. Some of the people from the street had come into the yard, but no one offered to help. I didn't expect them to. Clark was my responsibility.

The door opened and Shannon appeared in the light, still wearing her grass skirt and leis.

I said, "Call an ambulance."

She disappeared without a word. I pulled Clark's head way back until he almost faced the wall, then, holding his tongue down with the screwdriver, I took a deep breath and put my mouth against his.

My lips on another man's. You can be repulsed at the thought of something all your life and then not even think about it when the time comes to act. A minute ago touching a man on the face was the least likely thing I would ever do.

A shadow crossed the rectangle of light and Eugene knelt beside me. He was dressed in a gorilla costume with no head.

"Who is it?" he asked.

Clark's chest rose when I blew into him, but when I stopped, so did he. "Clark Gaines. Billy's boy."

"Why isn't he breathing?"

"Electrocuted himself."

I don't know if the information meant anything to Eugene or not. He probably didn't remember the name Billy Gaines, and if he did, I doubt if he connected his attempt at finding me something to do with this body on the porch.

Eugene used his teeth to pull off his gorilla paws. "Move up closer to the head," he said. He put his palms on Clark's chest and pumped. I went into a three exhalations, then listen pattern. Clark's lungs would work one or two breaths, then stop again. He wasn't dead, but he couldn't stay alive on his own.

Shannon reappeared with jeans, a T-shirt, and a pair of sneakers. "You'll need them in the ambulance," she said.

"Call Billy Gaines and tell him to meet us at the hospital. Moses Cone is closest, so I guess that's where they'll take him."

"Okay."

"Billy was at Gilia Prescott's a half hour ago. He might still be there."

Shannon started to ask a question, but didn't. She moved to go inside, then turned back to me again. "He'll want to know what happened; what do I tell him?"

I had no answer.

27

The ambulance attendants stuck paddles onto Clark's chest and jolted him with a battery and got him going, then at the hospital he stopped again in the emergency room. I watched him start and stop until a nurse spotted me in the corner and chased me into the waiting room.

Billy, Skip, Cameron, and a woman I didn't know sat on pastel chairs like you see in institutional cafeterias. The waiting room walls were legal pad yellow and the tube lighting buzzed. "Hart to Hart" played on an elevated TV with a bad picture and no sound. Robert Wagner wore a tuxedo while Stephanie Powers pounded out her next best-seller.

Skip glared at me in blatant hatred, but Billy came over and shook my hand and thanked me for bringing Clark in. He introduced me to his wife, Daphne.

"I don't understand why Clark was at your house," she said.

Billy and I stared at the tile floor. He was still in shock at having a son who'd attempted suicide. He hadn't gotten around to blame yet.

Skip had. And Cameron. My fathers had hated me from the start and now they hated me with good reason, which made them more confident in their hatred. Cameron still wore the three-piece suit he'd been in when he came to threaten me earlier in the day. Skip had on the tennis shorts uniform. It was hard to see anything the two had in common besides Skip's sister and my mother.

"Hart to Hart" ended and the news came on and went off while we sat in silence. Every now and then an orderly or a nurse came through and everyone looked up expectantly. The nurses were professional at ignoring people in the waiting room. Billy cleaned his glasses. Twice he asked Daphne if she wanted a Coca-Cola and both times she said, "No." Skip smoked a cigarette.

I thought about how I would feel if Shannon killed herself. That's what fiction writers do—see someone in trouble and try to feel what they feel. If Shannon committed suicide, I couldn't conceive of ever recovering. People do live through it, but I don't know how. Maybe they have no choice.

I watched the side of Billy's face as he blinked, his attention on Daphne. His face wasn't sneaky or complicated; it accepted, like an animal. Innocent. I got in a fight once to stop a kid from killing kittens, but what I'd done to Billy was so much worse than killing kittens. All that pride I took in knowing right from wrong and refusing to do wrong had turned out nothing but hooey. Accidental cruelty is just as evil as doing it on purpose.

The emergency room doctor was Egyptian, I think. He looked Egyptian and wore a name tag that said DR. FAROUB. He walked with that straight-up way you never see in Americans.

He came toward me, fingering the stethoscope in his jacket pocket. "Your son, he will live."

My stomach unclenched. "Not my son. His."

Dr. Faroub turned to Billy. "The boy suffered a grand mal seizure, which brought on heart failure. He should lose weight and receive counseling. Counseling is a help for the children."

Billy shook the doctor's hand. "Thank you for saving him."

"Suicide is illegal, you know."

190

"How can you tell he did it on purpose?" Daphne asked, which might have been a meaningless question if anyone but Clark had stepped in a wired bucket of water and stuck their finger in a light socket.

Dr. Faroub looked from Daphne to Billy. "The boy had a note in his pocket saying he wanted his body going to the Duke Medical School . . . so his father couldn't touch him."

Daphne raised her hand to her cheek. Of all my extended family members, she was the one who'd been left in the dark. "Clark idolizes his father," she said.

Dr. Faroub shrugged and repeated, "Counseling is a help for the children. Will you proceed to the front, there are forms."

"I already gave them my insurance card," Daphne said.

"There are always more forms."

After the doctor clicked away, Billy's legs kind of went out from under him and he sat down quickly.

"It's my fault," he said.

Cameron looked at me. "No, it isn't."

"Why would Clark be mad at you, William?" Daphne asked.

Cameron stood up. "The doctor said something about forms, Daphne. Don't you think you should take care of that?"

Daphne's eyes traveled from Cameron to Billy to me, where they stayed a long time. The woman may have been dressed by Wal-Mart, but she wasn't stupid. She knew a story lay beneath the facts, only she was Southern enough not to demand explanations in public.

"Okay," she said. "Billy, you want a Coke?"

He shook his head, no.

I don't know if they'd been waiting for word on Clark or for Daphne to leave the room, but as soon as she left, Skip and Cameron turned nasty.

"I hope you're happy," Skip said.

Women use that sentence when they're pissed. Generally, men only say it when they mean it.

"Why should I be happy?" I said.

Cameron turned sideways, away from me. He seemed to be

addressing the television. "You wanted to place our lives in upheaval and now you have. Your goals are met, but I promise you, the price will be heavy."

"I never wanted to place your lives in upheaval."

"Then why seduce Skip's wife? Why drive Billy's son to suicide? There can be no motivation other than harming us."

"Skip's wife seduced me."

Skip doubled his fists and took a step toward me. "Katrina told us how you got her stinking drunk and had your way with her, then you blackmailed her into an affair."

"She made me eat her in the sauna."

Cameron turned to stare in my direction. "Your relationship with Gilia stops now."

"I'm afraid so," I said.

Billy suddenly let out a sob. "Why does Clark hate me?"

"Simple," Cameron said. "This . . . person turned him against you."

"I hope you're happy," Skip said. The evening had cut off his ability to vocalize bile.

I felt terrible about Clark and Gilia and everyone else who suffered because of my existence, but these men were persecuting me for events they had set in motion.

I said, "I'm not the only one to blame. None of this would have happened if you hadn't raped Lydia in the first place."

There was silence, then Billy said, "Raped?"

"Why can't any of you take responsibility for your actions? I'm nothing but the product of this crime, you're the cause."

"Nobody raped your mother," Cameron said.

"She was a slut," Skip said.

"Bullshit. You got her drunk on vodka shot into oranges with a hypodermic needle, then the five of you raped her over and over and when you were done you stood in a circle and urinated on her body."

Billy's face was twisted in pain. His voice came in a choke. "That's a lie."

"My mother wouldn't lie about something so important." A whitewater roar started in my ears. My mouth tasted of tin.

"Your mother was a slut," Skip repeated.

"Babe Carnisek admitted you all raped her."

Had he? I couldn't remember if the word *rape* was used or not. Cameron was watching me like an owl on a mouse. When he spoke, his voice was deliberate. "Your mother gave us each some fudge and a tumbler of her daddy's scotch. After we drank, she offered us two dollars apiece to have sex with her."

"No."

"We were sixteen- and seventeen-year-old boys. What did you expect us to do?"

"I don't believe you."

"We were all virgins," Billy said.

Skip said, "I wasn't."

Billy went on. "We were all virgins and scared to death, but she insisted. I was so frightened I couldn't get erect. She called me a 'worm' and made me give back the two dollars."

This didn't make sense. All the relationships of my life had been shaped by Lydia's rape. "Why didn't you tell me that when I came to your house?"

Billy looked down at his hands. "I couldn't admit I'm a worm."

"Your mother was a slut," Skip said for the third time.

"Face it," Cameron said. "You've been had."

"I need to use the telephone."

Didi answered on the eighth ring.

"What's wrong?" she said.

"Is Babe home?"

"Whenever the phone rings at midnight, somebody's died."

"No one died, Mrs. Carnisek. This is Sam Callahan, I need to ask Babe a question."

"He goes to sleep after the weather and sports."

"Could you wake him up? It's important."

The phone was silent a long time. A short black man in a white uniform came down the hall, sliding a floor buffer from side to side in rhythm to music only he could hear over a pair of earphones. He was smoking a cigarette, but instead of using the sand ashtrays at either end of the hall, he let the ash get long until it fell from its own

193

weight and was swept under the floor buffer. I concentrated on breathing.

"What?"

"I'm sorry to wake you, Babe, but I have to know what happened on Christmas Eve 1949."

"Who is this?"

"Sam Callahan. I was at your house the Saturday before last during the Washington-Detroit game. You might be my father."

"I remember."

"I need to know what happened the night I was conceived."

He hesitated a moment, then said, "A bunch of us screwed your mother."

"I was hoping for details."

"Let me think." The black guy came close to the pay phone and I put a finger in my ear to cover the *whish* of his buffer.

"I was at Skip Prescott's house listening to colored music on the record player," Babe said, "and a friend of his sister telephoned and asked us to a party."

"Yes."

"Your mom was mad at her daddy about something, so she screwed us."

I inhaled deeply. "Whose idea was it?"

"Was what?"

"Having sex. The five of you having sex with Lydia."

"Hell, we were such young punks none of us even knew what hole to go in."

"So the sex was her idea?"

"She paid us money to do her."

Everything that had happened in my life up to that point suddenly became void. I closed my eyes to block the nausea and leaned my head against the wall next to the phone.

Babe's voice was hesitant. "After you left the other day, I got to thinking, and I don't believe I was quite honest while you were here."

"You lied?"

"Didn't lie so much as forgot the whole truth. You can ask Didi, that's not like me."

194

"What's the truth?"

"I'm probably not your father after all."

I didn't say anything. I was beyond the ability to react.

"The truth is I squirted so quick I don't think I ever got far enough in to make her pregnant."

"Oh."

"She cussed me out for messing on her belly."

I walked all night. It must have been raining, but I don't remember. I don't remember feeling anything, inside or out. The police stopped me down by the interstate. I must have answered enough questions not to be taken in as a drunk, but I don't see how.

Dawn found me lying on Atalanta Williams' couch with my head in her lap, sobbing. Fingers ran through my hair. Her other hand rested on my shoulder.

She said, "I knew all along my Jake couldn't have done what your mama said."

Her bathrobe smelled like flowers. I could easily have stayed on that couch for years. Another day at home—waking up, looking out at the weather, deciding what to wear—was more than I could face. Going on was too much responsibility.

"I wish you were my mother," I said.

Atalanta gave me a squeeze on the shoulder and said, "So do I."

PART TWO

Wyoming

1

R ule Number One of Being Sam Callahan: In times of tor-
ment, fly to Maurey. The evening after Halloween, All Souls'
Night itself, I landed in the Jackson Hole Airport during the
first real snowstorm of the year. Because the flight attendant thought
I was handicapped, she helped me down the airplane steps and across
the runway to the terminal where Hank Elkrunner awaited. I did feel
arthritic, especially in the knees and feet. The world looked the way
I imagine it would if you'd just survived a plane crash where other
people were killed. Objects appeared brand new; I couldn't come up
with the word that went along with the thing.

Hank said, "Welcome home."

I said, "Oh."

He drove to the ranch through blowing snow and no heat in his
pickup. On the radio, Jimmy Buffett sang "Peanut Butter Conspir-
acy"—a song glorifying shoplifting. At the ranch, Hank led me to my
private cell in the barracks he and Pud built years ago for Maurey's
recovering legions. Without undressing, I crawled between the sheets

of a twin bed and lay on my back, neither awake nor asleep. The plywood ceiling had knot whorls in the wood grain that stared down at me like eyes. Pissed-off, judgmental eyes. Female eyes.

Maurey came through the door. She felt my forehead and took off my shoes. "You look like a wreck," she said.

"I am a wreck."

"You're in the right place, I'm a tow truck."

I closed my eyes, too tired for metaphors.

Every now and then I got up to pee, which meant going outside in the snow and around the building. Twice each day a pregnant teenager who told me her name was Toinette brought food. You can take it as a gauge of how far into my hole I'd sunk that I felt no curiosity as to how and when Toinette became pregnant.

On the third day, Maurey showed up at my bedside, straddling a chair backward, like a cowboy.

She said, "My brother is dying, his lover is losing a lover. I've got a pregnant girl disowned by her family and a little boy so traumatized he can't speak."

I pulled the sheet over my mouth; she reached across and yanked it back down.

"And you," she said, "are the only person on the ranch who feels sorry for yourself."

"Auburn can't talk?"

"Auburn's fine." She knocked wood on the chair. "Roger can't talk."

"Who's Roger?"

"Long story. Are you going to get up or waste away?"

"What about the recovering junkie?" I asked.

"What?"

"When we talked on the phone you had a recovering junkie."

"He stopped recovering and left."

"I'm sorry."

"Win some, lose some. The deal is, you're the lone refugee out here not pulling your weight in the cheerfulness department."

"Are you cheerful?" She looked worn out. The veins showed in her arms and her eyes crinkled like she'd been outside too much without sunglasses.

"Fuck, no, I'm not cheerful. Helping family die is hard work, but I'm faking it like a champ, and I can't do this unless you fake it too."

I sat up. "You want me to fake being cheerful?"

Maurey's blue eyes glistened, but she didn't cry. "I need you, Sam. You've got to get up and help me."

So I did. All I needed was someone to need me.

Mornings, Maurey drove or snowmobiled the boys six miles down to their bus stop while Hank hitched a team of half-breed draft horses to the hay sled, which he skidded around the pasture with Pud and me on back, throwing hay to a herd of forty horses and a half dozen semi-tame elk. I couldn't help but wonder what Gaylene and Shirley would say if they saw me feeding horses with horses. The TM Ranch was a long way from Callahan Golf Carts, in more than distance.

After feeding, I went back to bed with a carafe of coffee and *Madame Bovary* by Gustave Flaubert. Emma Bovary was the sort of woman I once would have found ripe for adultery—bored silly. So desperate for attention that she'll risk all for one interesting night. I have now sworn off the Emma Bovarys of the world.

I generally took a short nap after lunch, then strapped on the cross-country skis and shuffled up Miner Creek to the warm springs and back. This time segment was set aside for self-flagellation. Going up the hill I pined for Gilia, at the warm springs itself I dwelt on my shameful conduct toward Clark and Atalanta, and coming down I mourned my wasted talent as a novelist—the theory being the best way of coming to terms with guilt is to wallow in it.

Maurey gave me a choice between cooking supper and the daily cleaning of the stud stall. Food won't stomp you to death, so I chose supper. Cooking can be quite pleasant when it's cold outside and you're in a warm place that smells good. As I chopped and blended, Toinette sat in the family room or den or whatever it was called and played her viola. She warmed up with scales and finger exercises, then she practiced Irish Rhapsody by Victor Herbert—"We Roam Through the World" and "My Lodgings on the Cold Ground." The viola parts weren't something you'd whistle along with, but they made the day nicer.

Toinette had come from Belgium to Jackson Hole to play in our summer symphony. Under the full moon in the Tetons, she surrendered to love—Maurey suspects a percussionist—and a child was conceived. I can relate to that. When Toinette telephoned Papa he called her a whore in Flemish, French, and English and told her not to come home. He said, From this day forward my daughter is dead. The jerk.

Dinner was a sitcom written by Edgar Allan Poe.

Afterward, Pud and the boys cleaned up. I carried my decaf into the family room and looked through catalogs or read Zane Grey by the wood-burning heater while Chet and Pete played Scrabble and Toinette watched French-language TV off the Canadian satellite. Some nights, during old movies, I watched with her. The strange language wasn't nearly as disconcerting as seeing Jimmy Stewart open his mouth and speak in a totally non–Jimmy Stewart voice.

By ten-thirty I was back in bed with Madame Bovary.

The third day after I got out of bed, I came in from my afternoon ski and guilt orgy to find Maurey in the kitchen, aiming a hypodermic syringe at the ceiling. Pete sat on a stool beside the wood-block table, playing gin rummy with Chet. I checked out the score; Pete was way ahead.

"Where'd you learn to give shots?" I asked Maurey.

She tapped the syringe barrel with her index fingernail. "You'd be amazed how many doctors are alcoholic."

"I doubt it."

"They come here to start recovery and I make them teach me things. Who you think will deliver Toinette's baby if it comes during a blizzard?"

I opened the refrigerator to pull out a bottle of cranberry juice and perused the options for supper—leftover corned beef and applesauce.

Pete said, "Gin."

Chet said, "Hell." He gathered in the loose cards and shuffled. Chet was an adept card shuffler, which is a skill I've never been able to pick up. My shuffles tend to explode across the table.

"Roll up your sleeve," Maurey said to Pete.

As Pete rolled his sleeve up over his mop handle–thin arm, he turned on the stool to face me. "Maurey says you're paying my doctor bills."

I shrugged and drank juice straight from the bottle. It embarrasses me when people act like I'm being generous for giving away bits of the Callahan family fortune. I never did anything to deserve it, except being born.

"Thank you," Pete said.

"We're family," I said. "Family sticks together."

Pete continued staring at me, like he used to when he was ten and wanted to drive me crazy. I tried to look back at him, but it was difficult. He breathed with his mouth open and his gums were swollen to the point of cracking. His skin was a translucent yellow green, like zucchini pulp, and he'd lost so much weight the bones around his temples stood out from his face.

Chet slapped the deck on the table. "Cut."

Pete said, "Sam, you and I have never liked each other." It was a quiet statement of fact, not an accusation.

I said, "You were God's own brat as a child, but since you turned fifteen or so, I've liked you."

Maurey swabbed Pete's upper arm with rubbing alcohol. The smell filled the room.

"But I haven't liked you," Pete said.

"That's too bad. Why not?"

"To start with, you're homophobic."

"I like gay guys as much as the other kind."

"Can't argue with that," Maurey said.

"What else?" I asked.

"Your mother was a snob to my mother."

"My mother is a snob to everyone—even me. Especially me. It's not fair to turn on a person because they have snotty parents. What else?"

He blinked twice, thinking. "You knocked up my sister when she was thirteen."

I held up one hand like a cop stopping traffic. "She made me do it. Have you ever tried saying *no* to Maurey?"

Maurey pinched loose skin on Pete's upper arm. "He's right, Pete.

I seduced him. Poor little Sam didn't know the first thing about sex."

"That's not exactly true," I said.

"You thought you could make a girl pregnant with a French kiss."

No one ever got anywhere correcting Maurey's view of history, so I went back to Pete. "There's enough people in the world with good reason to dislike me, Pete, but you're not one of them. I'd be real happy if I could call myself your friend."

He smiled, showing much more of his swollen, bleeding gums. "Okay," he said, "let's kiss and make up."

My face must have shown terror because Chet and Maurey went into hoots of glee. Even Pete laughed. I don't mind being the butt of a joke if it relieves tension.

"Instead of kissing, how about if I deal you in," Chet said.

"Great."

But it never happened. As Chet dealt, Maurey sank the needle into what was left of Pete's muscle. He picked up his cards and studied them a moment, then his eyes turned dull, his chin dropped to his chest, and the cards in his hand fluttered to the floor. Gently Chet helped Pete walk into the bedroom.

Over the weeks, I got to know Chet fairly well. While Pete rested in the afternoons, Chet would come into the kitchen, sit at the block table, and smoke cigarettes while I cooked. Chet was tall with reddish blond hair. You could tell from how he smiled sometimes that he was basically a pretty happy person, or would have been if his partner hadn't got sick. He and Pete had met working lights at some theater in New York, Off Broadway, and Chet liked to talk about plays and who was hot and who was gliding on their past glory. He gave me the scoop on which actors were gay. A couple amazed me.

The only visible difference between Chet and the hetero males on the ranch was Chet tucked in his shirttail.

Hank and Maurey both hassled me for refusing to see Lydia.

"She's your mother," Maurey said.

"I've heard her deny that, many a time."

"She was young then. Now, she'll admit she has a child to almost anyone."

"She ruined my life."

"Everybody's mother ruins their life. That doesn't mean you can blow her off."

"Watch me."

Hank said Lydia wanted to apologize and reconcile our differences.

"Did she say that?"

"Not in words, but I know your mother. She never says what she feels in words."

"You mean she lies."

He shifted his weight from foot to foot. "Lydia doesn't lie, exactly. She expects you to see behind what she says."

A letter came from Gilia.

> Sam Callahan,
>
> You did a rotten thing. It hurt. I don't know which is worse, screwing Mrs. Prescott or running away. You could have at least given me the satisfaction of telling you to go to hell.
>
> Dad gave me a set of the photographs of you and Katrina. I told him he is as despicable as you are, which is a lot. I haven't had much luck with men in my life.
>
> Speaking of Katrina, she and Skip are now the lovey-dovey couple of the South. They neck in public. She compares their love to that of Prince Charles and Lady Di. Yesterday, I heard Katrina telling a table full of trust fund widows at the club that you date-raped her. It made me so mad, I walked over and threw the photo of you and her on the table—you know the one where you have a pom-pom on your penis and she has you tied to the wall. I said, "Does that look like date rape?"
>
> Sam, you're the only person who ever let me act like myself. I wish you hadn't turned out to be such a dip-shit.
>
> *Sincerely,*
> *Gilia*

Paper-clipped to the letter was the *Greensboro Record* "Births and Deaths" column from November 1, 1983. Midway down the births, Gilia had highlighted in yellow Magic Marker:

> Sam Lynn Paseneaux, a boy, 8 lbs., 1 oz., born to Babs Paseneaux and Sam Callahan.
> Sammi Babs Norloff, a girl, 6 lbs., 5 oz., born to Lynette Norloff and Sam Callahan.

In the margin, she had drawn a yellow exclamation point followed by a question mark—*!?*

I had no contact with Callahan Magic Golf Carts. They didn't need me. I called my lawyer to set up rent payments for Babs and Lynette and to get started hurling counterinjunctions at Wanda.

"I'll pay ten thousand dollars to make certain she doesn't get a penny."

"We can do that," my lawyer said.

Maurey overheard the conversation. Her comment was "Getting vindictive in our old age, aren't we?"

"I'm a man of principles."

"That's the nice word for it."

My only other conversation with anyone in North Carolina came after Thanksgiving dinner, when Shannon telephoned.

She asked, "Are you well yet?"

"No."

"Are you better?"

"I don't think in qualitative terms."

"Wanda tried to move in the other day."

"Good Lord."

"She brought two guys with tattoos and a pickup truck full of stuff. Gus blocked the door and wouldn't let them in."

"How'd Wanda handle it?"

"She cussed worse than I ever heard anyone cuss. She waved a tire iron in Gus's face and screamed, *'Nigger!'* Then she ordered the two guys to beat her up."

"Two guys with tattoos are no match for Gus."

"I sure am glad I never called Wanda Mama."

I looked over at Maurey, who was making cowboy cappuccino. She would enjoy this story. "What'd you and Eugene do?"

"I ran around and locked the other doors and windows. Eugene took notes. He wants to write his thesis on my family."

We chitchatted a few minutes, or Shannon chitchatted while I counted the number of holes in Maurey's phone mouthpiece—eighteen.

Shannon said, "Gilia and her parents aren't speaking to each other, so she spends the night here sometimes. We have a lot in common."

There was a long silence while I searched for a detail to study.

"Gilia Saunders," she said.

I guess she wanted a comment. I couldn't even breathe, much less comment.

"She and I are going to New York City over Spring Break. She wants to take me shopping and to art galleries and all that stuff you never would do with me."

I stared at the turkey remains on the table. Hank had gone to town to be with Lydia, and Pete only ate some dressing and gravy before lying down, but the six of us who remained had pretty much left the carcass in tatters.

I said, "That's nice of Gilia."

"We drove down to see Clark Gaines. He's back home now. He said to say 'hello.' "

"I have to hang up now."

"I love you, Daddy."

"Thank you."

> Dear Babs and Lynette,
>   Enclosed you will find two envelopes addressed to Gilia Saunders of 16 Corner Creek Drive in Greensboro. Would each of you mind dropping her a note explaining my relationship to Sam and Sammi and why my name is on the birth certificates instead of the real fathers?
>   This favor will save me from much groveling.
>
> *Yours,*
> *Sam Callahan*

Dear Gilia,

I'm surprised to hear that you don't know which is worse—what I did with Katrina Prescott or running away afterward. I ran because I had hurt you, I had confirmed all your worst opinions of men, and I didn't think you wanted to hear my excuses. Not that there are any. I told myself someday I would make a commitment to you and after that I would be true from now on, but in the meantime, it didn't matter what I did. That, of course, is a lie. Wanting to love someone means loving them now. Or not at all.

I went cross-country skiing today. The snow was beautiful and cold. As I skied, I thought about why I was a dip-shit to you, and here, near as I can see, is it:

Before we met I had two wives and an uncountable number of relationships, ranging from twenty minutes to four months, and every woman had this in common—she was desperate. I thought a woman had to be a drunk, crazy, extraordinarily young, unhappily married, or in big trouble before she would want me. She had to need what I have to give—sex and money. I thought no one desirable could love me. I married women I knew it wouldn't hurt to lose.

Then I met you, and you are desirable. You don't need me. We simply have fun being together and that scared me so much I had trouble breathing. When you have something that matters, you have something to lose.

Katrina couldn't touch me, so I slept with her. You could touch me, so I drove you away. And I regret it. And I am sorry.

Sam

Pete relapsed in early December. One evening he was tireder than usual and the next morning he didn't get out of bed. Maurey, Chet, and a doctor floated in and out of Maurey and Pud's old bedroom with exaggerated quietness and muffled tones. No one said it aloud, but the general feeling was this time was for keeps.

2

It was Tuesday, six days before Christmas. Maurey's son, Auburn, and Roger, who can't or won't speak, sat perched on a board, solemnly watching me flake hay off bales. Behind the boys, I could see Hank Elkrunner's ponytail and part of his right wrist, which snapped up and down as he turned the team toward the Gros Ventre River Road.

"Too fast," Auburn shouted. "Gristle will hog it all."

Gristle had two white feet and massive dingleberries hanging off her butt, and she'd appointed herself herd bully. Whenever I came near the equine bitch she would pull her lips off her teeth and lean toward my face. Hank said she smelled my fear, but I think she just enjoyed biting people.

"Let's shoot her for bear bait," I said. Auburn's face turned scared. He can't tell when I'm kidding yet, so he tends to take me literally, which sure as hell isn't how I care to be taken.

"Maybe I could read the others *Winning Through Intimidation*," I said. I looked at Roger and winked, but his expression didn't change.

The boy's expression never changed. Always the impassive observer. We weren't sure how old Roger was, but he looked younger than Auburn, who was soon to turn twelve. Roger had the eyes of a person considerably older and more world-weary than any of us, and that's saying a lot.

I slid the X-Acto knife under the bale twine and cut up, toward my face. The loose string went into a potato sack at my feet, then, as forty or so horses led by the selfish nag Gristle shuffled in our path, I shoved layers of lime-green-and-yellow grass onto the tracked-over snow. Way off to the south, the sun shone weakly through a smattering of high clouds. Up by the ranch buildings, aspens stood against the hill like gangly white skeletons with ooz-ing joints, while in creases along the foothills spruce and lodgepole pine made a kelly green mosaic on the snow, and way off alone an occasional limber pine declared its independence from everyone— animal or plant.

The propriety of the whole scene kind of got to me, like I was an important piece of a huge jigsaw puzzle or a character in an Amish movie. Working outdoors in weather will do that sometimes—give you the feeling of being minutely small yet still consequential.

I looked at the fenceline and saw 1966. Wyoming women. Broad shoulders, flat bellies, unafraid to look men in the eye. My Dodgers won the pennant, lost the World Series. That summer I'd gotten downwind of a grass fire in Curtis Canyon and the smoke stayed in my nose for weeks, so wherever I went I swore the immediate vicin-ity was smoldering. I slept with a shovel under the bed. I asked a girl named Tracy Goodman on a date and she said "Okay," but when I went to pick her up she'd gone shopping in Idaho Falls. I often dreamed of winning the Academy Award for Best Original Screen-play and when I stood at the podium to give my speech I would start out, *"Eat shit, Tracy Goodman."*

Auburn's voice cut through my vision. "Earth to Sam. Earth to Sam."

Maurey taught him to say that and he thinks it's hilarious. He turned to rap Hank on the shoulder. "Sam's left his body again."

Hank glanced back at me. "Tell Sam to close his mouth so his spirit can't escape while he's gone."

"Close your mouth so your spirit can't escape—"

"I heard him, Auburn."

Maurey doesn't mind, but Lydia throws a fit when Hank talks about turning into a bird and flying around the universe in front of Auburn. She's afraid Auburn will take him seriously, which Hank says is the point.

"I was daydreaming," I said.

Hank gave his Blackfeet chuckle. "Bad practice to daydream with a knife in your hand. It may bite you."

Auburn laughed and I pretended to. What I actually did was block thoughts of Lydia by studying a lone raven flying toward the red hills across the river.

Hank said, "Pud's coming."

Pud's white van with the TALBOT SATELLITE DISH SYSTEMS REPAIR magnetic sign on the passenger door picked its way through the ruts and slush. We're always the last county road plowed, so the ice base forms thickest, and when a rare December warm spell comes along it's like driving through Dairy Queen soft ice cream. Takes four-wheel drive and the faith to keep moving no matter what. Those who stop may not start again.

Hank angled the team—Luci and Desi—toward a semi-solid meeting place along the fence, where Pud wrestled the wheel until the van came to rest against the far snowbank. He opened the door and sat with his legs out of the van, waiting for us to skid up to the fence, then he hefted himself to the ground and crossed over the ruts.

Pud Talbot wears cowboy boots year-round and a yellow cap that reads DASH ROUSTABOUT SERVICE. He's no taller than me and has the famous chin that marks all the Talbots except Auburn. Pud's brother Dothan is Auburn's father, and I'm afraid I've allowed the deep animosity—read that as hatred—that runs between Dothan and me to color my feelings for Pud. Also Pud sleeps with Maurey, and whether Maurey and I have a brother-sister deal or first-lover nostalgia or we're simply best friends for life, my chosen role is to quietly resent anyone who sticks himself into her body.

Luci and Desi shuffled to the fence and stopped, and us five males waited there a moment in the winter silence, which is so much more silent than summer silence there ought to be a different word for it.

Pud put one boot up on the snowbank and said, "Pete died."

I looked away from Pud to the horses with their necks down, eating hay.

Hank said, "The doctors told us he had another month."

"The doctors missed the call," Pud said.

More silence. A white mare raised her head and stared directly at me. I couldn't meet her eyes.

"How're Maurey and Chet taking it?" Hank asked.

"About how you'd expect. They'll be along in a couple hours."

For some reason, I turned to look at Roger. His eyes were huge and terrified, like a panicked deer. His mouth opened and he screamed.

The secret to cornbread is in the oil. I would have used lard if I thought I could get away with it, but like everybody else in the drugs-and-alcohol generation, Maurey's gone health crazy. As it was, I spooned a couple glops of Crisco into the ten-inch Dutch oven and stuck the Dutch oven in the real oven set at 350 degrees. Oil started, I pried the lid off the ceramic crock of sourdough starter that according to legend was brought across the Missouri River in 1881 by Maurey's great-grandmother on her father's side. I'd be willing to bet the crock hadn't been washed since 1881. A thumb's-width of dry dough skin ringed the lip of the crock like the rubber seal on a gasket.

I measured two dippers of starter into a 1950s Art Deco bowl and broke in four eggs, double what the recipe called for. Then I went to the refrigerator for buttermilk, where I mused for about the eightieth time that no one drinks straight buttermilk these days and it seems more than a change of style but a degradation of American values. Wasn't that long ago you knew you could trust a man who drank buttermilk.

Toinette's viola music filtered comfortably in from the next room.

At the kitchen table, Roger and Auburn played a silent game of Risk. Roger's scream hadn't been one of those painful breakthroughs where the victim flashes onto what was repressed and starts talking again. From outward appearances, he didn't seem affected by his foray into the world of sound. He knelt in the chair on his knees, leaning forward toward the game board, concentrating on pushing blue armies back and forth across the continents.

Auburn also adopted the quiet method of warfare. Roger's coming to the ranch had been nothing but good for Auburn. He stopped whining at chores and his picky eating habits disappeared practically overnight. Childishness no longer washes when you're paired off with a true survivor.

Maurey's friend Mary Beth dropped Roger off at the TM a few days before my own arrival. Mary Beth said two men showed up at her apartment in the middle of the night, and when they left the boy stayed, and she didn't know what to do with him, so she brought him to Maurey. His father—who a long time ago was Mary Beth's boy-friend—had been killed in Nicaragua running drugs or guns or something else horrible. Mary Beth mentioned slavery. She didn't know how long Roger had been quiet. They thought he might be the half brother of Maurey's artist friend who lives in Paris, but even that wasn't certain. Maurey and Pud checked Roger over for scars and lice and no one had physically left marks on the boy, but one look in his soft brown eyes and it was clear he'd been through something that children shouldn't go through.

I lowered the heat on the huge pot of chicken soup simmering on the stove. Mealtimes the next few days were bound to be off kilter, so it seemed a good idea to have something continuously ready. Freud could go to town on why I chose chicken soup, but for the first time in my life, I didn't care what my motives were. I pulled the Dutch oven from the oven and carefully poured oil into the starter mix. This was the point where twice before I burned the bejesus out of myself. The rest was basically unskilled labor—mix in the whole-wheat flour, cornmeal, salt, baking powder, baking soda. I had a box of sugar hidden in the pot-holder drawer. Maurey called sugar white death, but she made an exception for my cornbread.

Roger's face jerked toward the dark window and his eyes widened and a moment later headlights flashed on the log gate out by the road. I opened the oven door with the toes of my left foot and fondled in the cornbread. In the yard, the Suburban engine coughed, doors slammed, boots knocked snow off against the porch.

Then Maurey was in the kitchen, hugging me. I felt her face on my neck. I patted the thick hair on the back of her head and smelled her jojoba shampoo. She cried a few seconds, less than a minute, as I looked across at Chet, standing inside the door with his hands at his side. Toinette's music stopped and she appeared at the other door, bow in hand.

Maurey pulled away and looked at my face. We're almost the same height.

She said, "Life is the shits."

I said, "I'm sorry."

"Me too. Thanks for being here." She moved off to hug Toinette.

I stepped toward Chet, then stopped, raised a hand, lowered it. I smiled a weak I-mean-well smile, and he smiled back "I know. It's okay."

There was more boot kicking at the front door before Pud and Hank came in. They must have been in the bunkhouse, waiting. Hank certainly wasn't shy about touching Chet. They bear-hugged like athletes. Pud held Maurey. Toinette looked sad and pregnant. Auburn carefully kept his eyes off the adults, but Roger was a camera. I got the definite feeling he could see right through emotions, that he knew every coloration of every relationship in the room— whose love was pure and whose tainted by self-interest—and I failed the test.

Chet hung his coat on the deer antler rack by the door. "I need to use the phone," he said. "There's friends in New York . . ."

Maurey broke from a muffled conversation with Pud. She said, "Use the one in our room," meaning Hank's old room, where she and Pud moved when Pete needed a bed. Maurey looked at me and said, "Come help me pick out Pete's clothes."

"I was fixing to make dumplings."

"Dumplings can wait."

~

I gave Toinette instructions on when to pull out the cornbread, then I followed my friend into her dead brother's room. I found her sitting on the dead brother's bed, staring glumly into the dead brother's open closet doors.

"Did you know it's illegal to cremate a body naked?" she said.

"That's not something I've thought about too often."

"You have to buy a coffin, too."

"I guess the funeral homes were afraid they'd lose money when burial went out of style."

"Why didn't you disagree with me when I said life is the shits?"

I almost had disagreed, but we were making such nice eye contact I couldn't spoil it. "Didn't seem like the time to argue," I said.

Maurey pooched her lower lip the way Shannon does when she doesn't get her way. "Life isn't the shits," she said. "Life is fun; it's all this death that's the shits."

I sat on the bed beside her. "It's not death either. It's loving people who die."

She doubled up her fists. "Death is boring. Boring, boring, boring. I hate death. It ruins everything." She looked at me fiercely. "You better not die on me."

"I won't if I can help it."

"Just don't." She started to cry again.

I took her hands and unclenched the fists, then held them. We sat silently, remembering other deaths.

"The doctors said he had another month," I said.

"Doctors say whatever they think you want to hear. That's why so many of them drink—they can't stand themselves."

"Roger screamed when he heard about Pete."

Maurey looked at me. "Aloud?"

"You wouldn't believe how loud. I was hoping he would talk after that, but he clammed right back up. I don't think he even remembers screaming."

Maurey extracted her hands from mine and looked down at her palms. She has extremely small hands. Twenty years of working outdoors had left them tough. "He's been stealing food."

"Roger?"

"He hides rolls and cheese in his box springs. I found half a chicken in the laundry bag."

Maurey blinked quickly and her voice caught on a sob sound. "I can't do anything for him, Sam. I say, 'Bring me your dried-up drunks, your abused babies, all those lost souls,' but I can't do a damn thing for any of them. I let my own brother die."

I waited a while and said, "You helped me."

"You don't need help. You need someone to convince you you're not a jerk."

So that was it. "You're not a savior."

"That makes us even." She laughed, but it wasn't the laugh of a person amused. "Now, if you were dead, what would you want to be cremated in?"

I thought. "My Los Angeles Dodgers boxer shorts."

"You would, wouldn't you? Pete doesn't even own boxer shorts. Didn't."

We chose a light blue Van Heusen shirt with short sleeves and a three-tone sweater Pete and Maurey's mom knitted while she was in rehab. One look at the sweater and you knew the creator was schizophrenic.

"Nobody'll see it," Maurey said. "Pete didn't want a viewing."

She chose a pair of white slacks and I accidentally said I wouldn't be caught dead in those. That got Maurey giggly, which happens to distraught people. Hysteria means the same thing with either laughter or tears.

I wanted Pete to wear dress J. Chisholm cowboy boots; Maurey couldn't see wasting a pair of boots.

"Pud can have them, he and Petey are the same shoe size."

"Pud doesn't want boots off a dead guy, even if Pete was your brother."

"Is."

"Why do women always give away dead people's clothes?"

"Bodies in caskets are barefoot. Everybody knows that."

"That's an eighth-grade myth. They're not going to put a suit on someone and leave off the shoes."

"Pete asked that you give his eulogy."

"Oh, Lord."

Nausea came on so fast I sat down. I clutched the boots to my chest, smelling the leather smell that carried a hint of after-shave. He must have packed toiletries in the boots to save room in his suitcase. The thought of standing up in front of a bunch of mourners and saying "Here's what Pete's life meant" scared the wadding out of me. I can't sum up a person. It's in my genes that whenever I try to be sincere I come off shallow. The mourners would look up at me and think *glib*.

"Why not you or Chet?" I asked.

"He didn't want to put us through that."

"And he did me?"

She smiled—like a cat. "You writers are supposed to be good with words."

Pete's pillow still had sweat stains where his head had lain. You could make out the form of his body in the mattress.

"This is his way of getting back at me for being heterosexual," I said.

"I'd say it's more like Pete's last joke."

"He always had a dry sense of humor."

Maurey held a beaded Arapaho belt up to the mirror. "You'll do it, won't you?"

"Sure."

She smiled at me in the mirror. "You think this belt goes with white slacks?"

Pud knocked at the open door. "Telephone for you guys."

I said, "Someone called us?"

"Not exactly."

"This is a trick to get me and Lydia talking."

"It's your daughter." Pud looked at Maurey. "Yours too. Hank telephoned her with the news about Pete and she wants to talk to both of you. Sam first."

I said, "I understand," even though I didn't.

There was a phone in Pete's room. I sat on the bed with it in my hand and one finger holding down the button, preparing myself to communicate. You have to be ready for these things. I'd missed Shannon terribly the last few weeks, but still, talking to her would be difficult. She knew about Katrina Prescott, Gilia, Atalanta, Clark Gaines, Lydia, and everything else I was ashamed of. Lydia had disappointed me so often when I was young, I'd sworn never to disappoint my daughter, and now I'd gone and done it, big time.

I released the button and said, "Hi."

Hank went through the *goodbyes* and *take cares*, then it was just Shannon and me.

She said, "I'm sorry about Uncle Pete."

"He was a nice man."

"I'd like to come to the funeral."

I hadn't expected that. "He wanted to be cremated."

"That's what Hank said."

"It's illegal to cremate a body naked."

Shannon coming to the funeral felt strange. Somehow, I had the idea that North Carolina was way down there and Wyoming way up here and I was the only one allowed to cross between them. I like keeping my separate lives separate.

"Can I come?" she asked.

"Of course you can come. I don't know what day the funeral is."

"Friday."

"Hank told you?"

"He said Thursday is too soon for arrangements and they didn't want it on Christmas Eve or Day because that would spoil Christmases from now on."

"That's true."

"So I can catch a flight out tomorrow."

"Put the ticket on my Visa." I counted to ten. "And bring Eugene if you want to."

Shannon must have counted to ten also; it took that long before she answered. "Eugene dumped me."

I held the phone with both hands. "I'm sorry," I said.

"No, you're not."

The worst thing a parent can say at this point is *I told you so*, yet, "I told you he was a swine."

Her voice was flat. "Eugene is okay. He just can't handle my family."

Hell—more guilt. "Eugene left because of me?"

"You were part of it, but Lydia mailed him a thermos jug of buffalo balls."

Good for Lydia. She'd done the same thing to me after I married Wanda, and Hank told me she had him put together similar packages for Wyoming's two Republican senators. The balls meant something symbolic to her. I never bothered to ask what.

"Lydia scared off a few of my girlfriends too," I said.

"Eugene wants children someday; he said our family shouldn't procreate."

The pompous bastard. "You're better off without him," I said, even though I shouldn't have.

"It still hurts." I didn't say anything. Shannon added, "He has impotency issues to deal with anyway. He's almost thirty."

Wasn't much I could say to that one.

"Gilia's here," Shannon said.

"Oh."

"You want to talk to her?"

Gilia. Sweet, big-boned Gilia. The lifeline I had cut off. "I better not."

"C'mon, Daddy. If I can get her to talk to you will you talk back?"

"It's your mom's turn. I'll go find her."

"I'm right here," Maurey said.

"You were on the extension? Some might call that bad manners."

"Bad manners is not talking to the girl, Sam."

"I'm getting off now. You and Shannon can trash me in private."

Is it unnatural when your masturbation fantasy is a fictional character from the nineteenth century? Maurey says I waste time worrying about what is natural and what isn't. At some point in my low twenties, I looked at myself as others see me and realized I'm odd, and since then I've held my actions and thoughts up to a normalcy standard. Normalcy is hard to standardize. I mean, is it abnormal to fantasize licking Madame Bovary between the thighs as we pass through the dark streets of Rouen in a carriage pulled by matching palomino stallions? And, when does abnormalcy become perversion? We all agree it would be perverted to go down on a 127-year-old woman in a public conveyance, but is it equally perverted to lie on your bunk in the mountain silence and fantasize to the point of holographic hallucination?

While working on the Bucky books, I often dream about sex with Samantha Lindell. We do it the normal way—crotch to crotch. She lifts her feet onto my shoulders like the women in Chinese erotica. She whispers *"My man"* in my ear.

Since Halloween, I was no longer part of my own dreams. Emma Bovary did it with some hairy-backed geek I never saw before. Or pioneers fought off waves of attacking Cubans. Guys in white suits murdered children. But I wasn't the murderer or the one being murdered. I was a movie audience with access to varied camera angles and hidden microphones. What I couldn't do was touch or be heard or influence actions. The effect was disassociative.

The night Pete died I dreamed about Gilia Saunders, which is abnormal for me because I never dream about people I know. Maybe it's normal for others. Gilia stood next to an Appomattox Courthouse, barefoot, wearing an old-time Cattle Kate dress. Her hair was clean, her eyes bright. She chose a five iron from the leather bag in the cart. She approached the ball and pulled her dress sleeves up above her wrists.

Gilia swung and the ball soared into a faultless Wyoming sky. I kept the camera on her face a moment as she shaded her eyes with one hand, then I swung around to follow the ball. An osprey suddenly swooped down and snatched the ball in mid-flight. The osprey rose on an air current, flapped its wings three times, and, from a great altitude, dropped the golf ball on Gilia's head. Gilia pitched forward onto the ladies' tee and died.

I awoke with an erection.

3

In the morning, Chet, Maurey, and I went to Mountain Mortuary to make what are called the final arrangements: Chet, as partner; Maurey, as next of kin; me, as the one paying the bill. Mountain Mortuary is a ranch-style log cabin with heavy double doors and abandoned swallow nests in the eaves. Abandoned for the winter, anyway, they hang like lairs of mutant wasps. Inside, the floor is oak, a right-hand door leads into the chapel and a left-hand door into an office, where a young man about Gilia's age in a blue sweater, slacks, and sandals stood looking out the window with his hands clasped behind his back.

At the sound of me setting the suitcase full of Pete's clothes on the floor, the young man turned to face us and shake hands.

"Ron Mildren," he said. "You must be the family and friends of Pete Pierce."

Maurey and I nodded.

"Have a seat. You'll find us more informal and personal than your city funeral homes. Can I bring anyone coffee?"

Maurey said "No," I said "Yes," and Chet didn't say anything. While Ron went for coffee, Maurey and I flipped through a three-spiral binder marked CREMATION OPTIONS. It was divided into "Showing and Service," "Service Only," and "No Showing, No Service," with two more chapters at the back filled with photographs of special-order caskets and urns.

The urns were mostly either boxes or vases, but they had a few ceramic statues—leaping dolphins and a Greek woman without arms. One was five books that looked real but were hollow, so you could hide your loved one on a shelf. I studied an urn shaped like Cowboy Joe, the squatty University of Wyoming mascot I always thought was ripped off from Yosemite Sam.

Ron put my coffee on a coaster. "Did Peter go to UW?" he asked. I said, "No."

Maurey said, "Pete. Not Peter."

"Sorry." He handed her a clipboard with a questionnaire on birthdate, parents' names, length of time in the armed forces, that sort of thing. As Ron outlined our options, his hands touched his earlobes and hair, nervously, and his left dimple twitched. We told him no showing, services at the Episcopal Church in Jackson, and Chet was to receive the ashes.

Maurey looked up from the form. "Why does it want to know if Pete had a pacemaker?"

A cloud crossed Ron's face. "They run on a nuclear battery. You cremate a pacemaker and *blooey*"—his hands flew—"you can level a city block." He nodded quickly. "It happened in St. Augustine, Florida."

Chet spoke for the first time. "Is it just me, or does this strike anyone else as bizarre?"

Ron cracked. He'd held it together while everyone played their parts, but as soon as Chet vocalized the ironic weirdness of death, Ron's face collapsed and his shoulders dropped as if he'd taken a blow in the back from a baseball bat.

His voice shook. "My wife was raised in the funeral business. She loves it, but I married in."

Maurey glanced at me. I shrugged.

"It's not the cadavers," Ron went on. "I don't want you thinking

223

I'm squeamish over dead bodies." His eyes begged us to believe him.

"I don't think you're squeamish," I said.

"It's dealing with the bereaved. I can't help feeling what they feel."

"You're in the wrong job," Maurey said.

"People come to me at the saddest moment of their lives and, instead of offering comfort, I'm expected to make retail sales. 'That'll be ten thousand dollars, ma'am. I know you're penniless and your husband left you all alone, but we do take Visa and MasterCard.'" Tears dribbled down his cheeks. He made no move to stop the flow.

"We're not penniless," I said.

"And I'm not really alone," Chet said. "I have friends."

Ron sniffed. "You're just trying to make me feel better."

Maurey stood and went to a Kleenex box on the desk. She handed him a tissue and said, "Buck up. You don't want your wife to see you like this."

He stared at her. "How did you know?"

We met Gloria Mildren herself downstairs in the showroom. Urns filled a shelf on the left with caskets in the middle of the room and on the right. Each casket had a card giving the price and number of years on the warranty. Naturally, I drifted right over to the children's casket. They only had one on hand, sized for about a six-year-old. It sold for eighteen hundred dollars and had a twelve-year warranty. I was afraid to ask what the warranty covered. I immediately imagined the child in the box, her little arms crossed over her chest, her hair brushed till it glowed. I could see the expression on her mother's face. I knew her father's helplessness. Sometimes being a novelist is a curse.

Chet and Maurey chose a bois d'arc box with ivory inlay for the ashes and a simple pine cremation casket. Cremation caskets are much like the burial kind, only they don't have handles.

A woman's voice came from a back hallway. "Orifices plugged up *tight*." She walked into the showroom wearing a yoked shirt and 701 jeans, drying her hands on a Motel 6 towel. On seeing us, she had a moment's embarrassment, but she recovered nicely. "Gloria Mildren," she said, shaking hands all around. "My prayers are with you."

We pretty much looked at the floor on that one.

Gloria's eyes traveled the circle from us to her husband's face. "Has Ronny been crying in front of the mourners again?"

I said, "No."

"He cried in front of some folks from Pennsylvania last week. Their son skied into a tree and, if that wasn't enough, when they came to view the body their funeral director bawled like a baby." She turned to me. "How would you like it if that happened to you?"

"Ron was totally professional with us." I looked to Chet and Maurey for confirmation.

Maurey nodded and said, "Totally," but I don't think Chet heard.

The woman put her hands on her hips. She had the classic Western body of a barrel racer—wide shoulders, small breasts, tiny waist, strong thighs. "Do you want to see him?"

I said, "Pete didn't want a showing."

She seemed disappointed. "Are you the lover?"

"What?"

"We heard he had a male lover."

"I'm . . . that's me," Chet said.

"Oh." She studied him a moment. "Anything we can do to make your time of grief easier, let us know. I lost a lover once. I know how rough it can be."

"Thank you," Chet said.

"You two weren't married? I suppose not."

"No."

"Being married makes it more bearable. Everyone admits you're worthy of sympathy. My lover's wife got the condolences, the money, and the name, and I had to keep up the act."

"I'm sorry," Chet said.

"I know what you're going through. Believe me."

"I do."

Maurey blew across the surface of her coffee. "There's nothing worse than a shallow person trying to be thoughtful," she said.

"Pete and I are used to it." Chet inhaled on his cigarette. "She meant well."

"That's what I'm talking about. Artificially deep people are worse when they mean well than when they don't."

We were sitting in a window booth at Dot's Dine Out and I was nervous because when we walked in Hank waved at us from the far booth by the jukebox, where he sat facing Lydia. All I could see was the back of her head, but that was enough to pull my trigger.

Maurey continued. "Take 'He Ain't Heavy, He's My Brother.' Whoever wrote that was actually trying to be profound."

"Listen to the Warm," Chet said.

"There's something rotten in the state of Denmark."

I figured it was my turn. "Never take a rattlesnake by its tail or a woman by her word."

Maurey poured creamer and stirred. "Doesn't count. The author knew he was being cynical. We're talking about sincere froth."

"How about 'Have a nice day'?"

Maurey smiled. "I can just hear Gloria Mildren chirping that as the hearse pulls away."

Chet stared out the window. "Jesus loves me, this I know."

Maurey and I glanced at each other, then down at our cups. I wondered if Lydia could hear us. I couldn't hear her, but that didn't mean anything.

Dot's Dine Out may be the closest I have to a place that feels like home. It had a different name back then, but throughout junior high and high school I spent at least part of each day swilling coffee and trying to flirt with Dot Pollard, who was considerably more a mom than Lydia. Whenever the defeats and heartaches of puberty got me down, Dot was the woman I ran to, and I'd probably have starved to death if I had to depend on my own mother to feed me. That's why when the owner, Max, died of hardened arteries, I loaned Dot the money to buy the cafe.

"Isn't that your former husband?" Chet nodded toward Dothan Talbot coming from his real estate office across the street. "Pete pointed him out to me once."

"I wish Pete wouldn't go around exposing my shameful past," Maurey said.

Dothan wore a camouflage jacket and light blue cowboy boots. He got into a new Ford pickup truck that sported an NRA decal and a bumper sticker reading 👁 ♡ EX WIFE 🌲 ♪ . I didn't get it.

"What's the bumper sticker mean?" I asked.

"Filth," Maurey said.

"Perhaps you should sue him," Chet said.

"Oh, it's okay. There's been two ex-wives since me. Besides, it's not considered cowboy to sue people in Wyoming. If he offends me bad enough, I'll shoot his gas tank."

"I still don't get it," I said.

Dot approached, carrying my chicken strip platter and Maurey's chocolate malt. Chet was sticking to coffee. As far as I knew, he'd had nothing but coffee for two days, and it was starting to show on his face. Yesterday's shock was being overwhelmed by today's grief.

Dot watched with us as the truck pulled out of a handicapped parking space. She laughed and said, "Dothan tried to sell me a time share the other day. Took a lot of nerve, considering the grapevine says he's bringing in a Roy Rogers roast beef franchise." Except for adding twenty pounds, Dot hasn't changed in two decades. She's the only consistently cheerful person in my life.

"Where'd you hear that?" I asked.

"Where I hear ever'thing. Right here."

"GroVont doesn't need another restaurant. We've already got too many," Maurey said. Dot's Dine Out—under various names and disguises—and the Dairy Queen next to the Forest Service headquarters had been the only eating establishments in GroVont since the Second World War, until last summer, when a couple from Santa Barbara opened The Whole Grain out on the Jackson Highway. The Whole Grain specialized in hummus paninis and vinaigrettes.

"Hear from Jacob lately?" I asked. Dot's son, Jacob, tends to go off on tangents, so it's always risky to ask about him. You never know what you're going to get. But if you haven't seen Dot in a while, not asking about him is a pointed comment in itself.

Dot slid into the booth beside me and stole a French fry. "Jacob wrote a letter, said I was pedestrian and ruled by temporal lust and he's chosen a new mother. Says she nurtures his inner spirit."

Maurey stared me down. "Don't you hate kids who turn on their mother?"

Dot dipped my fry in ketchup and went on, unaware of the arrow I'd just taken in the chest. "Ft. Worth Jones saw him in the Salt Lake Airport last month. Jacob was wearing a sheet and passing out free flowers. His head is shaved."

If anyone deserves to be treated right by their son, it's Dot. Had she been my mother, I'd buy her chocolates every day and a condo when she retires.

"Maybe we ought to drive down there and drag his cosmic butt home," I said.

Dot laughed like I was kidding. "Lydia says it's nothing but a phase they all go through and he'll outgrow it."

"I never went through an airport beggar phase."

Dot popped the fry into her mouth. "Speaking of Lydia."

"We weren't," I said.

"She's sitting over there at Hank's table. Maybe you should go visit with her."

"Not likely."

Maurey pointed her straw at my face. "When a loved one dies, all grudges are called off, Sam. That's the rules."

"Lydia doesn't play by the rules."

"If I can forgive her for mailing poison to Ronald Reagan's dog, you can forgive her for faking rape."

"The two sins aren't equal."

"How would you feel if Shannon refused to speak to you? Lord knows you've pulled stunts not everybody's child would forgive."

I considered this carefully. "At least if I ruin my daughter's life, I won't do it on purpose."

"Nobody's ruined your life on purpose."

I stared down at my plate on the table. "Could of fooled me."

At the top of my line of vision, Maurey's hands doubled into fists. "You got a lot of nerve sitting in the same room with Chet and saying your life is ruined."

"You guys are capable of a loving partnership. I'm not."

Everybody ate or looked out the window in silence. I felt bad about saying my life was more ruined than Chet's. It obviously wasn't. He'd lost someone close and I hadn't because I didn't seem capable of having someone close. Up until Halloween, my purpose had been to give pleasure to women, and I'd been fairly good at it, but while I was busy giving women pleasure, I'd been unable to fall in love with one. I could love women I wasn't romantically linked with—Shannon, Gus, Maurey as an adult—but the moment I found a clitoris I forgot the person it went with.

Dot unscrewed the salt shaker lid and began poking a toothpick through it from the underside. She said, "Oly's licking salt shakers again. He drools all over the top and spit gets in the little holes."

"I wish you'd told me that before I salted my French fries," I said.

Dot polished the lid with her apron. "He must have a salt deficiency. Why else would anyone go around licking salt shakers?"

I snuck a look at Maurey to see if she was still angry, and she was. A dime-size red circle burned under each cheekbone. Her eyes had drifted far away. I said, "I could have sworn Oly Pederson was the oldest man in the valley when we moved here twenty years ago."

"He turned ninety last summer," Dot said. "He's holding out for a hundred so Paul Harvey will say his name on the radio. I don't think he'll make it with a salt deficiency."

"Oly's going to outlive us all," Maurey said with some bitterness.

"I guess I don't mind so much." Dot screwed the more or less clean top back on the salt. "This way I don't have to fill the shakers half as often as I used to."

"Every cloud has a silver lining," Chet said. I noticed he was falling into the habit of dry irony. That's not a habit you want to fall into permanently.

Dot went on. "Lydia says he's doing a public service. The collective blood pressure of the county is going down from lack of salt."

"I thought we weren't talking about Lydia," I said.

"Why aren't we talking about Lydia?" Lydia hovered, the other side of Dot. I kept my head down. No one answered her question, so she went right on.

"Sam. Son of mine. The county plowed in my car last week and now it's almost buried. I'd like you to come by and shovel my car out. Are you willing to cooperate?"

The secret was to study details. Count my remaining fries. Quantify the slaw. The white gravy next to my last chicken strip had congealed. The surface shone like a bald head.

"I'll do it," Chet said.

Lydia made a *click* sound in her throat. "Thank you, no. Shoveling out a car is a son's duty."

I compared the ketchup glint to the gravy glisten. The ketchup shone brighter. By moving my spoon an inch, I could reflect the fluorescent ceiling tube into the ketchup gleam.

Lydia said, "Hey, big shot, I'm talking to you."

I said, "I am not prepared to deal with you at this time."

She used her ugly voice. *"I am not prepared to deal with you at this time."*

I risked a glance at Maurey and Chet. They'd opted for false deafness. "Lydia," I said. "I will never be able to compete with you at sarcastic banter. I doubt if anyone can be as verbally cruel as you, so I choose to shut up."

She slammed her fists on the table. Both Dot and my plate jumped an inch. "I'll show you verbal cruelty, you little ingrate. Look at me when I'm talking to you."

I slowly turned my head. She wore tight jeans and a blouse that had been popular back in the fifties. She carried a leather purse shaped like a Western saddle. Because of my low angle and her eye makeup, she came off as fierce and forthright—the proud holder of righteous indignation.

I said, "I destroyed three families and a boy tried to kill himself."

"And that's my fault?" The vein in her forehead bulged out, pulsating in an almost sexual manner.

"Yes."

"Sam, you're thirty-three years old. You haven't lived at home since you were eighteen."

"Seventeen."

"It's time to stop blaming me every time you wet the bed."

"What?"

"My not breast-feeding you had nothing to do with that boy resorting to suicide."

Breast-feeding? The woman's self-delusions floored me. "You said my fathers raped you when it was you who paid them two dollars each."

"So I forgot some details."

I studied Lydia's face. As she'd aged, her neck got stringier, and a network of lines came off her mouth, but the eyes were the same. Did she not know what that lie had done to me? Did she honestly feel no remorse? "Mom, those details affect the way I see men. Women. Myself. Because of the rape story, I don't think I'm capable of love. And I'm afraid it's too late to change."

She stared at me for a two-count, then she snapped open her purse and pulled out a Kleenex. "Here. Cry on something that cares."

4

By early afternoon the bunkhouse twenty-gallon water heater had recovered from the morning rush and it was my turn to shower. I like showers. Generally, they make me feel renewed, as if a clean body equals a clean slate, but TM Ranch bunkhouse showers leave a lot to be desired. That's because the stall has rusted seams that turn the water brown as it passes over your feet, and after you dry off you have to go back outside and circle around to your room. Nobody much minds in summer when all it takes is flip-flops and boxer shorts, but winter means completely redressing, boots included.

During the rinse cycle I went into a daydream where Shannon wins the first Nobel Prize in Anthropology. The Swedish government flies both of us to Stockholm and puts us up in the finest hotel in Europe, one of those places where the maid turns down your bed at night so you don't have to fluff your own pillow. At the ceremony, Shannon, vibrant and beautiful as she is, stands before the hall of intellectuals and gives me all the credit.

"I never would have discovered the lost civilization of Borneo if not for the continued love and support of my dad," Shannon says, "and I am here to announce that I have named the era that these people flourished as the Samcallahantic Period."

Then Shannon kisses me on both cheeks and my stomach goes soppy nauseous. The nausea-from-love stomach part actually happened in the shower. Just thinking about my daughter could do that to me.

When I turned off the water the pipes made a painful shuddering sound. I stepped from the stall to find Hank standing between me and my towel, holding a chain saw.

He said, "The boys and I are going after a Christmas tree."

I don't do well when I'm naked and other people aren't. "Won't a Christmas tree be kind of maudlin, what with Pete dying and all?"

"Maurey decided Auburn and Roger deserve a Christmas. There hasn't been much cheer the last few months. She gave orders no one is to be depressed from after the funeral through New Year's."

I shifted to slide past him to my towel on the nail on the wall, but Hank didn't take the hint. Instead, he averted his eyes the way Blackfeet are supposed to when they have something serious to say.

"Your mother cried this morning," he said.

"Lydia hasn't cried since the day she was born, and that was only a rumor."

He nodded. "After the two of you shouted at one another in Dot's, I drove her home and she cried in the truck."

I considered what this might mean. "Regret or manipulation?"

"It appeared as regret."

"How would you know with Lydia?"

"She feels badly about what she did."

"Then why doesn't she say so?"

The outside door opened and Chet entered. He said, "It's getting cold out there."

Hank said, "Should be zero tonight."

Great. Now I'm naked if front of a Blackfoot with a chain saw and a known homosexual. Chet sat on the changing bench and lit a cigarette, cool and calm as if he were waiting for a bus. I have this recurring dream where I'm in a crowd of well-dressed people and I'm nude but no one seems to notice. Must be a primal fear thing because the dream shrivels my penis.

"How's Pete's eulogy coming along?" Chet asked.

"What?"

"We truly appreciate you taking care of it. I know you and Pete didn't always see eye to eye, but he respected your creative drive. Even though he never read one, I heard him say more than once that your novels are an achievement."

I tried holding my hands, casually, so they covered me without it appearing that I was covering myself on purpose.

Chet lifted his face to look straight into my eyes. "I know you'll do Pete right by your eulogy."

Behind my back, the toilet flushed. The commode stall door opened and closed and Toinette said, "Can I tag along when you go to cut the Christmas tree?"

My manhood disappeared in a black forest of pubic hair.

"Looking at a woman as an object you can give pleasure to is just as bogus as looking at a woman as an object that can give pleasure to you. It's still looking at the woman as an object."

Maurey downshifted on a grade, then hit the flats and punched the gears back into fourth. The woman was fearless in four-wheel drive. Ice meant nothing.

"But it makes me feel worthwhile when I save a woman."

She rammed back into third for a corner. "You can't save a woman by giving her an orgasm."

Words to live by. "Even if she isn't getting them in her normal life?"

"Right. Have you slept with this Gilia girl?"

"Of course not."

"What 'of course not'? You've slept with half the heifers in the Confederacy. It shouldn't be unreasonable to ask if you've slept with someone you actually like."

"Gilia's a friend."

"Since when are friends off limits?"

I looked out at the red willow wands sprouting from the snow crust and tried to come up with an explanation. "Friendship love is real; romantic love is conditional—don't sleep with anyone else, don't be a constant drunk, get a job, don't commit social blunders in front of my parents, love me back—and romantic lovers are based on chemical attraction; to me that isn't very important compared to real love."

Maurey ripped back into fourth and shot around a snow plow. She said, "I can see now why your wife left you."

"Me too."

Far to the south, the sun was setting with all the power of a weak flashlight beam. The dash clock said 4:30 and I remembered from some book that this was the shortest day of the year. Across the valley, green lights flickered on as an outline for the runway. I said a small prayer to Whomever to bring my daughter safely out of the sky.

"Do you think it's possible for people to change?" I asked.

Maurey glanced at me, then back at the road. In the soft pink light of the alpenglow her face was the same as I pictured it from twenty years past, when we were lovers.

"I did," she said.

"But you had alcohol you could quit. People with concrete problems like alcoholism or obesity or an abusive husband can solve the problem and, ultimately, change themselves. What about us poor stooges who are vaguely miserable, but don't have any real monsters to battle against?"

Maurey downshifted and hit the blinker behind a line of cars turning into the airport. "Everybody's vaguely miserable sometimes," she said, "and most people are vaguely miserable most of the time. The trick is to scrap your way from the most-of-the-time to the some-of-the-time category."

"How?"

She ticked off on her fingers. "True love, kids, mountains, exercise, and work you think matters. If none of that does it, I'd consider antidepressants."

Maurey flashed on her brights and pulled to within a car's length of a new Ford pickup, seemingly intent on blinding its driver. She said, "Speaking of vaguely miserable, that's Dothan ahead of us."

I peered at the spotlessly clean truck with the bumper sticker I still didn't get. "You think Dothan's miserable?"

"Deep down inside, Dothan can't stand himself."

"He hides it well."

"None of the valley women will touch him with a stick. Dot says he's flying in some bimbo from Denver whose husband is in chemotherapy. Even you never sank that low."

"Thanks, I guess."

Dothan Talbot beat me up in the seventh grade. He rubbed my face in the snow and twisted my arm around my back, then he became Maurey's boyfriend after I had already impregnated her. He knew I had impregnated her and I knew he was touching her with his grubby fingers, so it was only natural for us to evolve into lifelong enemies. Plus, Dothan was, and still is, a Class A jerk. He'd have been in the Mafia if he had come from a town of over five hundred people. As it is, he sells real estate.

I ran into him in the airport bathroom. Shannon's plane was late, like they all are in winter here, and I was nervous about seeing her. Up until then, I'd been fairly numb over what a mess I'd made of life, but now with Shannon's arrival I was going to have to start feeling again, and I wasn't sure I was ready.

When I'm nervous I need to pee every five minutes, so I left Maurey in the terminal and went to the bathroom, where I found Dothan standing in front of a mirror, combing Brylcreem into his hair. He's worn his hair the same way for as long as I've known him, which means he must have greased out ten thousand pillows since junior high.

He glanced at me in the mirror and grinned the way people will when they hate your guts. "Hello, Callahan."

"Yeah, right." I needed to go pretty bad but I wasn't about to pull out my pecker in front of Dothan. Standing in the middle of the room doing nothing felt stupid. The only alternative was washing my hands at the sink next to him.

"Still Maurey's puppy, I see," Dothan said.

It was one of those water-saving sinks where you push a button to get water but the moment you let go of the button a spring or something pops it back up and the water flow stops. This works fine if only one hand is dirty.

"You know the whole town laughs at you behind your back," Dothan said.

I pushed the button with my right hand and squeezed soap from the dispenser with my left. Dothan's primping style also took two hands—one for combing and one for patting grease.

He said, "I'm telling you as a favor. No one else in the valley will tell you the truth but I can give it to you straight. They all know you slipped the meat to Maurey once twenty years ago and you've been following her around sniffing her panties and being pitiful ever since."

I lathered my hands.

Dothan stared at me in the mirror. "Maurey'll never let you have sloppy seconds. Everyone knows she takes your money and doesn't give shit back."

I held the button with my left hand and rinsed the right, then switched off the other way.

"If I paid for her queer brother's funeral, I'd at least get a blow job," Dothan said.

Holding my hands up, I walked to the hot-air dryer and punched it on with my elbow. Over the *whir* of blowing air, I said, "Dothan, you're never going to have a friend in your whole life."

Dothan laughed heartily as he headed for the door. Halfway through, he turned back and said, "Maurey's laughing at you, son. Just like me and everybody else."

Dothan's bimbo was first off the plane and across the runway. She had zit-red hair with black roots and wore a yellow halter thing and tight pants that were totally inappropriate for winter. The two of them kissed and rubbed against each other in a disgusting public display of affection made all the more poignant by the fact her husband was off in a hospital somewhere with cancer.

"Are we friends?" I asked Maurey.

She was watching Dothan and the tramp. "Of course we're friends."

"You aren't laughing at me behind my back?"

Maurey touched my arm. "You've been listening to Dothan again. When are you going to learn he's nothing but a dildo with ears."

"You're right."

"There she is."

Shannon came off the plane, wearing a yoked down jacket and some kind of jeans that weren't Levi's or Wranglers. As she made her way down the steps, she was talking to an older, gentlemanly type with a mustache and a cane. Shannon looked confident and composed, at home in her element. Nineteen-year-old women weren't composed when I was nineteen.

Maurey said, "Airport scenes are so much nicer when the passengers walk down the steps and across the runway. Those tunnels took the romance out of flight."

Shannon said goodbye to the old man and came bouncing across the runway and I had that *Jesus, shit, I created this* feeling I always get when I see her for the first time after a separation. Shannon didn't seem any less a miracle now than the day she was born.

Then she burst through the double doors, all smiles and laughs. I think for a moment she forgot she was here for a funeral. She gave me a two-handed hug and a kiss on the cheek, then she moved on to Maurey. They hadn't seen each other since summer, and Shannon finally remembered Pete and the purpose of the trip, so the hugs were spirited and meaningful.

"I appreciate you coming," Maurey said.

Shannon's brown eyes went smoky. "Uncle Pete was always nice to me. When I was little he used to send me flowers on Valentine's."

I didn't remember that. It seemed like something I should remember.

Maurey said, "More than once Pete told me you were the only thing I ever got right," and they hugged again.

Shannon had brought two suitcases plus her carry-on, so we had to wait at the conveyor belt surrounded by skiers in off-colored clothes. They talked loudly about inches and runs. I glared at boys who were checking out my daughter. Maurey got as many looks as Shannon, but I figured I had no right to glare at Maurey's bunch. She was old enough to handle oglers without my help.

As often as they talked on the telephone, you'd think Shannon and Maurey wouldn't have that much left to catch up on, but the moment I finished the how-was-your-flight formalities they launched into mother-daughter gossip. Shannon gave a detailed description of a pair of boots she almost bought for the trip, Maurey talked about horses and how successful Pud was in the satellite dish repair business. Shannon gave a Eugene report.

"He wants us to date each other and other people at the same time. Says it would be values affirming. I said, 'Fat chance.' "

"You can't date a guy after you've lived with him," Maurey said.

"At your age I think you should still be playing the field," I said.

They both stared at me until I volunteered to go pluck her suitcases off the conveyor carrel. As I made my way through the skier jam, I heard Shannon say, "Play the field?"

Maurey said, "You'll have to excuse your father. He learned his parenting skills from 'Leave It to Beaver.' "

At the ranch, we found a Douglas fir lying on its side in the living room. Pud and Hank were crouched on the floor with a measuring tape. Toinette, Auburn, and Roger sat at a card table, stringing popcorn and chokecherries while Chet was off in Pete's room, talking to New Yorkers on the telephone.

"Our tree's too big!" Auburn shouted.

Hank and Pud studied the situation.

"We could cut a hole in the ceiling," Hank said.

"Or the floor," Pud said.

"Or take thirty inches off the middle and splice the tree together," Hank added.

This is your typical example of Native American humor. As a kid, it drove me crazy, but now it was Auburn's turn.

He crowed. "That's the dumbest thing I ever heard."

Hank's face was dead serious. "You got a better idea?"

Maurey introduced Shannon to Toinette and Roger. Toinette offered her supper, but Shannon said she had eaten on the plane. Shan-

239

non complimented Roger on his chokecherry necklace and asked him to show her how it was done.

"What's Gus up to?" I asked.

"Gus is on a cleaning binge. She's throwing out everything she doesn't consider vital to survival."

"My baseball cards?"

"They went the first day."

Chet came from Pete's room. "Our friends are coming in tomorrow."

"Do they need a place to stay?" Maurey asked.

"I made reservations at Snow King Inn."

Shannon and Chet shook hands and Shannon said she was sorry about Pete. Chet said Pete spoke of her often; Maurey went to the kitchen and brought back lemonade and these little crackers shaped like fish. Everything was going fine—I'd just taken my place at the popcorn-stringing station—when Shannon said, "I expected Grandma Lydia to be here."

I stuck a needle through a popped kernel and the kernel broke in half, leaving me with nothing on my needle.

"Your father and grandmother aren't speaking," Maurey said.

Shannon looked at me. "Why not?"

Maurey answered. "He says she ruined his life."

I set the needle next to my lemonade and gave up on Christmas decorating. There's no use trying to be constructive when you're ganged up on by women.

"That was weeks ago," Shannon said. "You be nice to your mother."

"She's not nice to me."

"Jeeze, Louise, who's the grown-up around here? Dad, I want you to march down to her house and make up. Right now."

"No."

Maurey said, "Forgive your mother, Sam."

Hank said, "You have the power to make her Christmas bright."

"I won't do it."

No one would look at me, except Roger who had an expression on his face like I'd stolen his teddy bear.

The silence didn't last long. Shannon laid down an ultimatum. "Forgive Lydia or I won't forgive you."

I hate ultimatums. "For what?"

"For hurting my friend Gilia. For messing up Halloween by making that boy try to kill himself on our front porch."

"Don't forget he was creepy to your boyfriend," Maurey said.

"That too."

I stood up. All day I'd been looking forward to my daughter's arrival, and now this.

"I'm being persecuted," I said.

Chet's face was the saddest thing I'd ever seen. He said, "People you love die. Don't waste precious time holding grudges."

I searched the room for an ally—Chet to Roger to Auburn to Hank to Shannon to Maurey. They were all accusing me and they were all wrong.

I said, "I'm going to bed."

She threw back her white neck, swelling with a sigh, and faltering, in tears, with a long shudder and hiding her face, she gave herself to him.

Ah, Madame Bovary. If only someone would throw back her white neck for me. Emma was so happy there for a moment, not knowing that she, like Anna Karenina and Oedipus's mother and so many other lovely yet loose women created by male novelists, would soon die a cruel death at her own hand.

On Lydia's fortieth birthday, Shannon and I flew up from North Carolina to surprise her. Hank arranged for us and practically everyone else who knew Lydia to meet at this hoity-toity restaurant in Teton Village. Surprise birthday parties carry a high risk. Take Katrina's as an example. Anyway, Hank told Lydia the two of them were going out to eat, and when she walked into the dining room we all yelled "*Surprise!*" and broke into that awful song. Lydia's face turned to wax, she looked at the massive cake Dot had baked, and she looked at me; then, calmly, she left. I didn't see her again for two years.

They—my family and friends—were probably right about Lydia. I've found there are few instances where I'm right and everybody else is wrong. In the morning I would drive into GroVont and do whatever it took to reestablish a relationship with my mother.

A knock came at the door, which is always interesting in the middle of the night. I welcome late night knocks. I marked my place in *Madame Bovary* with a Kleenex strip as Shannon walked through the door wearing her pac boots without socks and her cold weather flannel nightgown.

She held out two wrapped Fudgsicles. "You hungry?"

I nodded even though I wasn't, particularly.

She gave me a Fudgsicle, then pushed my feet over under the blanket, clearing a spot so she could sit on the end of the bed. I could see her looking around at my living situation, critically. Even though the room had been home for over six weeks, it wasn't much more personal than a monk's cell. I had a bedside stump for my Kleenex box and *Madame Bovary* and a length of clothesline between two nails for a closet. Five or six dirty coffee cups sat mired in dust bunnies under the bed.

"I'm planning to fix the place up after Christmas," I said.

Shannon said, "Don't go out of your way on my account." From somewhere in the flannel nightgown she produced a baby blue envelope. "Gilia sent you a letter."

She must have originally planned to mail it because the letter had been addressed and stamped. It was one of those personalized stationery envelopes women give each other as gifts, the kind with the return address embossed in white. The uncancelled stamp was a painting of a Baltimore oriole—it said so under the picture—but best of all the envelope smelled ever so lightly of Gilia.

"What did you do to her?" Shannon asked.

"How do you mean that?"

Shannon tore the top off her Fudgsicle wrapper and pulled the paper down over the stick. I don't do it that way. I pull the wrap up over the top, like a sweater.

"Gilia's been moping around ever since you dumped on her. I asked what was the matter and she said you two connected intellec-

242

tually and emotionally." Shannon did this arch thing with her right eyebrow. "You didn't screw her, did you?"

"Of course not."

I turned the letter over and looked at the back. It didn't have any of those Xs and Os most women put on letters.

"She'd be nuts to give you another chance." Shannon sucked the curved tip of her Fudgsicle. "But if she does, you better not blow it again, Daddy."

"Yes."

"I don't want a parade of Wandas in and out of my life."

"Me either."

We each slurped our ice cream bars in silence for a while. I poked my fingertips with the sharp corners of the envelope and hefted it for weight—didn't feel like more than one page. I wondered if it would be rude to read it in front of Shannon. She seemed lost in thought. She was staring at her Fudgsicle the way I stare into coffee when I've got something intense on my mind.

Suddenly, with no warning, Shannon raised her head and hit me with the full force of her brown eyes. "Dad, we need to talk."

I bit off a chunk of chocolate ice and waited, in no hurry. Whenever a woman says "We need to talk," it means she's reached a decision and it's already too late for you to talk back.

She said, "A couple of girls from UNC-G have an apartment on Carr Street, there across from the school. They needed a roommate and I applied and they took me."

I didn't understand at first. "But that would mean moving out of the Manor House."

"Yes, moving in with them means moving out on you."

"All your stuff is at home."

She reached over and patted my shin under the blanket. "I'm getting a new home."

Pretend your sacred daughter sticks a knife between your ribs into your heart and twists it and you'll get an inkling of how I felt. "Why would you want to leave our house? You need more space? I'll give you more space."

"I'm nineteen, Daddy. I'll be twenty next summer. It's time I got out on my own."

"You can be on your own at home. Ask the girls to move in with us. There's plenty of room and they won't even have to pay rent."

"Living with girls isn't the point. It's a matter of independence. I'm leaving the nest and you have to let me."

"I do?"

"Yes."

Melted chocolate ran down the stick onto my fingers. Shannon was staring at me hard, the way Gilia used to. It's not fair women can do that and men can't.

"Will you be living with Eugene?" I asked. "Is this an excuse for unbridled sex?"

When I said *unbridled*, Shannon smiled. She knew in my imagination I was picturing her as a debauched harlot. "I'm done with Eugene, and this doesn't have anything to do with sex. It's my freedom."

She was too young to talk about freedom. Only yesterday, she'd held my hand when we crossed the street. She used to run all the way home from first grade because she missed me. Hell, I used to run all the way home from eighth grade because I missed her.

"What am I supposed to do?" I asked.

"We'll see each other." Shannon's laugh was a clear bell. "I'm bound to be over with dirty laundry."

Maurey was right: Life is the shits. "But all I've ever done is take care of you."

"Maybe it's time for you to do something else." Shannon leaned forward to kiss my cheek and take the stick out of my hand. "See you in the morning," she said. Then she was gone.

Dear Sam,

Shannon says you don't conquer females the way my ex-husband did. She says you have an obsessive compulsion to save lost women, that you meet miserable women who need love which you translate as sex and you convince yourself their lives wouldn't be miserable anymore if only you would do them the favor of sleeping with them.

According to your letter, you were planning to commit to me at some unnamed point in the future, but I don't see how you can commit to anyone if you have an obsessive compulsion that forces you to sleep with sluts.

Atalanta Williams says you have never been loved by a good woman and if a good woman were to ever love you, you would straighten up.

My father says you are a truthless satyrmaniac and Skip Prescott says you're a "pussy hound," among other things.

I don't know what I say. All I know is I miss our talks and you are a villain.

Sincerely,
Gilia

5

I dreamed I was trapped in an elevator with thirteen Greco-Roman wrestlers. Their nude bodies glistened in virgin olive oil. Testicles hung down like baseballs in the toes of full-figure panty hose. I was wearing a Victoria's Secret crepe chemise with nothing on underneath. The wrestlers milled back and forth, moaning and jostling me with their shoulders, thighs, and slick buttocks. Suddenly, over by the elevator controls, an Indian pull-started a Poulan chain saw. Lydia shouted, "Castrate the homophobe!" and the wrestlers rushed to the opposite corner of the elevator, crushing me between layers of naked male flesh.

In the morning, I dropped Maurey and Shannon off in Jackson so they could Christmas shop for the boys. The plan was for me to drive back to GroVont, reconcile with my mother, then pick the women up around noon and go back to the ranch, where Maurey had a job lined up for me and Pud—something about elk in the hay.

The plan reminded me of when I used to write lists of what to do today:

Take a shower.
Buy socks.
Write great American novel.
Pick up film at Wal-Mart.

It's like if you sneak the big chore in, maybe you'll check it off without noticing, only this would be harder because I'd written novels before; I'd never reconciled with my mother.

"Go to her with your heart in your hand," Maurey said. "Lydia can't deal with open vulnerability."

"Beg her forgiveness," Shannon said.

"Beg her forgiveness for what? She's the one who lied."

Shannon patted me on the back of the head. "Jesus, Daddy, you're so naive."

The morning was beautiful—fresh snow on the Tetons, royal blue sky above, robin's-egg blue sky on the horizon. Winter can be real nice from inside a warm Suburban with two wonderful women by your side.

When I stopped at the Jackson Town Square, Maurey said, "Don't lose your temper. Remember, she's the childish one, you're the adult."

"Yes."

Shannon giggled. "I'm lots more mature than Daddy, who's lots more mature than Grandma. Our family must run in reverse."

"The Callahan clan does everything backward," Maurey said, opening her door. "Let's go to the bank first so I can get some money."

"No need, I still have Dad's credit card."

Instead of driving away, I sat with both hands on the steering wheel watching Maurey and Shannon walk toward the nearest tourist trap. From the backside, they not only could have been sisters, they could have been twins. Same dark hair—Shannon's short, Maurey's long—same shoulders, as they walked their arms swung the same distance from their look-alike hips. Maurey said something and touched Shannon on the elbow, then Shannon looked back at me and burst into laughter.

I imagine Maurey had said words to the effect of "What do you bet he's still sitting there, mooney-eyed with sentimentality." Words to that effect anyway. Women love to think men are predictable; I try not to let them down.

As I made my way across the frozen valley back along the highway to GroVont, I rehearsed possibilities of the upcoming scene with Lydia. What was I supposed to say? You don't erase twenty years of pain by quoting the back cover of a self-help book.

"Gee, Mom, it's fine you raised me thinking I was a child of rape when I wasn't. I can validate the empowerment that motivated your disinformation response."

"Thank you, Son, I accept responsibility for my actions."

Then we would cry cathartic tears and join arms around a campfire and sing "Kumbaya, My Lord" in perfect harmony.

Fat chance.

You could tell from several houses down the street that something had happened at Lydia's. Hank's truck was backed in the driveway and the tailgate was down. Possessions were piled around the sides—skis, snowshoes, Lydia's swivel work chair. When I pulled up next to the truck, I saw it was partially loaded with book boxes, a stereo, a painting of Martha Washington burning a bra over the Delaware, and Lydia's computer.

The cabin door opened and Hank came out, carrying two file boxes. I stood between the Suburban and his truck while he carefully stacked the boxes against the back of the cab.

"What's this?" I asked.

Hank studied the label on the end of a box. *"The Castration Solution."*

"Why is Lydia moving Oothoon?"

Hank turned to me and held his hands up, waist high, in a Blackfoot don't-ask-me gesture. He said, "She's joining the feminist underground."

"Is it because of me?"

"A man from Federal Express telephoned. Said her lost overnight packet had been found under the short leg of a dispatcher's desk in Hannibal, Missouri. Said the dispatcher is fired, Lydia's money will be returned, and the packet will be delivered by ten A.M. today."

"The poisoned chew toy."

"We'll hide out on the reservation until whatever happens blows over."

"I don't think assassination attempts on the President's dog blow over."

Hank shrugged. "Your mother always wanted to be an outlaw."

"What about you?"

The door slammed and Lydia appeared with two pairs of boots and a lamp made from an elk horn and semi-translucent rawhide. One pair of boots was normal brown with dark stitching, but the other pair had been painted yellow. Lydia herself wore sneakers, jeans, and a Patagonia jacket.

She said, "I'm leaving the TV, the Atari, and my car. You better take good care of her—oil changes every spring and fall. You'll need new tires if you plan on driving this winter."

I looked at the lump of snow in the front yard that hid Lydia's twelve-year-old BMW with something like 180,000 miles on the engine. The two cars she'd owned before this had also been over-the-hill BMWs. Don't ask me why.

She talked as she transferred her load to Hank. "Periodically while we're in Canada I shall be mailing manifestos for you to release to the media. Don't let those twits at *Newsweek* edit my copy."

"I thought you were disappearing on the reservation."

Lydia glared at Hank, who hung his head, shy dog–style. "Somebody's got a big mouth," she said, which may be the least true statement anyone ever made about Hank Elkrunner. "Tell the Secret Service we're in Mexico. Don't mention Canada until they break out the persuasion devices."

"Persuasion devices?"

Hank fit the lamp and boots into the back end like pieces into a jigsaw puzzle. He said, "I'll walk to Zion's Grocery and pick up some food for the road. You two can finish loading."

A look of dismay flitted across Lydia's narrow face. "You're leaving me alone with him on purpose, aren't you?" Hank gave his near smile.

Lydia said, "Rat."

Hank walked up the street, toward what passed for downtown GroVont. Lydia and I stood next to the truck, watching Hank's back as an alternative to looking at each other.

I said, "Don't you think making Hank into a fugitive is a lot to ask?"

Lydia turned, her hands on her hips, thumbs forward, fingers back. "Hank believes in loyalty—unlike other members of my immediate family."

"What's the chances of us having this discussion without snide sarcasm?"

Her hands dropped to her sides, and for one fleeting moment, Lydia looked profoundly depressed. "Slim. Or none."

Her first unguarded statement since I don't remember when—I took it as a good sign.

She looked at the truck and sighed. "Men have forced women to fall back on whatever weapons they have, and I'm afraid I'm down to sarcasm. Come on in and warm up. You may as well be of some use while you're here."

Whenever the television screen shows long lines of refugees running from a natural or manmade disaster, it's always interesting to see what possessions they deem important enough to flee with on short notice. Cooking utensils and bedding seem to head the list, followed by edible animals. Lydia hadn't packed any of that stuff. Instead, she went into hiding with her Oothoon Press files, most of her Ann Coe art collection, and a suitcase full of Danskins. A pile of political books. An exercise trampoline.

While Lydia finished packing, I wandered the house, taking in cracks in the logs and stains in the kitchen sink. When you grow up in a house, each square foot of wall and floor carries a memory, or not so much a memory as the emotion of one. I couldn't recall what event caused my strange stirrings at standing in my former closet, but I felt the strange stirrings just the same, as if the past had turned into its own shadow.

Lydia found me standing in the closet and told me to disconnect the VCR in her bedroom and take it to the truck, but to leave the TV. I guess wherever she and Hank planned to hide out already had a television.

As I walked down the hall with the VCR in my hands, I passed the open bathroom door and looked in to see Lydia staring at herself in the medicine cabinet mirror. Maybe it was a dimple in the mirror, or maybe leaving home after twenty years got to her, but I thought I saw a tear hanging off her lower eyelid. I thought her lip trembled. When she saw me in the doorway behind her, she focused her eyes on mine. Finally we were eye to eye, even if her back was to me.

"Remember when we moved in here?" she said. "That doctor Caspar rented from had dead animals on every wall."

"You slept on the couch for three months."

"Until Hank got me into bed."

"Why the lie, Lydia?"

She blinked once and whipped open the medicine cabinet. One hand held a paper bag while the other hand scooped in pill bottles, aspirin tins, and boxes of Q-Tips. "You're not going to let it drop, are you?"

"I can't."

A plastic jar of Mary Kay night cream missed the bag and hit the floor, where it rolled under the club-footed bathtub. Lydia's back rose and fell, then she turned to face me.

"Okay, shoot. Accuse me of child abuse."

I sat on the side of the tub with the VCR in my lap. Lydia closed the toilet lid and sat on it. The déjà vu element was amazing. We could have been mother and son in 1965, settling in for one of our sink-side bull sessions.

I repeated, "Why the lie?"

She blinked twice more. "I couldn't very well tell the truth."

"You didn't have to tell me anything."

She did the maneuver where she blew air straight up, lifting her bangs off her forehead. It translated as *Give me a break.*

"You kept hounding me for information, and then you found those pictures in my panty box. What were you doing in my panty box in the first place?"

Typical ploy—shift the defensiveness to me. "Don't change the subject."

"Times like this I would give anything to still smoke."

The stall technique. I said, "Lydia."

She crossed the right ankle over her left shin. "Sooner or later I had to come up with a story."

"But gang rape?"

She dropped her eyes to the floor. Her voice was small. "That's the story I told myself. After you tell yourself something a thousand times, you forget it's not true." She seemed to be drifting back in time, growing younger as I watched. "When you called to ask if their names matched Shannon's list, I didn't remember at first what really happened." She looked up, willing me to believe her. "I was scared to death. I didn't know what to do."

"The truth might have worked."

She uncrossed her legs. "I thought the truth would make you hate me. You may not believe it, but I don't want you to hate me."

I'd come prepared for anger and screams and gotten what I least expected—sincerity from my mother. Maybe. When you've grown up with the queen of manipulation, you learn to distrust anything that seems straightforward. My great fear was that someday Lydia would break down and speak the truth and I'd be too suspicious to listen.

She must have seen the doubt in my face. "What do you want from me, Sam?"

I stared at the VCR. "Remorse. Some indication that you're sorry you screwed up my life."

"One social blunder of mine did not screw up your life."

"It's not just the lie. You were never a mother. From the time we left your daddy's house, I cooked all the meals, did the laundry, tucked you in at night."

"You volunteered to cook and clean."

"You never once told me to do my homework or pick up my socks. I was the only kid in seventh grade who could stay out all night without calling home."

"Some boys would like that."

"No, they wouldn't."

She snapped. "Okay. I'm sorry. Are you satisfied now?"

The vein in Lydia's forehead beat a blue rhythm. She couldn't help who she was. You can no more force your parents to change than you can teach a cat to stop killing songbirds.

I said, "There's a big gap between apology and condescending glibness."

Lydia almost fired off an angry retort, but something changed her mind, and she slipped back into sadness. She pouted. "I'm not the type for guilt."

"I know." My reflection in the VCR control panel was distorted by knobs and switches. If I moved my head a bit to the side, my nose looked like a pig's snout. "I wonder why I'm nothing but a huge glob of guilt."

"It must skip generations."

What did that mean for Shannon? Lydia leaned forward on the toilet seat and laced her fingers into a web. She spoke to her palms. "I had you right after I turned fifteen, the poor little rich girl who'd never made a decision in her life. Pregnancy doesn't give you instant maturity. It just makes you fat."

She raised her hands to her face, thumbs on cheekbones, and looked at me through the web. "I'm sorry I did such a shitty job raising you."

Maybe she meant it. Maybe not. I like to think she did. Either way, I'd gotten what I came for.

"I'm sorry I lied about the rape. I'm sorry I didn't bake cookies and sing lullabies to you in your crib. I'm sorry you did the laundry. I'm sorry I let you stay out all night—what was the other thing?"

"Homework."

"I'm sorry I never made you do homework." She dropped her hands. "Anything else?"

"I guess not."

"Can you get on with your life now?"

"Yes, I can get on with my life."

" 'Bout damn time."

We celebrated with a conciliatory cup of coffee at the kitchen table. It's a wonderful old table Lydia found at the estate sale of an old dude ranch where Owen Wister was supposed to have written *The Virginian*. I liked to imagine Owen writing, "When you call me that, *smile!*" then spilling his whiskey on this very wood. As soon as Lydia went underground and left me in charge of the house, I planned to steal the table and take it back to Carolina.

Lydia held the cup with both hands and blew steam from the surface. Ever since I can remember, Lydia's held her coffee cup with both hands. She said, "Did you ever wonder what I did that pissed Caspar off so much he sent us west?"

"Only twice a day for twenty years."

Lydia glanced at me, then back at her coffee. "Right after you turned twelve, I started seeing Skip."

"Seeing?"

Her lips flattened in disgust at my stupid question. "Okay, fucking."

Someday I meant to price lie detector tests. "Funny he didn't mention it," I said.

"Skip didn't know who I was. We had to sneak around on account of his bitchy little wife and my father, so Skip never saw the house. He'd forgotten my name by then, if he ever knew it."

Lydia with Skip and me with Skip's wife made for a number of abstract equations.

"Whoever invented the term *Southern peckerhead* must have been thinking of Skip," I said.

"Don't I know it. I only saw him to upset Caspar." Lydia smiled into her cup. "Upsetting Daddy was the prime directive of my childhood. I can't tell you how many jerks I did nasty with trying to get his attention."

"Caspar knew about my fathers?"

"I told him the rape story first, but he threatened to cane them in public, so I had to come clean."

"You told your father the truth, but not me?"

"I already said that, Sam. Repeating it won't change the facts."

When I was young I had this strange feeling everyone around me knew something I didn't know. Turns out I was right.

"So you screwed Skip, again, and Caspar found out—"

"Caspar always found out."

"And he shipped us as far away as he could imagine."

She nodded. "This house. Now that I'm leaving, I think I'll miss it."

"C'mon, Lydia. The bureaucrat in charge of dog gifts will open the FedEx packet, throw the toy in the trash, and that will be the end of it."

Lydia looked dubious. Outside, a truck door slammed. Lydia clicked down her cup.

"Hank's back," she said. "Are we done with accusations and recriminations, because I have to hit the trail?"

"I guess so. Shouldn't we break some glass or scream at each other first? That's how I was brought up."

Lydia carried her coffee dregs to the sink. "I'm tired of breaking glass. Cleaning up afterward is undignified."

"Is this literal or metaphoric?"

Lydia looked at me a long time, then she sighed. "Sam, all your life I've never been able to decide if you walk around with your head in the clouds or up your ass."

Hank balanced on the truck's back bumper to strap a blue tarp over the amassed possessions. Even though Lydia's saddle purse and bottle of water were already in place in the front seat, ready to take to the highway, this driving into the sunset thing still didn't seem real to me, I guess because it's hard to conceive of your mother as a fugitive from justice.

"Wait a day so you don't miss Pete's funeral," I said.

Lydia had found a blue-and-yellow necktie left over from her Annie Hall phase. She held the folded tie up to my neck to check the color coordination between it and my skin. "I never was much for funerals," she said. "Tell Maurey and Chet we're sorry we couldn't be there."

I appealed to Hank. "What's a day going to matter?"

Hank grunted from the strain of tightening the rope around the tarp.

Lydia said, "Women's prisons are grossly underfunded. They must be avoided at all costs." She stuffed the necktie into my coat pocket. "Have Maurey tie it, you'll botch the job if you do it yourself."

255

This was happening too fast. It seemed wrong to have finally made up with my mother, sort of, anyway, and fifteen minutes later lose her for God knows how long. We should be bonding or interfacing or whatever being nice is called these days.

She said, "Leaving you in charge of the house doesn't mean some woman can waltz in here and change everything. I want the walls where I left them."

"I'm done with women."

"I'll believe that when moose fly."

Then Lydia did something completely uncharacteristic. She hugged me. I felt her head on my shoulder and her arms on my back. She was thinner than I'd imagined, and she smelled a bit like ink.

"Take care of yourself out there in the underground," I said.

She leaned back with her hands on my elbows and looked into my face. "I'll be fine. The government's not big enough to touch women like me. You take care of my granddaughter."

"I will."

"Promise me you won't raise her the way I raised you."

"I wouldn't dream of it."

After Lydia got into the truck, Hank came around and hugged me too. It didn't feel a bit weird.

"Feed the horses while I'm gone," he said.

"Maurey's not going to be happy," I said.

"You'll have to take my place."

"Yeah, right."

Hank grinned. *Nach-ki-tach-sa-po-auach-kach-pinna.*

"What's that?"

"Blackfoot for 'Keep your nose clean.'"

I stood in the snow, watching Hank's truck slowly drive away. Just before he turned west onto the Yellowstone Highway, an arm came from the passenger's window, fingers fluttered a goodbye wave, then they were gone.

6

Maurey was more than unhappy over Hank going underground with Lydia.

"We're talking last straw," she said.

I stood there, hands at my sides, wondering how I could save her. These crises are the times I'm supposed to take command.

Anger flashed in her eyes. "Who's going to run the ranch?"

"It could be worse. I've lost my mother. Temporarily anyway."

"I need Hank a lot more than you need a mother."

That was true. At my age, a mother is more symbolic than nurturing, not that mine ever was nurturing. "I can help with the ranch."

Maurey made a nasal sound indicating minor disgust. "Sam, this is a horse ranch; you're afraid of horses."

I hate it when people say that. "The ranch isn't only a horse ranch. I can fix fence, and I've always wanted to learn irrigation. Moving water where it's needed seems like a satisfying way to spend your time."

Maurey sat in her stuffed rocking chair and stared at a spot in the air several feet in front of and slightly below her face. She said, "I have to call my sponsor."

"Your sponsor?"

"Go find Pud. He needs your help in the hay shed."

"Are you turning to God?" I asked.

"I'm turning to the telephone. You go help Pud and don't come back for a couple of hours."

Here's my problem with Pud: Today, he seems nice enough and Maurey loves him and she's past that stage women go through where they fall in love with creeps, so he must be okay, but way back when Pud was seven or eight his mother told him to drown a litter of kittens. As an alternative to drowning, Pud decided to let his God-ugly dog kill them. Maurey and I came upon the gory scene, there was a fight, the dog bit me, I bit the dog, and in the end we saved one kitten. That kitten was Alice, my closest pal for the next eighteen years.

Okay. Pud had excuses. He was only a child and his family was a bunch of ignorant yahoos, and back then everyone thought Pud was retarded so they treated him cruelly. I understand the excuses; but the fact is I can't forget he once fed kittens to a dog. That was the same winter Lydia told me the rape story. People who can't forget lead fetid lives.

I found Pud in the barn, grooming the stud.

"Molly's in the hay," Pud said. "We fed her three Marches ago when the snow was nose deep and the elk were starving, and now she thinks we owe her lunch all winter."

"She's a welfare chiseler elk," I said.

"There's a lesson to be learned, I guess."

As Pud and I walked in silence up the sled track to the shed, it dawned on me for the hundredth time that I owed it to Maurey to be friends with him. Or, at least, friendly. They'd been together six years and Pud and I had yet to carry on a conversation between just the two of us.

I wasn't certain where to begin. "Pud," I said, "how'd you come to get into the satellite dish repair business?"

He was as surprised to hear me ask as I was to be asking. He kind of slid the corners of his eyes at me to see if I was putting him on.

"Maurey and I were up the Ramshorn one July, delivering horses to the Bar Double R, and they had a dish. I didn't even know what it was."

"And that's how you decided on a career?"

"I decided on a career when I saw eight full-grown cowboys hanging on every word of 'Jeopardy.' Those old men had lived long, happy lives without TV, but three weeks after putting in the dish, they were junkies."

"So, you look at your job as servicing junkies?"

"Heck, you should see the panic when a bandpass filter goes down. I charge seventy an hour, including travel time, which can be four or five hours back in the mountains."

This was a bigger scam than golf carts.

"I could get two hundred if I wanted," Pud said, "but that would be gouging." He slid his eyes over at me again. "I'm no gouger."

"I believe you."

The hay shed wasn't a shed in the North Carolina sense of the word. It was actually a large roof, larger than the roof on most houses, held up by telephone pole–looking logs about twenty feet high. The summer's hay crop—or in drought years like this one, hay bought from Idaho farmers—was stacked in bales under the roof to keep dry, and a twelve-foot double-posted mesh fence surrounded the hay to keep out horses, porcupines, deer, moose, and elk, and anything else with a taste for grass.

The system worked fairly well except when someone forgot to close the gate properly, which is what happened the day Pete died. An elk—Molly—had gone through the fence and was eating her way around the stack, costing the ranch money it didn't have to spare.

Pud stationed me just inside the open gate, which wasn't any more a real gate than the shed was a real shed. It was a section of fence held in by push screws. Each side of the enclosure had a removable section so Hank could take bales from anywhere without having a long haul.

"Stand here and when she comes your way, turn her out the open hole," Pud said.

"Turn her?"

259

"Only don't get under her feet. Molly's stomped three cowdogs to death in her career."

"How do I turn her without getting under her feet?"

"Wave your arms and holler."

"She's bigger than me."

"She doesn't know that."

Pud walked off counterclockwise around the hay bales. From the northwest corner, Molly raised her head and chewed a mouthful of hay. She regarded me disdainfully—with good reason. She was wild, strong, and noble. I wasn't. That animal knew I wasn't bigger than her. She wasn't stupid.

I looked across the white pasture to the river and wondered idly if I was fixing to get killed. The thought didn't disturb me as much as I would have expected. Mostly, I considered the uniqueness in a modern society of being killed by a wild animal. I always wanted to go out in a unique way. I also thought about how lousy Shannon would feel. She would wonder if her desertion last night caused me to flaunt risks.

"Scat! Move it!" Pud's voice came from around the corner of the stack.

Molly ignored him. Six-hundred-pound animals don't respond to *Scat*.

A firecracker exploded at Molly's feet. *Pop*. She jumped back and hit the fence, but didn't move any closer to me. A string of firecrackers went off—*Pop! Pop! PopPop!* Molly walked ten feet or so down the aisle toward me, enough to clear the line of fire, then she stopped and went back to feeding.

Pud appeared on the far side of the elk. "Black Cats aren't motivational enough," he said.

By leaning toward the fence, I could see him working something out of his coat pocket. Pud is wiry and no taller than me. I'd always thought Maurey didn't love me in the romantic way because I wasn't tall, so it came as a shock when she took a boyfriend my size.

"Pud," I said, "when we were kids, everyone thought you were retarded. Why was that?"

He stopped fiddling with whatever he'd been fiddling with and looked at me. "I'm dyslexic."

His eyes have always been so soft and open, not angry like Dothan's, that I used to suspect something other than a demented home life made him different.

He went on. "I couldn't learn to read. My family and everyone treated me like a retard, so I believed them."

"I remember how mean the kids were to you at school."

"Maurey had me tested. All those years I thought I was stupider than everyone else, and then I found out I wasn't."

"Must have had an amazing effect on your self-image."

"Like waking up and discovering you're a different person." He held up a round object. "You ready?"

"For what?"

"Cherry bomb."

I glanced from him to Molly. "Are you sure that's a good idea?"

Her nose reacted first. The nostrils flared and her head jerked, then *BLAM!*—thirty times louder than a Black Cat. She leaped backward into the fence and bounced and came down running. I doubt if Molly even saw me before the collision. Her eyes were panicky wild, bugging pink whites and huge pupils. It happened way too fast for me to wave my hands and holler, or be smart and climb the fence. I think her inside shoulder hit me; whatever it was, I flew into the hay and she went out the fence gap.

Pud pulled me to my feet. "That was great," he said. "I don't know if I could have stood my ground like you did."

After a few minutes, my lungs accepted air and my vision cleared somewhat. I almost convinced myself I'd been brave from choice; maybe I did stand my ground; maybe I had had time to jump. Bravery isn't what you do so much as how you look back at what you did. I was so happy about surviving Molly, I tripped over barbwire under the snow and cut the living bejesus out of my hand.

So I walked into the living room with my fist above my head, clenching a hard-packed snowball. The blood trickled down my arm and off my elbow.

Maurey was still on the phone. She took one look at me and said,

"I have to go, Lloyd, there's another emergency." She listened a few seconds and said, "I'll call you back."

After she hung up I said, "You didn't have to stop on account of me."

"I'm supposed to chat while you bleed on the floor?"

Maurey got up and led me into the kitchen, where she kept one of the most complete first-aid kits a nonprofessional ever owned. It filled an old army mule pannier. A lot of doctors must have dried out on the TM because Maurey was prepared for any emergency. She had me stand at the sink and run cold water over the cut. It was at the base of my thumb and hard to see, what with the flow of blood, but there seemed to be a penny-size skin flap over a deep, ragged hole.

"This'll take stitches," Maurey said.

"Should we call an ambulance?"

"I can handle it."

She dug through the pannier and came up with a sealed Baggie containing a sponge and this frothy brown liquid. As she leaned over my hand, her hair fell across her line of vision and she brushed it back over her ear in my favorite Maurey gesture.

"Was that your sponsor on the phone?" I asked.

She nodded. "Lloyd. Have you had a tetanus shot lately?"

"Last year when a Vicksburg battery mount fell on my foot. Am I supposed to know Lloyd?"

"Yes, you dip." The brown liquid was some kind of alcohol and it hurt like the dickens. I gritted my teeth as Maurey scrubbed and talked. "I've told you about Lloyd and Sharon Carbonneau at least twenty times. They own a sports paraphernalia shop in Denver."

Even though the pain was tremendous, I resolved to follow the expected male code of toughness. "Sports paraphernalia?"

"Caps and coolers. You can make a killing off any piece of plastic with a Denver Broncos logo on the side."

" 'Sponsor' is an AA term, isn't it?"

"Your sponsor is the person you turn to when you're in trouble."

"That makes you my sponsor."

She gave one last squeeze of brown antiseptic. "Are you still in trouble, sugar booger?"

Was I in trouble, or was this despair the daily routine of going on? "Shannon's moving out," I said.

Holding my sterile hand palm up, Maurey led me back to the kitchen table. "I know."

"She always tells you everything before me."

Maurey found a preloaded syringe and broke off the seal. "Shannon's worried. She thinks you'll fall apart without her at home to fuss over."

I stared at the syringe. Nobody had told me about a shot. "What did you advise?"

"I said, 'Birds gotta fly.' If you fall apart that's your fault. She can't spend her whole life being needy so you have something to do."

When Shannon was little we had this ritual where I came in every night to tuck her into bed. The covers would be an awful mess and I would say, "What would you do without me?" and she would say, "Freeze in my sleep," or something to that effect. But then one night I went into her room in my socked feet and found her reading *Yertle the Turtle* in a perfectly tucked bed. She didn't see me at the door, so I returned to my room, put on shoes, and clumped back up the hall. When I re-entered Shannon's bedroom, the covers were tangled up around her feet.

I couldn't decide if the trick to make me feel needed was touching or manipulative. Either way, finding out the truth took some of the glow off night-night.

"This may sting," Maurey said, and she stabbed me right in the cut.

"*Aighgh! Jesus!*"

"What a wienie," she said.

"Wienie? Let me poke a hole in you and see how it feels."

"Hank didn't scream when I deadened his wrist."

"Hank's stoic. It runs in his genes."

"Wieniehood runs in your genes. That'll numb up in a minute."

My pain threshold has never been up to cowboy standards. The Callahan nerves are more sensitive than theirs, I think. Some people can see or hear better than other people, it only follows that senses of touch vary also, and mine is highly developed.

"Doctors just give you all these medical supplies?"

"They leave things with me when they go away."

Another plastic bag held a curved needle, like cobblers use on shoe soles, pre-threaded from a little bobbin of nylon thread. I said, "A doctor recovers from alcoholism and he's so grateful he leaves behind a home clinic."

Maurey held the needle between her thumb and index finger as she studied my cut. "Actually, this particular doctor committed suicide."

She slid the needle into the flap and pulled it out of clean skin. It felt icky. No pain—just icky, like the ultimate in fingernails across a blackboard. "He couldn't live with or without alcohol," she went on, "so he hung himself in the barn."

"And you kept his stuff."

Maurey tied a complicated knot by dipping the needle through a loop and turning it sideways or something. I couldn't follow the process. Afterward she snipped the thread and went back into my thumb for a second stitch.

Without looking up, she said, "Pud asked me to marry him."

"Ouch!"

"Don't jerk your hand while the needle's in it."

"You purposely waited until I was helpless to break the news."

"I was going to tell you. He only asked last night."

"I hope you said no."

Maurey drew the thread through and tied the knot. She pretended to be concentrating so hard I knew she wasn't concentrating at all. She could easily have sewn my fingers together.

"I said okay."

"Okay? The kid asks you to marry him and all you can say is 'Okay.' Isn't that a bit halfhearted?"

"Don't be tacky with me, Sam."

"But you already married one Talbot and he was a shit."

"I've got the good brother this time."

Maurey and I had been best friends since before puberty. I thought we would always be the way we had always been, with our romantic lives a hobby we take seriously, but nevertheless, still a hobby. The nuclear family would always be each other.

"You've lived with Pud for years. Why change what works?"

Maurey pulled the third stitch. "Why are you freaking out?"

"I think he's taking advantage of your vulnerability over losing Pete."

She tied the knot hard and snipped the loose end with her scissors in a crisp *snip* of anger.

"You've been married twice."

"But that was different. Neither of those women was as vital to me as you are."

"And they knew that. I don't blame them for hating me. Did it ever occur to you that maybe—just maybe—putting me first over your wives had something to do with why your marriages failed?"

"They were both emotional cripples. It had nothing to do with you."

Maurey's eyes met mine fiercely. "Pud is my partner, Sam. My mate. You are my very good friend. You are important, yet secondary."

"But we always said friends matter more than lovers."

"You always said that. Pud is the number-one man in my life, Sam. You have to accept that."

"Fat chance."

7

I kicked on my cross-country skis and headed up the creek. Got to get away. Got to go. Movement eases turmoil. The warm days earlier in the week had softened the snow and today's cold hardened it, so basically I was skiing on ice. I fell twice before the back fence. A single rail showed above the snow and it was easy to sidestep over. Once across, I made my way into the aspens, where the going was a bit easier.

How could she do this to me? When I got married I didn't flaunt my true love in her face. I didn't call her *secondary*. The first time I sent a postcard: "Got married. Wish you were here." The second time, Shannon told her.

When Wanda ran off with the illiterate pool man I thought I had a rock-solid support system—mother, daughter, closest friend—stable as a three-legged stool. Okay, the mother wasn't too supportive, but I knew where she was. If I felt like talking to her, all I had to do was hold on to a check for a couple of days. I never dreamed Shannon would leave so soon. Maybe if I'd stayed in Greensboro after the

Katrina fiasco she wouldn't have discovered how easy I am to live without.

What was I going to do? I couldn't go back to North Carolina. The Manor House would be an empty tomb without Shannon. Besides, I'd had it with golf carts and serial sex. Gilia changed all that.

For sure, I couldn't stay in my cell at the TM Ranch forever. Spring would come; Madame Bovary would eat arsenic and die; Maurey would marry Pud.

What I ought to do was move to a small Western town and find a log cabin within walking distance of a video store and a coffee shop, and do nothing for ten years but write novels. Not teenage sports fiction, but literature—*Death in Steamboat Springs*, *Bucky Redux*, a rewrite of the New Testament. I would be as serious as Richard Ford. Psychiatrists and doctors take sick people and bring them up to normal. I could take normal and make it better. My readers would stop being miserable; they would tolerate themselves and each other.

Or if that was too ambitious, I could bring Babs and Lynette to Wyoming and set them up with their own Dairy Queen. They'd like that.

The options were boundless. Almost too boundless, like the night I was left alone at the ranch and I tried to watch satellite TV. Four hundred channels gave me so many choices I spent the entire evening switching from satellite to satellite and didn't watch anything for fear of missing something. When all choices are possible, realistic and unrealistic lose their edges. Here I was torn between writing a book that would make unhappy people happy and opening a Dairy Queen.

When had I been happy in life? When Maurey was pregnant. When Shannon was young and needed me. Looking back at the recent past, I realized helping Babs and Lynette had given me a gut-level satisfaction that had been missing lately from Young Adult novels and sex acts on lost women.

I was almost to the warm springs when I came through a gap in the aspens into a wide clearing covered by virgin snow, and I had a vision. Maybe not a vision in the Cheyenne sense, more like a waking dream—a visualization. It wasn't something I could ever tell Maurey or Shannon about. They would laugh. Lydia would hoot.

What I saw was a log lodge with a rock chimney next to a white clinic. Individual cabins lay scattered around the clearing connected by smooth paths. Golf carts hummed quietly back and forth between the cabins and the main lodge, carrying my women. A long driveway lined by cottonwoods and red willows looped up from the ranch. At a quaint wooden bridge spanning the brook, a tastefully small sign read CALLAHAN HOME FOR UNWED MOTHERS.

Why not? I could hire nurses. We'd need a helicopter for hospital runs, but, hell, I had money. Nothing on Earth sounded nicer than to surround myself with pregnant teenagers.

A doughnut of green clover about three feet wide encircles the warm springs all winter. The north side of the doughnut is the actual spring, which steams from the earth like a scene from Shakespeare—one of those Scottish moors haunted by witches. The hot water gurgles into a moss-lined pool, thigh deep at its deepest point, then, already cooling, it empties west into Miner Creek. The Miner Creek approach involves skiing across a log high above the rocks and ice, so my rest and meditation spot was on the east side, the gentle bank.

I popped boots off bindings and planted my skis upright in the snow, then I sat on the clover and waited. I didn't touch the water. When you first start visiting a warm springs on a regular basis, you check the temperature each time you return to see if the water really is as warm as you remember it. The TM spring was a tad cooler than I like bath water, warm enough to melt the surrounding snow but not so hot as to scald the tropical fish Maurey and other kids had released into it over the years. Back in early high school Maurey talked me into a full-moon skinny dip at twenty below zero. The water itself was cozy, warm and foggy as a Jacuzzi, but the seconds between leaving the water and drying off were among the most painful of my childhood. Seeing her naked was not worth hypothermia.

I came to the warm springs mainly for the dirt. Winter in Jackson Hole may be beautiful and spare beyond the Eastern Time Zone conception of beauty, but several months with no sight of dirt leaves me weird.

So I sat on the clover with my fingers in the dirt, watching tiny goldfish dart around the shallows' muck, my energy at an all-time low. I was too exhausted to be depressed. The truth is I'm only good for one intense, spine-wrenching emotional blowout a year, and when the scenes come stacked up on one another some sort of morphine response kicks in. My brain goes numb; my muscles fill up with lactic acid.

The high whine of a snowmobile wafted in from back along the fenceline, and I realized I'd been holding my breath, waiting for it. Maurey arrived in a powder blue snowsuit, gold metal-flake helmet, and her father's old Mickey Mouse boots. I averted my eyes as she dismounted. I heard her shake out her hair and wade down the snowbank, then felt her sit beside me. Neither of us spoke for a while. I underhand tossed a pebble into the water and we both took what life lessons we could from the concentric, spreading ripples.

"You knew I would come," she said.

"Yes."

Our shoulders were a half-inch apart. I sat cross-legged while Maurey stretched her legs in a V. She leaned back on her hands and said, "Remember the day I fell in the creek and went into labor?"

"I've never been that scared since." Maurey broke her leg, Shannon was born, and I became a father three weeks before my fourteenth birthday.

Maurey exhaled a sigh. The fog from her breath looked like punctuation. "Sam, it's time we got a divorce."

I said, "I know. It's a pain in the ass."

Maurey pulled off her left glove and laced her fingers into mine. "You think you're incapable of loving a woman, and you blame Lydia, but maybe the problem isn't her, maybe it's my fault."

"You're honest with me, I'm honest with you. How could there be a problem?"

"There's worse things than dishonesty, Sam."

My automatic response was cynical, but I clamped down before it got out.

Maurey said, "Ever since we were kids, we've had each other, so neither of us has had to learn how to take care of ourselves."

A flock of small black birds twittered through the willows across the creek, making the bushes seem to crawl in a DT effect. I looked from the birds to the fish to Maurey's hand in mine.

"I have this test I give myself," I said, "whenever I fall for a new woman. I pretend she and I are about to be married. The families are there in their best clothes, the minister stands with his back to the cross, the organist breaks into the 'Wedding March,' and you telephone to ask if I want to go out for coffee."

"Why wasn't I invited to the wedding?"

"If I say no to you, I don't want to go for coffee right now, it proves I'm serious about the woman. Falling for her is for real."

There was a moment's quiet, then Maurey said, "That's either silly or sick. Give me a minute to decide which." She used her right hand, the hand I wasn't holding, to brush hair behind her ear. "Tell me, how many have you married in this fantasy?"

"None. Not even the two I married in reality."

"That is not silly. It is definitely sick."

A face appeared in the steam over the spring—a face with high cheekbones and a freckle between the bridge of the nose and her right eye. I said, "Gilia."

"What?"

"I'd rather marry Gilia than go to coffee with you." I tossed a handful of pebbles, many concentric and overlapping circles. "But I blew that one."

Maurey and I went into our respective funks. It seemed to me that we were embarking on something inordinately stupid. We were chopping up our one dependable crutch. Friendship is so much healthier than other crutches—alcohol or TV or religious fanaticism. One healthy crutch shouldn't be against the rules.

"What exactly does this divorce mean?" I asked. "Are we still friends?"

She squeezed my hand hard, then let go. "Of course we're still friends. It just means we're no longer next of kin. We no longer save each other every time there's a crisis. The next woman breaks your heart, you have to handle it without me."

"There won't be a next woman."

"Yeah, right."

"I'm finished with romance."

"You could no more do without romance than air."

I decided not to fight with her. This would be a conversation to dwell on in my old age. I didn't want to dwell on a fight.

"What else?" I asked.

Maurey leaned toward the warm springs. "I can't accept any more of your money."

Dothan's ugly taunts ran through my mind. The gossip I'd heard and ignored. The fears I'd been afraid to think.

I looked at her. "Is money all you used me for?"

Maurey swung her right arm and punched me in the face.

"*Ow!*"

"How dare you say that, you snot. When Daddy died and Dothan took Auburn, I'd never have survived without you."

"I didn't mean it."

"This split-up is just as hard on me as it is on you, you stupid jerk."

I held both hands over my nose. "You hurt me."

"I meant to hurt you."

"Is my nose bleeding?"

She tipped my face to view the damage. "Six stitches should do it. Maybe seven."

I looked down at my hands. No blood. "Before we go apart, would you do me one last favor?" I asked.

"It better have nothing to do with sex."

"Let me pay Pete's bills, the doctors and funeral."

She frowned. "Wouldn't that be hypocritical? To say 'No more—after this last time'?"

"It's as much for Pete and Chet as it is for you."

She regarded me with her blue eyes. The first time I saw Maurey I was amazed at her blue eyes and black hair—like Hitler. Twenty years of history passed between us as we stared at one another. Twenty years of shared parenthood. I couldn't believe it was over, we would be casual from now on.

Maurey nodded once, to herself, and smiled. She said, "Okay."

271

8

A letter arrived the next morning:

Dear Mr. Callahan,

Rory Paseneaux returned to claim his position as head of the household and he is PO'ed because me and Babs named you as the father of our babies. He went so far as to talk to the woman at the hospital and she told him it is too late to change the papers.

Rory has said we can not have any more to do with you, even me, and if you come around he will kick your butt.

We also can not cover for you with your girlfriends any more. We have to call Sam and Sammi by their middle names which are Lynn and Babs.

So that is that. I thank you for what you did for us and I know Babs would too if she was allowed.

With respects,
Lynette Norloff

p.s. Rory Paseneaux did allow one thing. He says your lawyer can keep paying our rent.

Something kind of nasty happened before Pete's funeral. I was standing outside the Episcopal Church, on the sidewalk that had been cleared by a snow blower, talking to Chet and three of Pete's friends from New York City while Maurey and Pud parked the Suburban. The friends were nice-looking young men in New York City suits and shoes. I got the feeling they had been Ivy Leaguers because I couldn't tell them apart.

Dothan Talbot drove past, slowly, with the Denver bimbo scooted so close she was behind the steering wheel. He stared at me in this challenging look of his where he lowers his pointy chin and glares out the tops of his eyeballs. That look used to make Lauren Bacall incredibly alluring, but it did nothing at all for Dothan.

I ignored him and went on talking to the New Yorkers about the color of snow in Manhattan and the odds of them seeing a bear. One of the guys said it's not the temperature that makes you cold, it's the humidity. Chet lit a cigarette. Pretty soon Dothan cruised back the other way. The bimbo had a possessive scowl on her face, probably because married women fooling around are the most jealous creatures on Earth. I didn't envy Dothan a bit.

He eased his truck up to the curb next to me, got out, and slammed the door. The three New Yorkers instinctively sensed tension and leaned away. I doubt if Wyoming men would have been that sensitive to the possibility of ugliness.

Dothan's voice dripped with smugness. He said, "I always knew you'd end up with the fairies."

I glanced at Pete's friends to see how they handled being called fairies. Their faces had gone mask. I said, "Who are you trying to insult, Dothan, me or them?"

"I'm not trying to insult anyone. I came to pay my last respects to Maurey's queer brother."

I slugged Dothan in the stomach. He doubled over and I hit him in the face, then he was down on the snow and I was kicking him.

I lost control, which is something I'd never done before. A kidney stomp immobilized him long enough for me to go for the head. There was a rush of memories—of Sonny and Ryan beating me up in October; of Dothan beating me up in the seventh grade; of him fucking

Maurey when I couldn't; of Maurey, Shannon, and Lydia dismissing me. I kicked the living bejesus out of that bastard.

Then hands were pulling me off him and the bimbo was screaming. The New Yorkers looked aghast. I guess they weren't used to personal violence.

Chet was saying, "He's not worth it, Sam. Back off."

Maurey was saying, "You split your stitches, tiger."

She borrowed handkerchiefs from the New Yorkers and wrapped my hand tightly. I watched Dothan's woman hold his head in her lap and pat his lips with snow. His eyes blinked, but didn't focus.

As we walked into the church, Maurey said, "I wish you'd let me get to him first."

"It was my turn."

"Blessed are the dead who die in the Lord; even so saith the spirit, for they rest from their labors."

The priest, whose name was Father Jack, held his arms out about sternum high, with the thumbs and forefingers made into Os. Blond beard, thinning hair, thick forearms—Father Jack looked like Edward Abbey in a ghost costume.

"The Lord be with you," he said.

Chet and a smattering of people at the back said, "And with thy spirit."

"Let us pray."

Chet kneeled and after a few false starts, the rest of us followed. Chet was Episcopalian, which was why we were having the funeral service in the Episcopal Church. That, and AA met in the parish hall, so Maurey knew Father Jack. But the rest of us in the family's pews weren't Episcopalian, or much of any other denomination, so we were lost when it came time to sit, kneel, or stand. On top of saying goodbye to his partner, Chet must have felt like he was leading a very slow aerobics class.

The church was a dark log building with two lines of pews wide enough for four people or five if they scrunched up. Pud sat against the north window with Roger at his side. Then it went Auburn,

Maurey, Chet, the aisle, me, Shannon in her new outfit, and Toinette. Dot Pollard was behind me, with the three friends from New York behind her.

The rest of the church was maybe three-quarters full of Pete's high school friends and people who go to funerals to prove they're not dead yet. I heard sniffling from the far back and sneaked a look to see who it was—Ron Mildren, being glared at by his wife, Gloria.

Pete was in the bois d'arc box with ivory inlay on top of a walnut table a few feet in front of Chet. My theory that dead people know what's going on around them for four days after they die applies just as much to ashes as bodies. Pete knew what I was thinking, so I'd best be careful.

Father Jack announced he was going to read to us from the Book of Job. Not my favorite book. God tests Job by killing his children, then says, "You passed. Here, have some more children." If God killed Shannon, then said, "That was a test, I'll replace her," I would say, "Forget it, you jerk."

As the Father read, "And though after my skin worms destroy this body," I leaned forward to check out the front pew's handle on the grief process. As usual in groups, I felt responsible for everyone's peace of mind. Roger sat pale and unblinking; Auburn was restless. Chet was tremendously sad, yet he had dignity. He didn't jump up and bash the priest in the mouth, which is what I probably would have done.

Maurey looked both beautiful and beat up by life. Her eyes were muddy and the scar on her chin seemed whiter, but she was still concerned about the others. One hand touched Chet's shoulder and the other arm extended over Auburn and rested on Roger's leg.

Shannon's shoulder touched mine; I leaned my weight toward her in case she needed support.

Job's part ended and Toinette went to the front with her viola. She played a wonderfully wistful song I'd never heard before, which she told me later was a "Romanze" by Max Bruch. Toinette's face was golden and her belly was huge. When she ran her bow across the viola strings, they seemed not so much to weep in the tragic keening of a violin, but to cry out a deeper, more elemental pain. The viola mourned not only Pete, but all loss everywhere. After Toinette finished, she gave Father Jack a shy smile and walked to her pew, and he sat there on his bench, looking poleaxed.

Shannon put her fingers over my good hand.

After that, Father Jack read another Bible verse, this one from Revelations, the book hippies used to quote in North Carolina. I tried to follow, but when he read the part about no more death, sorrow, crying, or pain, I drifted off. I'm not sure a world with no pain at all would be that desirable. The boredom would be debilitating. I could write a novel about it sometime.

When Maurey and Pete were kids their mother drove them into Jackson to the Baptist Church every Sunday while their father went fishing or hunting or read detective stories by the woodstove. If anyone asked Buddy where you go after you die, he always said, "San Francisco." It was a family proverb: *Stick by Mom and spend eternity in heaven or stick with Dad and go to San Francisco.* His version made as much sense as heaven. What good are streets of gold?

Shannon jabbed an elbow in my ribs. Everyone was looking at me. Maurey mouthed, "Go on up."

The eulogy. In the excitement of the last couple of days, I'd forgotten the eulogy.

Father Jack said, "Mr. Callahan."

I was careful not to touch anything because my hand was starting to throb and I was afraid blood might ooze through the handkerchiefs and stain the oiled wood of the pulpit or the cloth that hung over the top. I said, "I met Pete Pierce the day President Kennedy was killed."

Chet stared at me, unblinking. So did Roger, but his unblinking face sucked in light while Chet's glowed with emotion. Like the difference between the moon and a black hole.

Nothing to do but plow ahead. "Pete must have been six or seven. He wanted to watch cartoons, but they weren't on because of the assassination coverage. He and Maurey got into a fight and she smacked him in the nose."

Maurey was frowning. It seemed awfully important not to disappoint her in this, which meant the story had to go somewhere, mean something.

"I realized then how a family works; the members of a family may fight like cats and dogs, and they almost never understand what the others want or feel, or who they are, but that doesn't matter. What matters is the love that flows without reservation. Without doubt."

Father Jack shifted his weight on the bench. I wondered what he thought of us behind that beard. Was it just another day's work for him, like me at the golf cart plant?

"What else do I remember about Pete?" I asked myself and the congregation. Had to be something. "His mother. When Pete's mother was sick all those years, he took care of her. Pete loved his mother very much."

The people looked up at me, expecting more. I hadn't yet said enough to quit. "After she died, he went to New York City and got a job in the theater, managing lights for plays and musicals."

Chet had stopped watching me and was staring at the box of ashes. His eyes were striking. They showed more than the grief of separation. You could see that he'd received something permanent from Pete, something I had never felt with a woman—friend or lover. It came to me that the funeral wasn't for Pete; it was for Chet.

"Pete Pierce was gay," I said.

Maurey moved her hands into her lap. The three guys from New York rustled in their seats. I could tell from some faces farther back that not everyone had known. Instead of addressing the group, I spoke directly to Chet.

"Pete was proud of being gay, and I think that pride is why he chose me to say words about him today. He knew I wouldn't pretend he was someone he wasn't. He knew I wouldn't skip over one of the central elements of his life."

Almost imperceptibly, Chet nodded. I knew I was going in the right direction.

"We can't talk about who Pete was without acknowledging his love for Chet, here. They were partners, mates. Lovers in every sense of the word."

Chet's lips parted in almost, but not quite, a smile.

I said, "His love for Chet was the truth that made Pete feel unique."

I looked at Pud over against the window. His face was turned ever so slightly toward Maurey's, and hers toward him.

"A person would like to think his or her life has significance," I said.

Shannon's face was turned to the window, as if she were listening to something outside the rest of us couldn't hear. She was daydreaming.

"To me, significance means to love, and to be cherished, and to impact creatively the world—large or small—that one occupies. Pete found significance. Through his work and his love he left a legacy that will live into the future with each of us he touched."

I turned to Father Jack. "Where's the nearest phone?"

He shifted forward on the bench, confusion in his eyes. "The church offices. Next door."

I left by the door behind the pulpit. Crossing the snowy yard, I saw that Dothan and the bimbo were gone. Love wasn't everything. Neither was friendship and family. What I wanted and couldn't get, even from the three legs of my support stool, was someone to take my dreams seriously.

Gilia answered on the third ring.

"Hello."

"What do you think of a home for unwed mothers? We could run it. You and I."

There was a long silence and quiet breathing, then Gilia said, "Where?"

The End

Words After

Social Blunders is the third novel I've written about the good folks of GroVont, Wyoming, and several reviewers and letter writers have told me I am misspelling the name of my fictional town. This hardly seems fair since I created the place. There once was a real town named and spelled Gro Vont on almost the same spot where I put my version. The real Gro Vont was settled in 1894 near the Gros Ventre River at the base of the Gros Ventre Mountains, which, together with the Gros Ventre Indian tribe, are pronounced the same as the town. Gros Ventre is a French term meaning Big Belly. A translation more in keeping with the spirit of the tribes who named the Gros Ventre Indians would be the Hippy Derelicts.

One group of old-timers claims the early settlers of Gro Vont changed the spelling because they sere sick and tired of correcting outsiders who pronounced it Gross Ven-tray. Another faction, pointing to various maps that spell it Grovont, Gro Vont, or GroVont, say the early settlers couldn't spell for squat and painted the post office sign in ignorance. No one but the Postal Service evcr called the town

Gro Vont anyway; to the people who lived there and those in the surrounding valley, it was always Mormon Row.

Gro Vont's population peaked in the mid-1920s at more or less fifty, then when the Depression trickled down to Wyoming, John Rockefeller's agents bought all the land they could get their hands on for thirty-seven dollars an acre. Rockefeller gave the land to the government so they could form what is now Grand Teton National Park. Those who wouldn't sell were forced to sign life leases. A life lease means when the current title holder dies, the land goes to the government and the children go elsewhere. As the old-timers died or were run off their ranches by the Park Service, Gro Vont's numbers dwindled until now only Clark and Veda Moulton are left. The Mormon Church was hauled twenty miles closer to the ski area and made into a pizza parlor, the old school is now the shower house at a yurt village, and the last post office was taken to a nearby dude ranch. Interestingly enough, the Park Service is working on a plan to hire actors and actresses to go out on Mormon Row and pretend to do what the real ranchers were doing before the government chased them off the ranches. Only in America.

After finishing *Skipped Parts*, I discovered I was the third novelist to set books in a fictional town named GroVont or Gros Ventre—a remarkable coincidence when you think about it. How many Yoknapatawpha Counties sprang up independently of each other? The first Gros Ventre belonged to H. L. Davis, whose book *Honey in the Horn* won a Pulitzer Prize in 1936. Ivan Doig created Gros Ventre number two—three if the real one counts—for his Montana trilogy. Mr. Doig's Montanans pronounce it GROVE-on. Don't ask me why. Even God doesn't understand native Montanans.

In the summer and fall, I live a stone's throw (if you have a great arm) from the Gros Ventre River in two one-room cabins. I need two cabins because one has the refrigerator and the other has the stove. My outhouse has an amazing view, a guest register, and a copy of *Madame Bovary*. Last summer it had *Anna Karenina* and the two summers before that *Under the Volcano*. I recommend reading fat classics with your pants down.

During the winter and mud season I live in practically the only suburb in Wyoming, a neighborhood called Cottonwood Park. People shovel their driveways and walk dogs on leashes and there's a committee that sends you letters if your canoe is stored within sight of the street. The cabins border a Wilderness Area while Cottonwood Park is less than a mile from McDonald's and Kmart, but just last week a grizzly bear and three cubs were captured over across from the school bus stop. Novelists call that ironic.

In his introduction to *Down the River*, Edward Abbey made what I call a shameless plea for mail. Most of my mail comes from people in prison. They offer to tell me their story, which they swear is a best-seller waiting to be typed. "I'll give you the facts, you write the book, and we'll split the money." I send them Norman Mailer's address.

But I would enjoy hearing from readers who aren't necessarily in jail. Old friends would be nice. People I lost along the way. Anyone who connects with the characters living in my head. Hate mail isn't personally satisfying, but do what you've got to do.

Anyhow, the address is Box 1974, Jackson, Wyoming 83001. Unless you come off sounding like a stalker or I lose your letter you will receive a picture post card of the Tetons and a short but sincere thank-you note. I won't write your story and I won't split the money with you, but we will have communicated, and along today's information highway, that's about the best we can hope for.

OCTOBER 1994

A B O U T   T H E   A U T H O R

In addition to his GroVont Trilogy—*Skipped Parts, Sorrow Floats,* and *Social Blunders*—Tim Sandlin is the author of *Sex and Sunsets* and *Western Swing,* and a collection of his columns from the *Jackson Hole News* called *The Pyms: Unauthorized Tales of Jackson Hole.* To support his writing habit, Mr. Sandlin has taken on many jobs, including elk-skinner and pizza-parlor manager, dishwasher and cook in a Chinese restaurant. Despite all, he continues to write, live, and thrive in Jackson Hole, Wyoming.